Love Affairs

Love Affairs

A Collection of Contemporary,
Historical and Paranormal Novellas

SYLVIA DAY

LOVE AFFAIRS: A Collection of Contemporary, Historical and Paranormal Novellas

Library of Congress Control Number: 2015906094
ISBN-10: 1626509948
ISBN-13: 978-1-62650-994-8

Cover design by Croco Designs.
Interior design by VMC Art & Design, LLC.

Published by Sylvia Day, LLC
5130 S. Fort Apache Rd., Ste. #215-447
Las Vegas, NV 89148
www.sylviaday.com

Table of Contents

Wish
List

Chapter One

NICHOLAS JAMES, THE HOTTEST man on the planet, was bare-assed naked with a bow covering his cock.

Steph gaped. And not just any kind of gape, but a "bug-eyed, mouth hanging open to catch flies" kind of gape. Before she could even think twice, she flipped up the red bow and then drooled at what was under it. *Oh. My. God.*

"Jesus, Steph," muttered her paralegal Elaine, bringing her sharply back to the festive conference room and the sounds of Frank Sinatra singing holiday songs. "Your Secret Santa gift can't be that bad. Let me see it." She held out her hand and beckoned with her fingers, showing off long acrylic nails with airbrushed snowmen.

Hugging the silver foil box to her chest, Steph thrust over the restaurant gift certificate that had concealed the photo beneath—the photo with the clever little bow strategically glued with just enough hinge to afford her an eyeful.

"Ooohhh, nice. I love Dominico's." Elaine's red painted mouth curved in a smile. "You should take me. All of my dates are too cheap to go there."

"Uh." Turning her head, Steph searched the crowded conference room for the naked man of her dreams. Of course, Nicholas wasn't naked right now. Not at the Mitchell, Jones, and Cline annual holiday party. No, right now he was wearing beautifully tailored slacks in dark blue, a crisp white shirt with blue tie and white silk vest. She loved that he wore three-piece suits. Somehow, the urbanity of his clothing only served to accentuate the raw masculine power of his body. He was single and gorgeous, and like most single and gorgeous men, he led an active lifestyle which kept him in fine shape.

Just the sort of man most women were wildly attracted to. She, however, avoided him like the plague. She'd learned her lesson the first time.

Her breath caught.

There he was. By the door.

You could hardly miss him. Not when he was so tall and broad shouldered. His dark hair gleamed under the glow of blinking strings of Christmas lights as he leaned his lanky frame casually against the doorjamb. He was staring at her with a wicked half smile.

Then he winked.

Realization hit her hard and made her gasp.

Somehow, he'd found her wish list. The fantasy one. The silly stupid *naughty* wish list.

Oh. My. God!

Nick knew the exact moment Steph caught on. The flush spread up from the low V of her teal silk blouse and then colored her cheeks.

Finally! After almost a year of flirting that got him nothing more than the occasional inconvenient hard-on, he was getting what he really wanted for Christmas—the opportunity to prove he was the man for her. He wished he could say it was his charm that won Stephanie over, but that wasn't the case. No, he'd had to wait for fate to step in and slip her name into his hand for their law firm's annual Secret Santa draw. He'd opened up the folded slip of paper, saw *Stephanie Martin* and grinned like an idiot.

For about one second.

Then he'd realized he'd have to come up with not only a great gift, but a great gift she'd have to share with *him*, and not one of the other drooling Lotharios around their firm. He'd walked through endless crowded malls, surfed a hundred on-line shopping sites, grilled every one of his ex-girlfriends and female relatives—all to no avail. They couldn't understand why he didn't just ask Stephanie out, instead of trying to plan something elaborate to make his point.

The answer was really very simple. He had a reputation as a ladies' man. She'd heard about it and didn't want anything to do with him because of it. So straight up asking for a date wouldn't work. He had to show her he was serious first.

Steph's reticence wasn't a new experience for Nick. Most of the women who were strictly platonic friends were ones who'd made it clear they were looking for Mr. Right. Not Mr. Right Now. Starting in high school, Nick had learned how to give the "not going to settle down" vibe pretty well. Not that he didn't have committed relationships. He did. They just weren't the forever kind of commitment.

So he'd tried to respect Steph's obvious non-interest, but the gnawing craving in his gut wouldn't go away. He wanted her—wanted that long dark hair wrapped around his fist, wanted those dark brown eyes burning with lust, wanted that lushly curved body out of the business suits and arching naked beneath him. And even though he knew it was never going to happen, Nick couldn't stop dreaming about it.

Steph was gorgeous, beautifully built, confident and

intelligent. She knew her assets and showed them off. She also knew her worth and wanted a man who did. What had she said to him once?

Any man who has one foot planted firmly outside the door never really comes in.

But he wasn't a fly-by-night kind of boyfriend. He took damn good care of the women he dated. He paid attention to what they liked and didn't like. It wasn't so hard. It just took a little effort, and Nick enjoyed making that effort. Enjoyed watching their surprise when he remembered their favorite author, favorite song, favorite places to be touched and caressed. Because of this, most of his exes were still his friends.

"You're staring," teased a soft voice beside him.

He tore his gaze away from Steph's wide eyes to look at the woman next to him.

"Looks like she liked your gift," Amanda said with a fond smile. "Why didn't I ever get naked pics of you when we were dating?"

"You never asked."

Stephanie hadn't either, at least not in the verbal sense. He'd been staying late one night working on his billable hours. The goal was twofold—to get a decent cushion for the holiday time off work and also to forget about how he couldn't find a damn thing to give Steph that would get his foot in her door. The ploy wasn't working, so he'd stood and began to pace the hall that formed a ring around the center receptionist's desk and elevators.

That was when it caught his eye. The small, crumpled ball of paper missed or dropped by the nighttime cleaning crew. It was wedged next to the polished wood leg of their waiting room sofa. He'd picked it up with the intention of tossing it when a bit of red and green caught his eye. Steph had been using a cute little stocking-shaped notepad ever since the first of the month. Christmas was obviously one of her favorite holidays, if the tiny decorated tree on her desk was any indication. He knew instantly the festive bit of trash had once belonged to her, and it took on new meaning just because of that.

So feeling a bit guilty but unable to help himself, Nick opened the bit of trash…

And he'd been thanking his lucky stars ever since.

At the top of the striped paper were the words *Wish List* printed in a font designed to resemble a child's scrawl. Below that were the beautifully formed letters he recognized as Steph's handwriting.

Mom – new bread maker

Dad – deep sea fishing

Sam – gift card

And then she'd run a slash through that list and begun a new one.

My Wish List – (naughty)

Nicholas James naked and wrapped in a bow.

Nick kissing me senseless.

Nick cooking me dinner naked. (so I can stare at his ass)

Going down on Nick. (yum)

Nick going down on me. (double yum)

Fucking Nick until he can't walk.

The shock of that list had hit him so hard he'd stumbled into the nearby couch. He'd understood then that Stephanie had been fooling him the whole time, just like she would a jury. Acting unaffected when she was really as hot for him as he was for her. No woman had such detailed sexual thoughts about a guy she wasn't totally into. She'd obviously been thinking about him for a while.

Images inspired by her words filled his mind. His dick swelled and he wondered how he'd make it back to his office, let alone the parking garage eighteen floors below.

He needn't have worried. Her next shakily written line took all the heat out of him and left him cold.

My Wish List – (good)

Forget about Nicholas James or transfer.

In that moment he'd discovered two things. One—no matter how much she wanted his body, she still didn't want anything to do with *him*. To the point where she was considering transferring to their firm's other office across town.

Two—the thought of not seeing her nearly every day struck him like a physical blow. Too painful for his interest to be merely casual. He'd realized then what the tight knot in his gut was trying to tell him.

Somewhere along the way, the purely sexual desire he had for her had become something more. Maybe it'd happened when they'd worked that last case together and she kept blowing his mind with her brains. Or maybe it was when she'd cried over a verdict and hadn't tried to hide it from him. Whatever it was, he'd be damned if his past got in the way of what they both wanted.

This Christmas, not so saintly Nick was making sure all of Stephanie Martin's wishes came true.

Chapter Two

STEPH LEFT THE CONFERENCE room party the moment Nick's attention was drawn away. She had the next two weeks off. If she could just slip out of the office, she could get out of this mortifying situation.

She'd had a feeling when she threw out that stupid scrap of paper that she should rip it up first. Or burn it. But then she'd told herself she was just being paranoid. The damn thing was in the trash. Who was going to see it? Certainly not Nick. He didn't dig in trashcans. Or so she'd thought.

As her temper rose, her step quickened and she reached her office in record time. This was ridiculous. Those were private scribblings made during an especially boring meeting. She hadn't been able to concentrate with Nick sitting across from her and looking as impossibly gorgeous as ever. Instead, she'd been totally absorbed in staring at the small part of his wrist visible at the edge of his cuff—hair-dusted dark skin next to the gold of his watchband and the white of his shirt. That little flash of *nothing* had made her hot and damp between the thighs.

There was just something about Nicholas James. Maybe it was the dangerous beauty of his face. Or that tall, well-honed body. Perhaps it was his amazing intelligence and aggressive stance in the courtroom. Or maybe it was his pro bono work for the Abused Women's Program… Shit, she didn't know why. She just knew his track record with women was bad news and she'd already had enough bad news to last a lifetime.

She growled. That damn list had been a form of purging therapy. None of it was ever meant literally. Still, as she shoved documents into her briefcase, she grabbed the silver box with the X-rated photo of Nick and shoved it in too.

"Merry Christmas to me," she muttered.

"I'm just getting started," purred a deep voice in her ear. The delicious sound hit the top of her spine and then curled all the way down.

Mouth open to protest, she spun to face her tormentor.

And found herself hauled up against a rock-hard body and kissed senseless.

Taken completely off guard, by the time her addled brain figured out who was accosting her and what he was doing, she didn't want him to stop. As her senses filled with the scent of aroused male, the hands pushing against Nick's shoulders slipped around them instead.

God, he was good. Equal parts demanding and tender. His lips were warm, the inside of his mouth soft. His hands slipped between her jacket and blouse, splaying on either side of her spine and pulling her closer. When his touch slipped lower to cup her ass, heat flared outward and flushed her skin.

"Don't," she whispered against his mouth.

Groaning softly in answer, Nick tilted his head and deepened his already drowning kiss. He tugged, stealing her balance so that she tumbled into him. Taking the advantage, he lifted her and sat her on the desk, wedging his lean hips intimately between her thighs. Instantly the throbbing that had begun the minute he touched her turned into an all-consuming ache. "Nick…"

His damp forehead rested against hers, his panting breaths hot against her swollen lips. "Let me give you what you want for Christmas, Steph."

"I don't want you."

"Liar." His hand came up and cupped her breast. Expert fingertips found the hardened nipple that betrayed her. Kissing his way to her ear, he whispered, "I bet you're creamy for me."

"Jesus, Nick!" She shivered but couldn't deny it.

"I locked the door…"

"Are you crazy?" she shot back, pushing his wandering hand away.

Nick caught her hips, pulled her to the edge of the desk and fit the hard length of his cock directly against her pussy.

"Yes." He moved his hips, nudging her clit through the soft fabric of their dress pants. She whimpered.

"Don't you know how crazy I am about you?"

"You're crazy about all women."

"No," he argued, thrusting against her with greater urgency. "I *like* women. I'm crazy about you."

The sweet friction of his dry fucking made her sex spasm with need. With her heart racing and her breathing labored, she pushed at him weakly. "Stop that… I can't think…"

"You think too much." He held her in place as he rubbed his cock against her. She hadn't bothered with the lights when she'd entered, since moonlight lit the room through the floor-to-ceiling window. But even in the semi-dark, his eyes burned with a hunger that made her throat tight. Holding her still, he stroked the impressive length of his erection up and down her slit. He was so gorgeous, so determined, just watching him pleasuring them both was nearly orgasmic by itself. "I want you, Steph. I've wanted you a long time. And you want me too."

On the verge of coming, Steph set her hands on the desk and swiveled her hips into that large straining bulge, stroking him with her pussy. Nick's raw, pained moan was the impetus that pushed her over. Crying out, she rode the waves of pleasure that spread through her veins and made her dizzy.

"That's it," he praised hoarsely, rocking into her, making it last. "Ah, sweetheart. You're so beautiful."

She sagged into his chest as the tension fled. With her hot face pressed against his throat, the scent of his skin was nearly overwhelming. She groaned, wishing the earth would open up and swallow her whole. The last thing Nick's ego needed was her hair-trigger orgasm.

"It's been awhile for you, hasn't it?" His large hands stroked the length of her back, gentling her.

"You're not going to take credit for that?" She couldn't hide her surprise.

"Me?" He pulled back slightly. "I wish. That was all you. But the next one's on me."

A laugh escaped against her will and she buried her face in his shoulder to hide her smile. He was charming, she'd never denied that. "There's not going to be a next time."

His embrace was nearly crushing. "Whatever. You really had me fooled. Until I saw that wish list, I thought you didn't like me."

"It's not about whether I like you or not, Nick. In fact, I think you're a great guy, but—"

"You're looking for someone to get serious."

"Actually, I'm not looking for anyone."

"I could get serious." Cupping her face in his hands, he used his thumbs to stroke her cheeks. "There's no reason I can't. But we'll never know if you don't give me a chance."

"Why?" She pushed him away. "Because we have the hots for each other? Being horny isn't the basis for a relationship and I don't want to be your experiment in monogamy."

"There she is," he said softly, stepping back so she could slide off the desk. "The exterior woman who doesn't want me, while the real Steph inside does."

She winced. The real Steph had learned to give up some of the things she wanted. It was a sacrifice she'd accepted gladly when she made it. "Are we done here?"

"No way. Not nearly." He ran his hand through his thick, glossy hair.

She regretted that she hadn't touched it when she had the chance. "You didn't get off, but I don't feel too guilty about that. You can have any of the girls in the conference room."

"Fuck you, Steph," he said gruffly. "This isn't about getting laid and you know it."

She snorted. "This is all about getting laid."

Suddenly he straightened, his eyes lit with a dangerous glint. "Give me a couple days to go through your wish list. Then, once you've lived out your fantasies—all of which happen to be mine as well—we can get back to business as usual. Minus all this sexual tension."

"That's not going to work." But her stomach did a little flip at the thought.

"Then you switch offices anyway, like you planned. But at least we got to have wild, sweaty, dirty sex before you go. If this is all about getting laid, let's do it."

Oooh, he was good at arguing a case. He knew he'd had her from the word "wild" too. She could see it in his eyes. "A hotel?" she suggested, resigned. A girl had only so much willpower and faced with a watertight argument, what else could she do?

At least that's what her inner devil said.

"My place," he said smoothly, having the grace not to gloat. "I've got everything I need to cook dinner—" He flashed a dazzling grin. "Naked."

"Oh, Lord…" She was blushing, she could feel it. That he knew her secret longings was embarrassing in the extreme. And a major turn-on, which was dangerous. She had to keep the two separate—the lawyer she admired and the playboy she wanted to fuck. "Let's just keep this simple."

He reached into his pocket and pulled out a folded slip of paper. Tucking it in her hand, he brushed his lips across hers. "No. You've been a good girl, so you deserve to have your wishes come true." He kissed her again and it didn't escape her for a second that he was the star of her sex dreams. "Come on, Steph, play along. It'll be fun."

Fun. Guys like Nick were always having fun.

"That's directions to my condo. I'll be waiting."

By the time Steph got to Nick's place, she was balls to the wall committed to having a good time. If she was going to binge, she was gorging. Period. So when she rang the doorbell and Nick answered wearing nothing but a Santa hat and an apron that said "Kiss the Cook", she didn't hesitate. She dropped her mini-duffle at his feet and jumped him.

"Shit." He stumbled backward in surprise but managed to shove the door closed before spinning his way to the nearest couch. They fell into black leather in a puddle of semi-naked gorgeous male and determined female.

Straddling him, Steph leaned forward and kissed him hard and deep. His scent inundated her senses and her nipples hardened into aching points.

Nick groaned.

She sat up atop the hard ridge of his erection, an obvious sign that he was as ready as she. Digging into the pocket of her billowy gauze skirt, she pulled out a condom and tossed it on his chest. "Hurry up and put that on."

Blinking up at her, Nick sputtered, "Just like that? Wham, bam, let's fuck?"

"You complaining?"

"Hell, no." As she lifted to her knees to pull up her skirt, he fumbled for the foil package with comical haste. Then he glanced up and stilled, his gaze riveted between her legs. "Oh man. Steph... You're not wearing panties."

"Ooops. Must have forgotten those." She tucked the trailing hem into the elastic waistband.

Dropping the condom, he licked his lips. "Whose wish list are we working on here?"

The heat banked in his heavy-lidded eyes made her shiver. His Santa hat was askew, his dark hair pushed over his forehead. Adding in the apron, he should have looked silly. Instead, he looked edible. His arms were sexy as hell, the skin still bearing the remnants of a dark summer tan, the muscles beneath beautifully defined.

"Come here." The command was issued in a seductively husky voice that made goose bumps cover her skin despite the fire crackling in the fireplace.

"Come where?" she teased softly.

"Come in my mouth, sweetheart. I want to lap you up."

Yes, please...

Forcing herself to crawl over him slowly so she didn't look desperate, Steph kneeled astride his head. With one knee on the sofa armrest and the other on the very edge of the couch, she was spread wide, affording him an unhindered view. His warm hands slid up her thighs, his breath gusted over her sex. He squeezed her ass. She whimpered her excitement...

And then he licked her pussy in a long deliberate lap.

She clutched the back of the sofa like a lifeline and moaned. Kneading the backs of her thighs, he settled in to feast, gliding his tongue through her slit. Dipping inside her. Finding all the places that made her cry out and concentrating there before drifting away to find somewhere else. And then returning to stroke back and forth across her clit.

"Don't come too soon," he murmured as her legs began to shake.

"Are you kidding?" she gasped, her hips rocking into his busy mouth. "Don't be so good at this."

His chuckle was filled with pure masculine satisfaction. "I want to be fucking you when you come."

She shuddered violently. "You better hurry up with that condom then."

"I'm ready whenever you are."

"Huh?"

Nick's grin was pure wickedness. "I guess you were a little distracted."

Glancing down the couch, her eyes widened. He'd flipped up the apron and sheathed the object of her day and night dreams. Long, thick and arching up to his stomach, his erection made her mouth water. No wonder the man had that air about him that screamed *I know how to fuck your brains out.* The picture hadn't done him justice.

She swallowed hard and moved to straddle his hips. He angled his cock upward solicitously. Her chest tight and heart racing, Steph paused just above him. It was the point of no return. Nothing would ever be the same between them once they had sex. Could she handle that? Could she keep the distance she needed?

"Steph."

Her gaze shot up to meet his.

"Remember your list?" Nick's handsome face was flushed and his lips were slick with her cream, but despite the blatantly sexual look about him, his blue eyes shimmered with just as much compassion as lust. "It's okay to take what you want," he said softly. "Especially when it's given to you."

She took a deep breath. Suddenly, she registered the holiday music playing softly and the smell of pine from the small, undecorated tree in the corner. If she went home, she'd be alone right now. Or she could spend the night with Nicholas James.

She'd wanted this, wanted him. It was Christmas, damn it!

Slick with desire, she sank onto him slowly, taking the only thing she'd asked for this year. The only thing she'd asked for in many years. To be touched and held. To be wanted.

"Oh yeah," he groaned, his hands stroking along her thighs, his back arching. "Christ, you feel good."

Steph bit her lower lip as the languorous glide continued. He filled her too full. The heat and hardness of him stole her breath. The wonderful length and width… As her buttocks hit his muscular thighs and the head of his cock struck deep, the sound that was torn from her was raw and needy.

"I've got you," he soothed gruffly as she leaned over him, shaking. He stroked the length of her spine, murmuring, "Lift up a little… Shh, I'll give it to you… Right there. Now don't move."

His hips lifted, stroking her with a breathless thrust.

"*Nick.*" She buried her face in his neck, her pussy spasming around him. "Ah!"

He lowered and lifted again, fucking upward into her greedy depths. "How's that feel?" he panted.

"Like I'm losing my mind." She lifted her head and looked at him. His chest rose and fell harshly against her breasts, making her wish she'd taken the time to get naked so she could feel him skin to skin.

"Good. I'd hate to be the only one." Holding her hips steady, he quickened his pace, surging upward in a relentless rhythm, withdrawing until only the thick crest breached her and then plunging balls deep with primal grunts.

Keening softly, she clutched his shoulders and braced herself for the slap of his hips against hers. He felt so good… He smelled delicious…

Nick spoke through gritted teeth, "Don't wait for me." He punctuated his order with a brutally hard thrust that caught her clit in just the right spot.

Her orgasm was stunning. She was paralyzed, unable to move, every cell in her body focused on the rippling of her pussy along his endless length of hard cock. He jerked beneath her then crushed her to his chest, growling in her ear as he came.

Holding him, she listened to the violent beating of his heart and the soft sounds of music, and she felt cared for.

For the first time in a long time it felt like Christmas.

Chapter Three

NICK HELD STEPHANIE CLOSE and tried to focus his eyesight on the cobweb that hung in the corner. It was almost impossible. His brain and body felt like mush, which was really saying something considering how energized he'd been while waiting for her to arrive. He'd been worried she might not show and if that happened, there would be no way he could track her down until the office was open again. He had no idea how to reach her outside of work.

Then she'd rang the bell and he'd run to the door, feeling like a kid on his first date. And when she'd tackled him, he felt like a king.

He'd always known she would be like that, warm and open and sexy as hell. No shyness about her when it came to getting down and dirty. Just like when she argued a case, she gave one hundred percent to everything she did. Lucky for him, he got to be on the receiving end of that attention to detail.

And he wanted it to stay that way.

Steph wiggled just a tiny bit and it was enough to remind them both that his cock was still buried inside her. His balls gave a last weary twitch and his eyes slid closed in contentment. It'd been a long time since he'd come that hard and even longer since he'd cared this deeply about the woman he did it with.

"Nick?"

"Hmm?" He nuzzled against her neck.

"You didn't have anything on the stove, did you?"

Groaning, he said, "Nah, but the oven's on for the breadsticks."

She sighed. "We should probably go check on that."

It was the "*we*" that got to him. He'd wanted to be a "*we*" with Stephanie Martin for the last several months. Looking back now, he thought he knew when it'd hit him. She'd been standing in the break room talking to Charles from Entertainment and while laughing at something said to her, she'd met Nick's gaze and winked.

In that little blink of an eye, he'd fallen hard.

That tiny wink had said so much. It was playful and affectionate, and it had warmed him on the inside enough to know that out of all the women in his world, she was the one he wanted to spend his down time with.

Sliding off him carefully, Steph rose to her feet and wobbled a bit. When he stood, the same thing happened. His legs felt like jelly.

"Christ, Steph." He laughed and clutched her close. "You wrung me out."

Her blush was lovely and he hated to let her go, but he had dinner to cook. He needed to charm her with more than his bedroom skills. So after a quick kiss on the nose, he moved toward the kitchen. Catching up her duffle on the way, he set it on a dining chair and took note of the luggage tag.

"Stephanie Donovan?" he asked, as he pulled off the condom and tossed it.

She was righting her skirt and didn't look up. "My maiden name."

"I didn't know you were divorced." He turned on the faucet and studied her as he washed his hands.

"It's not something that comes up and I don't like to talk about it."

"That bad, huh?"

Nick dried his hands then turned to light the burner beneath the waiting pot of water. "Want some wine? A beer?"

"A beer would be nice, thanks." Steph took a seat on a barstool at the breakfast bar. "It wasn't bad. It just wasn't good."

He grabbed a couple longnecks out of the fridge, twisted off the tops and set one in front of her. "How long ago did you break up?"

"A couple years. Should have been sooner, but we were both too stubborn to admit it wasn't working."

Catching up her hand, he gave it a squeeze. "You hate to give up. It's what makes you such a damn good lawyer."

"Thanks." Her dark eyes sparkled with warmth at his compliment. "Tom and I never should have gotten married. We were friends in law school, nothing more. He was such a player, I never took him seriously. Then somehow we ended up together and I still can't figure out how or why."

"Love?"

"I thought so, but really I think we did it just because it was 'time', you know? Tom felt like he was at the age where he should get married. All of his colleagues were married and I think he started to feel a little out of place."

"I can see that," he admitted, resting his elbows on the granite countertop.

She wrinkled her nose and it hit him suddenly that he'd just been inside her, holding her, touching her however he wanted. It was the first time he could remember where he didn't forget the sex as soon as it was done. Fucking Steph was an addition to an already established relationship and not the entire reason for it.

Now if he could only change their professional relationship into a personal one. He had to admit, he was usually actively working to do just the opposite so he was out of his depth.

"Do guys have a marriage clock?"

He laughed. "Like a biological clock?"

"Yes."

"I guess there is some peer pressure after awhile. If you're thirty-something and single, even women start to think there must be something wrong with you or else some chick would've snapped you up." Turning away, he opened the fridge and pulled out the produce he'd chosen to make a salad with. He was a simple guy. Spaghetti, salad and breadsticks were about as much as he could do with confidence in a tasty outcome. "I personally don't care what people think."

"I would say that's pretty obvious."

The humor in her tone had him looking over his shoulder at her.

Steph was grinning. "This whole wish list thing is really a bad idea, but I have to admit, it's worth it to see you dressed like that."

"You're not laughing at me, are you?" He'd been a little nervous. Like anyone, he didn't want to look stupid in front of someone he wanted to sleep with. Bent over like he was, he knew she was getting an eyeful of every damn thing he had to offer.

"No." Her gaze was mischievous and warm. "I'm actually really impressed with you. You have enough confidence to wear that. I know I wouldn't be able to do it."

"Personally," —he turned with an armful of vegetables, which he dumped on the counter— "I'd like you in just the hat. That's my Christmas wish."

"You know…" Her fingers toyed with her beer.

"I know what?"

She sighed. "I really thought getting the sex out of the way would make me more comfortable."

"The sex isn't '*out of the way*'," he retorted, pulling a knife out of the wooden block next to him. "Just say what you're thinking.

I'm the one wearing nothing but a Santa hat, apron and a smile, so you've got no business being shy about anything."

"Thank you," she blurted, her gaze focused on the beer label she was removing from the bottle. "I don't care why you did it. I don't care if you just want to get laid. I'm flattered you went to all this trouble."

Nick paused with his knife halfway through a cucumber and stared at her. "It wasn't any trouble, Steph. I like giving you what you want, I like seeing you smile."

She blew out her breath and fiddled with her collar. "Do you need my help with anything?"

It wasn't like her to be so nervous or to switch subjects because she was uncomfortable, which told him she wasn't dealing too well with tonight's events. He knew it was a lot to throw at her—the photo, the wish list, the sex. Before the Secret Santa exchange they'd been nothing but distant co-workers. Now they were lovers. He'd had a couple months to adapt to his changing feelings for her. She's had a couple hours. She was asking for a little space and he had no problem giving it to her.

"No, I've got it covered. Go watch TV or something. It won't be too much longer."

"Okay. I'm going to wash up then."

He gestured toward the hallway with a toss of his chin. "First door on the right."

Steph locked gazes with Nick for a long moment and knew she was in trouble. He didn't have that air about him that said, *Thanks for the fuck, you can go now.* No, his vibe was very homey and relaxed. And she was falling for it like a ton of bricks.

Somehow she made it down the short hallway to the bathroom, where she leaned against the vanity and stared in the mirror. The glazed look in her eyes and the flush on her cheeks made her wince.

Damn it, she didn't need this right now! A relationship was completely out of the question on a good day, but to fall for a guy who had "temporary" written all over him was just plain stupid. Hadn't she learned anything at all from her years with Tom?

Apparently not.

When dinner was done, she was going home. They'd both gotten what they wanted.

It was time to minimize the damage.

"That was wonderful."

Steph smiled at Nick as she set her fork down, not the least bit concerned that she'd cleaned her plate. They'd eaten together many times over the last year and after the first time he'd praised her hearty appetite, she'd ceased being concerned about appearances.

"You're either too generous or you were really hungry." He stood and picked up her plate from the small oak dining table. Featuring a pine centerpiece lit by three red tapers, it was both inviting and unexpected. There was so much about him she didn't know. But she wanted to learn. Nick wasn't good relationship material, but he was a fascinating guy, a great lawyer and a good friend from what she'd heard.

She watched him walk into the kitchen, his fine ass flexing as he took each step. Occasional glimpses of his cock and balls kept her hot, and she grabbed her napkin to dab at the fine sheen of sweat that misted her forehead. He was also a fantastic and generous lover, but then she'd always suspected that and heard innuendo to the same.

The urge to bolt she'd felt in the bathroom earlier was now suddenly overwhelming.

It was time to go.

Standing, she reached for her duffle. It was rude to leave without offering to clean, but maybe a little animosity between them would be a good thing.

"What are you doing?" he asked behind her, the volume of his voice telling her that he was still some distance away.

"I'm going to head out," she said with forced casualness, even as her heart raced. "Thanks for a great evening."

Suddenly, she was crowded into the table from behind by a very hard body. "Talk to me, Steph." His palms flattened on the surface, caging her in place.

"We've been talking all through dinner."

"About everything except us."

"There is no '*us*'."

One of his hands reached into the pocket of her skirt.

"How many condoms did you bring? Feels like you've got half a dozen in here." He tossed one onto the tabletop. "You were planning for a busy night. Now, all of a sudden, you're done?"

"Yeah, well." She took a deep breath. "I didn't expect you to be so good. You took care of things the first go-round."

"Bullshit. You're as hot for it now as you were when you jumped me." Wrapping a hand around her throat, he tilted her head back. He nipped her ear with his teeth and she shivered. "What's got you running scared?"

She stiffened. "I'm not scared. I just think we both got what we wanted and it's best to end the night before it gets complicated."

"Guess what?" Nick bent his knees and rubbed the hard

length of his cock between the cheeks of her ass. Somewhere between the kitchen and the dining room he'd lost the apron. With only the thin layer of her gauze skirt between them, she felt every millimeter of his arousal. "I'm not finished getting what I wanted and it's already complicated."

"Nick…" Her eyes closed on a whimper as he cupped the weight of one breast. Heat flared across her skin. She was suddenly more than hot, she was burning up, melting. He smelled like heaven and felt even better. She'd had a ton of daydreams about him, but they'd always been raw. Carnal. Fucking on her desk or his. Buttons flying everywhere. Rough hands and bruising lips. Never had there been this gentleness, this concern for her feelings and pleasure.

"You had a wish list, Steph. Fantasies about me. Tell me why you don't want to live them out anymore." The pads of his fingers brushed across her nipple and it peaked into a hard, aching tip.

"Fantasies aren't meant to come true."

"Mine did. Yours too."

"That's the problem," she muttered.

His hand left her breast and lifted her skirt, bunching it in his fists. She should stop him, wiggle away. He wouldn't keep her against her will, despite the forearm that crossed between her breasts and the grip that held her neck. But the energy she needed to escape just wasn't there. It had been so long since she'd been held with such tender lust, she didn't have the heart to reject it.

"Did I become too real?" he breathed in her ear. "Do you like me, Steph? Just a little?"

A little too much.

Cool air hit her buttocks the moment before he stepped closer. His cock was so hard, so hot against her skin.

His open mouth nuzzled against her throat. "Stay with me." Reaching beneath her skirt, he parted her and stroked her clit. A soft fluttering touch, circling then pressing. Rubbing. "Be with me."

"Nick." Her eyes drifted closed on a soft moan. She was wet, nearly soaked, and she ached for him. She was starving for the affection he gave so freely. It scared her how needy she was. Until tonight, she hadn't realized how lonely her life had become.

"Open the packet," he urged, his voice like rough silk.

She reached blindly for the condom, steeling the reserve she'd had when she arrived. *Enjoy him*, her heart said, and she would. One last time.

"We're so good together, Steph." Nudging her legs apart, he slipped two fingers inside her, moving in and out in a deep glide. "In every way that matters." The hand at her throat lowered to cup her breast again. It was heavier, full with desire for him. Expert fingers stroked over her nipple, pinched it, fondled it through her thin shirt and satin bra. That teasing touch radiated outward and left her gasping.

"Here." She thrust her arm back with the open packet in her hand.

Nick reached for the condom with shaking fingers. Steph had been ready to leave. More than ready. She'd been nearly out the door. And he knew in his gut if he couldn't get through to her before she left, he never would.

"Bend over," he said gruffly.

When his fingers left her soaked cunt, she made a soft sound of protest. "Hush," he soothed, pushing gently on her lower back until she bent across the table. "Let me give you my cock instead."

He stared at the erotic view as he sheathed himself in latex. All the times he'd watched her at work and thought lewdly, he'd never quite pictured the view correctly. Her lips were flushed, swollen, glistening. He wanted to lick her again and did, a quick swipe of his tongue that had her writhing. Taking himself in hand, he used the tip of his cock to tease her clit, to make her cream, to see her squirm for him.

And then he caught her hips and slid deep into her.

"Oh!" she breathed, her fingers scratching at his table.

Her cunt was burning hot and tight as a fist. "Fuck, yeah," he groaned, his balls drawn up tight and aching. He withdrew and watched his thick shaft slide out of her, slick with her arousal, and then groaned as he pressed back in. Holding her hips, he stared at the place where they joined, arrested by the sight of him fucking her as he'd wanted to for so long.

"Nick."

The sound of his name spoken so morosely tugged at his heart. Hunching forward, he laced his fingers with hers and began thrusting in short shallow digs, his stomach rippling against her lower back. Her pleading gasps goaded him, incited him to bend his knees so he could stroke her pussy high and hard with the broad head of his dick.

With his cheek at her shoulder, he asked, "How can you give this up, Steph?"

She answered with a whimper and then hitched her hips up higher so he could pump deeper. Widening his legs, he gave her the long deep plunges that made her moan helplessly and drove him crazy. He released her hands, moving one of his to cup her breast and the other to pin her hips in place so he could swivel his pelvis and screw his cock through her grasping ripples.

"Give me a chance," he gasped, shuddering with the need to come, with the need to keep her close until he could change her mind.

"You don't…know…"

Reaching beneath her, he pinched her clit and thrust balls deep. With a cry she came, clutching his dick greedily, milking him in a sensual massage. "Give me a chance, damn you."

Her "*yes*" was a whisper, but he heard it. His release was silent, his teeth gritted, his cock jerking as it pumped his cum into her.

He should have felt relief. He should have felt some sense of security.

But he didn't.

Chapter Four

IT WAS THE SOUNDS of shuffling paper that woke her. Stretching on the black leather sofa, Steph opened her eyes and turned her head to find Nick wrapping gifts. Or trying to.

"You're mangling that wrap job," she murmured, vaguely remembering being lifted in the dining room and carried to the couch. The fire still crackled merrily, music still played softly. Despite the fact she was in a strange place, it felt like home.

Dressed in worn gray sweatpants, Nick sat within touching distance. He twisted at the waist and tossed his arm over her legs. "I'm trying not to, but the more effort I put into it, the worse I seem to do."

"Need some help?"

He nodded and gave her a boyish smile. With evening stubble along his jaw and finger-mussed hair, he was almost too gorgeous. Angled toward her like he was, the beautifully defined muscles of his chest and arms stood out in stark relief. She hesitated and then gave in to the urge to touch his hair. It was thick and silky, making her shiver with renewed desire. Then he turned his head to kiss her wrist and her stomach did a little flip.

It was going to take her a long time to get over him.

Blowing out a resigned breath, she sat up and maneuvered herself into position straddling his back. He leaned into her and yawned. Shooting a glance at the clock on the mantle, she saw it was two in the morning.

"Being tired might be the reason you're not wrapping well,"

she said dryly. "Why don't you go to sleep and we'll go over how to wrap in the morning?"

He linked his arms around her calves and looked at her upside down. "If I go to sleep, will you still be here in the morning?"

"Oh, Nick." Steph leaned her cheek against the top of his head. "Don't be silly."

"You're talking to a guy who cooked dinner naked."

Nuzzling her mouth into his hair, she changed the subject. "Do you have double-sided tape?"

"Huh? That sounds kinky."

She laughed and fell a little in love. "For your presents."

"Oh… Bummer. No. Just the regular clear stuff."

"Okay, sex maniac." She looked over his shoulder. "Let's see what you've got."

He turned his head and kissed her cheek.

Her heart clenched, and she had to clear her throat before she spoke. "You have too much paper on the ends. That's why it's hard for you to fold them without bunching it up."

Nick took up the scissors and cut. "Like that? Is that enough?"

"Yeah." She slipped her arms beneath his and demonstrated how to tuck the corners. "Now put some tape right there."

"Here?" His voice had deepened. With her breasts pressed to his back and her nose by his throat, their position was unbearably intimate.

"That's perfect," she breathed, releasing the gift and drawing back. He caught her hands before they left his lap.

Cupping her hands over his pecs, Nick whispered, "Touch me."

She swallowed hard as his skin heated under her hands. The tips of her fingers found the flat points of his nipples and rubbed gently. Groaning, his arms fell to his sides.

He leaned his head back into her lap and the sight of his face lost in pleasure was too much for her. Steph looked away, taking in the glass-topped coffee table, the flat-screen TV and the bare Christmas tree by the sliding glass door.

"Don't you have any ornaments?" she asked.

"No." His voice was a low whisper of sound. "I bought the tree for you and forgot the damn ornaments."

Her hands stilled. "For me?" *Oh my God, I'm going to cry.*

"Yeah, I knew from that notepad of yours and the little tree on your desk that you must really like Christmas. I do too, but since I'm going to my sister's for holiday dinner, I hadn't bought one for myself. For you, though, I figured it wouldn't be much of a Christmas wish if it didn't feel like Christmas around here."

Wiggling around, she switched from straddling his back to straddling his hips. Face to face, they stared at each other.

"I'm sorry I forgot the ornaments," he said.

And then he cupped the back of her neck and kissed her.

Unlike the deep possessive kiss he'd given her in her office, this kiss was coaxing, his lips brushing, his tongue flicking softly. Steph wrapped her arms around him and kissed him back with everything she had. In gratitude. In lust. In love.

She pulled away and gasped, "What do *you* want for Christmas?"

"This. You. Making love with you." He rocked his hips and she felt how aroused he was.

A gift that required no wrapping. No words. She lifted her skirt, he tugged down his sweats. She sheathed him. First in latex, then with her body. He groaned, she cried out. They moved together, without the haste that had marked their previous encounters. Her hands on his bare shoulders, she took him deep, rising and falling in tempo with the sounds he made. Clenching her muscles to stroke his thick length. Pulling off her shirt and bra to press her bare skin to his.

"I've wanted you," he said hoarsely, guiding her hips with shaking hands. "So badly… Christ, you feel amazing."

Steph made it last, in no hurry for their time together to end. But it did, of course.

Dawn came too swiftly. As the pink light of the early rising sun came into the room through the sliding glass door, she tucked a blanket around Nick and picked up her duffle.

"Merry Christmas," she whispered, pausing on the threshold a moment before shutting out the view of Nick asleep on the couch.

The clicking of the latch said the goodbye she couldn't.

"Well, this is a surprise," Amanda said as she pulled the door wide. "It's been over a year since you last darkened my doorstep, Nicholas James. And you looked a hell of a lot better then than you do now."

He gave a curt nod before dropping a kiss on her forehead. "I need a favor, Mandy, and I hope it doesn't make me an asshole for asking. Do you know where Stephanie lives?"

The petite blonde blinked up at him. "Wow. Okay, hang on a sec. That hurt a little." She blew out her breath and stepped out of the way. "Come in."

Nick stepped inside but hovered by the doorway. Three damn days had passed since he last touched Steph and if he didn't get to her soon, he was pretty sure he'd go insane.

Mandy stared at him a moment and then walked to the kitchen counter where her purse waited. "I'm over you, I swear I am." She pulled out her BlackBerry and a pen. While writing she said, "I still have to ask why Steph's the one that got to you."

"Hell. What kind of question is that?" He ran his hand through his hair.

"I don't know. I guess I'm just wondering if what they say

about *The Rules* is true. Is playing hard-to-get the way to land the great guys?" She came toward him and held out a business card with an address on the back.

Relief flooded him. He tucked the precious card in his pocket. "Maybe in the beginning the chase is fun. Now it just sucks. Thanks for this, Mandy. Really."

"Hey, Nick."

He paused on the threshold, his impatience nearly overwhelming. "What?"

"You're not heading over there now, are you? Steph and Kevin were—"

"Who the fuck is Kevin?" Every muscle tensed at the sound of Stephanie's name linked with another guy's.

Amanda's eyes widened. "Oh shit... You don't know."

"Obviously not." He strode back into the living room. "But you're going to tell me."

She sighed. "You better take a seat."

Nick watched out the window of his car as Stephanie exited her Grand Cherokee and started up the icy walkway from her driveway toward her front door. The house where she lived was quaint and cozy, with soft touches that were clearly Steph's that made the residence a home. She looked sad and he knew why. He'd watched her leave with Kevin Martin just an hour ago. Now she was alone.

Steph had a family.

He was the outsider.

Steeling himself inwardly, he stepped out into the chilly afternoon air and shut his door with enough force to catch her attention. She looked over her shoulder and came to an abrupt halt. He walked toward her with a purposeful stride, part angry and part really fucking hurt.

"What are you doing here?" she asked, her voice low and slightly panicked.

He didn't answer. Instead, he pulled his hands out his coat pockets and pulled her close, his mouth finding hers. The moment her lips met his, he groaned. When her momentary hesitation melted into desperate ardor, he knew he had a chance.

She still wanted him.

Lifting her feet from the ground, he carried her to the door. "Open it."

"Nick—"

"I suggest you hurry up if you don't want to shock your neighbors."

Fumbling nervously, Steph shoved the key in the lock and when the knob turned, he crowded in behind her, kicking the door shut with his booted foot. She turned and he pushed her against the foyer wall.

"I've missed you," he said hoarsely, his hands wandering restlessly in an attempt to feel her through the bulky jacket she wore. "Every goddamned minute since you left me, I've missed you."

"Don't do this, Nick." She leaned her head back and then gasped when his teeth scraped her neck. "We had a deal. The wish list, and then we'd be done."

"But we're not done," he argued. "We're nowhere near done. And if I have anything to say about it, we'll never be done."

"What?"

Stephanie stared up into Nick's gorgeous but pissed-off features and felt like she was going to pass out. His jaw was shadowed with stubble, his blue eyes rimmed with red. His hair was spiked from agitated fingers and his beautiful mouth was harshly drawn. He simply looked like hell, but her heart swelled with happiness at the sight of him.

"I love you, Steph." He caught her hand and pressed it over his heart. "Feel that? That's panic. I'm terrified you're going to say that's not enough, when that's all I've got to give you."

Tears welled and dripped from her lashes. "Kevin—"

"You should have told me about your son, Steph. I've been going nuts trying to figure out why I can't have you." Catching her zipper, Nick tugged it down and shoved her jacket to the floor.

"Now you know why this isn't going to work," she said, her voice shaky.

"I don't know shit, Steph. Because you didn't tell me." Shoving his hands beneath her top, he squeezed her breasts and she melted in his hands. "Think quick. The bed or right here on the floor."

"God."

She stumbled away, backing down the hallway as he stalked her. With wide eyes and a racing heart, she watched as he shed his jacket and then his shirt. When he reached for the button fly of his jeans, she swallowed hard. The tender lover she'd known three nights ago was gone and the thrill that coursed through her made her dizzy.

"Nick…"

"I'd lose the sweater if I were you. You'll be sweaty enough without it." He shoved his waistband just low enough to free his fully engorged cock and heavy balls. Then he reached into his back pocket for a condom and sheathed himself even as he stalked her.

Yanking her sweater over her head, she faced forward and nearly ran the remaining distance to her room. Nick was right on her heels. She was barely to the foot of her bed before she got her bra loose and then he was on top of her, his long lanky body sinking into hers. The crisp curls of his chest scraped her nipples and she gasped, opening her mouth to his questing tongue. A low groan rumbled deep in his chest and he tugged at her jogging pants.

"Off."

She squirmed desperately, kicking. "I'm trying."

"Try harder."

Laughing, she wiggled free and then his hand was between her legs, stroking her pussy and rubbing her clit. She wasn't laughing anymore—she was whimpering and arching up into his hard body.

"Did you miss me?" he growled, biting her earlobe.

"Yes... Ummm... too much."

Two fingers slipped inside her and stroked, making her cream.

"Spread your legs."

Nick came over her, nudging her thighs wider with his lean hips before he took her in a deep, breathtaking thrust. Then he wrapped his fist in her dark hair and began to fuck her within an inch of her life.

"Nick!" Steph writhed beneath him, trying to move but held still by the prison of her bound hair and his pumping cock.

He leaned his weight on one elbow and used his free hand to pull her leg over his hip so he could plunge to the hilt. She watched him, every nerve ending in her body hot and tingling, her breath panting. The waistband of his jeans rubbed against her inner thighs, a constant reminder that he couldn't bear another moment without being inside her.

"This isn't about getting laid," he insisted hoarsely.

"I know." Her hands clung to his straining, sweating back.

"This isn't temporary."

"I-I..." Her pussy fluttered along his cock. "I know."

Burying his face in her neck, he said, "I love you" against

her ear and she melted. Into the bed, into him, into an orgasm that made her cry out his name. And he filled her with love.

With hope.

Nick tucked her cheek against his damp shoulder and said, "Talk to me, Steph. Tell me what you're thinking so we both get on the same page."

She gave a lame shrug. "I don't know where to begin."

"Start with the ex," he suggested. "Tell me about him."

"Tom's a great guy. He's handsome and charming, a caring dad. But he couldn't commit to me. I think he really wanted to, but he couldn't."

"Sweetheart, I'm not like Tom. Just because I waited for you to come along doesn't mean I've got commitment issues."

"He's got a new girlfriend every month," she rushed on. "Kevin has a little notepad he takes to his dad's to write down their names so he doesn't mess up and use the wrong one. He did that once and it was a mess." She reached down and stroked his bare hip. "I can't do that to him, Nick."

He nuzzled against her. "I'm not asking you to do that. I'm asking you to let me in. Make room for me in your life, someplace permanent. Let me love you, be with you. You won't regret it."

As his blue eyes began to glisten, something inside her softened. "I'm scared. For my son. For me."

"I know. I'm scared too." He pressed his lips to hers. "I'm scared you're going to send me away because you can't trust me."

The last three nights without him had been hell. She'd missed the feel of him holding her, making love to her, making her feel special and cared for. She missed the way he made her laugh and how good she felt when she was with him. "I want to trust you," she whispered.

"Then do it! Listen to me, Steph." He rose up on his elbow to look down at her. "Being a single mom doesn't mean your life is over."

"It means my needs come second. I can't—" She closed her eyes. "You don't understand. It was hard for Kev. I was a wreck when Tom and I broke up. And I didn't even love him anymore."

"But you love me." Nick cupped her face in his hands. "A little. Enough to be scary. And I'm glad you love me because I'm head over heels for you."

The look in his eyes told her he was laying it all out there, making himself vulnerable.

"I-I don't know what to say."

"Say you'll give us a chance. You're used to running the show, and you can keep on running it. I just want to be the guy you lean on when you need to recharge. I want to be the guy who holds you when you're tired and makes love to you when you're not. I want to be the guy you come home to every day."

"There won't be any sleepovers for awhile," she warned, needing him to cast aside any romantic illusions.

"We'll take long lunches."

"A lot of nights you won't see me. I can't do the dinner and date thing often. Kevin only goes to his dad's every other weekend and part of every holiday."

"I know I'll take the backseat to your son. I'm okay with that. In fact, I love you for that."

The tears wouldn't quit and the knot in her throat made it hard to speak. "Kevin might not warm up to you right away."

Nick pulled her closer. "I know that too."

Steph frowned. "Have you dated a single mom before?"

"No. But my friend Chris just married into a similar

situation. We met for lunch today and talked about it. I talked to his wife, Denise, too so I could try to see things the way you do."

"You did?" The image in her mind of Nick approaching his friends to discuss his feelings and fears made her cry harder. She hugged him tight, silently conveying her endless gratitude.

"I wanted to know what to expect. I wouldn't have come here like this without doing my homework. That wouldn't be fair to any of us."

"So you know it won't be easy."

"I'm not asking for easy, sweetheart. I'm asking for a chance to make you happy."

She didn't know whether to laugh or keep crying. So she did both. "You're *The One*." Kissing his face, she pressed him back and climbed over him. "This whole year you've been right here and I couldn't see it."

"I love you, Steph." His lopsided smile made her heart race. With a lock of dark hair falling over his brow, he looked younger and vulnerable. Lying on her holiday quilt, he was the most perfect present she could ever imagine.

She pressed her lips to his. "You made all my wishes come true."

"Actually…" He grinned. "We missed one."

"Did we?" Thinking back, her eyes widened as her mouth curved. "Yes, we did."

Licking her lips, Stephanie slid down his body.

Nick closed his eyes with a contented sigh. "Merry Christmas to me."

What
Happened
in
Vegas

IT WAS 115 DEGREES in Las Vegas, but Paul Laurens could have sworn the temperature dropped from the chill in his former lover's gaze.

Robin Turner entered the Mondego Hotel's ground-floor lounge like a gust of arctic air. Her long blonde hair was restrained in a sleek chignon and her lush body was encased in a pale blue dress that wrapped around her curves and tied at the waist. Nude-colored heels gave the impression that she was barefoot, while a chunky aquamarine necklace circled her throat like ice cubes.

Paul's grip on his beer bottle tightened and his dick thickened in his jeans. How they'd ended up in bed together was still a mystery to him. One minute they were riding the same elevator and the next he was riding her, the attraction so fierce and immediate he couldn't remember how they reached his room or even shed their clothes.

Taking a long pull on his beer, his gaze followed Robin's progress across the barroom. She approached a booth where a guy in a suit stood to greet her. The man kissed each of her cheeks before they sat. Paul knew he couldn't stay in the same room with her and not have her, so he gestured for the bartender and ordered a martini extra-dirty to be sent to her table.

"Your brews are popular," one of the cocktail waitresses said as she collected the drink and placed it on her tray. Her smile was an invitation. The way she looked him over made sure he got the message.

"I'm glad to hear that," he replied, breaking eye contact to convey his lack of interest. Convincing the Mondego to carry his microbrews had been his first toehold in Vegas. The resort's contract funded his biweekly trips to pitch his product to other establishments in the area, which in turn had allowed him to have Robin for a year. His weekends with her had been the most valuable and treasured blocks of time in his life.

Until four months ago, when he'd fucked up and lost her.

Tossing some bills on the bar, Paul vacated his barstool and carried his beer out to the elevators. He'd left flowers for Robin with the front desk, along with his room number in a note. Although he knew she must have checked in yesterday, she hadn't contacted him. He'd tried to convince himself that she was busy getting ready for the jewelry trade show that opened today in the hotel, but that look she'd just shot him proved the lie. His only consolation was that she wasn't indifferent to him. He could only hope that meant she wasn't totally over him. He'd take whatever he could get from her right now—an argument, a slap to the face, anything at all. As long as it gave him the opportunity to say what needed to be said.

He was stepping into the elevator when he smelled her. Inhaling deeply, Paul pulled the fragrance of vanilla and something flowery deep into his lungs. Awareness sizzled down his spine and fisted his balls, his dormant sexual needs stirring after months without her. He hit the button for his floor, then moved to the back of the car and turned around. As Robin took up a position beside him, anticipation thrummed through his veins. He briefly wondered what excuses she'd made to her companion, then he pushed the thought aside. He didn't give a shit. The only thing that mattered was that she'd followed.

An elderly couple and three suit-clad gentlemen entered the car and faced the doors. As the elevator began its ascent, Robin balanced on one stiletto, drawing Paul's gaze. He watched as she pushed her underwear down, pulling one leg free and then the other.

Jesus. His dick throbbed with eagerness and fantasies of stepping behind her, lifting her dress, and pushing into her right there filled his mind.

A soft ding signaled the first stop. The businessmen got off and four teenagers in bathing suits got on. Training his gaze straight ahead, Paul reached over and slipped his hand between the overlapping front of Robin's dress. She sidestepped closer, putting him slightly in front of her, inviting his touch. He cupped her baby-soft hairless pussy, his fingers curling between her legs and finding her hot and damp. His dick swelled further and he finished his beer to hide a telling groan.

The car stopped again and the elderly couple exited. As the teenagers moved out of their way, the lone girl in the group glanced at Paul. Interest flared in her kohl-rimmed dark eyes. She checked him out, reading his brewery's logo on his T-shirt and eyeing the tattoo that peeked out from beneath the sleeve. She was following the line of his arm down to where he was parting the lips of Robin's cunt when the two boys with her spread out in the absence of the couple and cut off her view.

Robin sucked in a sharp breath when he pushed his middle finger inside her. Her tight, plush sex sucked at him greedily, and his eyes grew heavy-lidded, lust riding him hard. Pressing his heel to her clit, he massaged her, getting her ready for the pounding drives of his cock. He'd meant to talk with her first, but she was hot for it and God knew he was hot to give it to her. Stumbling through his life without her had been torture. At times, he thought he'd go insane from the need to hear her voice and feel her body against his.

The kids stepped off at the next stop. The car continued

its ascent to the forty-fifth floor with only the two of them on board.

"I've missed you," he said gruffly.

In answer, she thrust her desire-slick pussy into his hand. "You've missed this."

Her cool voice sliced into him, but her body betrayed her. She was scorching hot and delectably wet. As he finger-fucked her juicy cunt, soft sucking noises filled the car. Her composure lost, she gripped the brass handrail and moaned, shamelessly widening her stance.

The moment the car reached his floor, Paul pulled his fingers free and caught her up, tossing her over his shoulder and dropping his empty bottle in the trash can conveniently placed just outside the elevator. He had a condom between his teeth and his keycard in hand before he reached his suite. Kicking the door open, he propped Robin against the inside of the stationary half of the double-door entrance. His button fly was open before the latch clicked shut.

His jeans dropped to the entryway's tile, the weight of his chained wallet hitting the floor with a *thud*. A moment later, her lacy underwear fell from her fingers and fluttered down. As he sheathed his cock in latex, Robin pulled her dress up to take him. Paul paused to look at her, his chest tightening. She was unruffled elegance above the waist and a walking wet dream below it. Her legs were long and lithe, her sex pouty and glistening.

He'd been dead when she came into his life, frozen in grief over the death of his son and the subsequent dissolution of his already-broken marriage. That first elevator ride with Robin had been like a flipped switch, jolting him out of his coma. She'd forced the air back into his lungs and the blood back through his veins. He had begun to live for the weekends he spent with her, craving her laughter and smiles, her touch and her scent.

But when she'd suggested they take their relationship to the next level, he had panicked, prompting her to walk out on him with her head held high and his heart in her hands.

Reminded of how damned lucky he was to have her ready and willing again, Paul pinned her slender body against the door and took her mouth in a lush, hot kiss. His lips sealed over hers, his tongue gliding along the lower curve before slipping inside. She was stiff at first, resistant, which got his guard up. When it came to physical intimacy, they'd never had any barriers between them.

As he stroked his tongue along hers, Robin reached for his cock and slung one leg around his waist. She jacked him with both hands, making him so hard and thick he groaned into her mouth and slickened her fingers with pre-cum. She used him to prime herself, massaging the tiny knot of her clitoris with the head of his dick. Impatient, he brushed her hands aside and tucked his cockhead into her slit. She was so ready, he slipped through her wetness and sank an inch inside her. As her cunt fluttered around him, his chest heaved with the loss of his control. What he wanted was to nail her to the door with pounding thrusts; what she needed was to know that he was committed to making their relationship work.

"Hurry," she hissed.

Before he could rein himself in, her hands gripped his ass and yanked him into her. The unexpected thrust sent him tunneling deep. His palms hit the door on either side of her head and a curse burst from his lips.

"Robin, baby," he growled. "Give me a damn minute."

But she was already coming. With her head thrown back against the door and a purely erotic moan of pleasure, her cunt tightened around his aching dick like a tender fist. When the delicate muscles began milking his length in incredible ripples, he lost it.

"Ah, shit," he gasped, feeling his balls tighten and semen rush to the tip of his cock. Gripping her ass in the palms of his hands, Paul fucked her convulsing pussy like a mad man, banging her with hammering strokes. The violent orgasm was the rawest of his life, the pleasure so pure and hot he couldn't stop the growls that tore from his throat. Or the words. "Robin... fuck... I love you, baby. Love you..."

Dripping with sweat and shaking, he sagged into her as the white-hot ecstasy eased, his hips grinding mindlessly as he emptied himself inside her.

She shuddered in his arms and a soft sob escaped her. "God... You're an ass, Paul. You know that?"

Fucking brilliant. He finally told her how he felt and it lacked all grace or romance. She'd walked away thinking he just wanted to get laid, and he'd hardly redeemed himself by cursing out his feelings in the middle of a full-throttle, no-preliminaries screw that had probably been heard by every guest on the floor.

His forehead touched hers.

Her arms fell to her sides, her exhales gusting over the perspiration-damp skin of his throat. "I have to go."

Paul's gut knotted. He couldn't let her walk out again. He wouldn't survive it a second time. Gripping her behind the thighs, he hefted her up and kicked free of his boots and wide-legged jeans. In just his socks and shirt, with his dick still hard and buried in the sweetest pussy in the world, he carried her to the bedroom on shaky legs. "Not until you hear me out."

"I heard you loud and clear the last time."

Gritting his teeth, he pulled free of her and dropped her on the bed. Before she could scramble away, he caught her ankles and lifted her legs high and spread them wide. He looked down at her succulent pink pussy, the plump folds glistening with her desire. "I wasn't done. I'm not done."

"*I'm* done."

He licked his lips, hungry for the taste of her. "We'll see about that."

Recognizing the intent in Paul's hazel eyes, Robin struggled to back away before he destroyed her again. She loved a man who was damaged. She could work with that if Paul wanted to heal, but he didn't. The look on his face when she'd suggested they rendezvous in his hometown of Portland had told her all she needed to know—she was his biweekly screw, his hot piece in Vegas. And everyone knew what happened in Vegas stayed in Vegas.

She'd walked out of his hotel room that night with the intention of not looking back. She had told herself Paul Laurens was just a brief spate of madness in her life. But watching him leave the bar just now had been too much for her. She'd left her brother at the table without a word, chasing a man she couldn't recover from.

One last screw, she'd told herself. And then it would be over.

Idiot. She craved him like a junky, and one fix was never enough.

Paul sank to his knees between her legs, and her womb clenched greedily. Her pussy trembled with its eagerness to have his mouth on her; her clit throbbed with the need to feel his tongue stroking over it. He held her open with his hands on the backs of her thighs, his gaze riveted to her intimate flesh.

"I've been dying to eat you," he said gruffly. "I've jacked off a dozen times thinking about it. Get comfortable, baby. We'll be here awhile."

"I have meetings to attend!" she protested. "I can't—oh, god!"

The first stroke of his tongue stole her wits. It was a soft, slow lick that fired every sensitive nerve ending. The next pass was more deliberate, working her clit with the ball of his barbell piercing. His groan vibrated against her, making her pussy spasm in want of his cock to fill it.

Her hands fisted the comforter.

"You're so sweet," he praised hoarsely, his hands sliding down to her inner thighs. "Your cunt is so soft."

A soft noise escaped her.

His mouth sealed over her clit in a heated circle, his pierced tongue fluttering over the hard knot with devastating strokes. Her hips moved without her volition, thrusting and rocking as she chased another orgasm. In her past, she'd been lucky to come once with a partner. With Paul, the more he touched her, the more sensitized she became. Each climax came quicker than the one before it until she was coming in rolling waves that seemed to have no end or beginning.

"Fuck me with your tongue," she gasped, draping one leg over his powerful shoulder to urge him closer. Her back arched as he obliged her, teasing her quivering slit with shallow thrusts. Gripping his overlong hair, she rode his mouth, shameless in the extremity of her need.

She'd watched people dismiss Paul out of hand because of his appearance. Those who clung to stereotypes saw mobile homes and biker gangs when they looked him. They couldn't see past the stubble-shadowed jaw and visible tattoos. But beneath the body jewelry, ink, and shaggy hair was a gorgeous face that was classical in its lines and features. Paul could have graced an ancient coin or inspired a statue in a temple, and he was far wealthier than people would ascertain from his laid-back style.

Cupping her buttocks, he lifted her hips and tilted his head. His tongue pushed deeper, and her pussy clutched helplessly around the rhythmic impalement.

Robin squeezed her aching breasts inside her bra, pinching her nipples to ease their tightness. Her hips churning restlessly, she begged, "Make me come."

Latching on, he kissed her pussy, drawing softly with gentle suction while he rubbed her clit with his tongue. She cried out and fell apart beneath his avid and tender mouth, her body melting into a boneless, breathless, teary puddle on his bed.

"I love you." He pushed to his feet and tossed the condom in the trash.

"You love fucking me," she whispered, knowing that when the passion was sated and reality intruded, he would withdraw again as he'd done before.

Paul leaned over her, pressing his hands into the mattress on either side of her waist. "I'm in this for the long haul."

"You think same time, same place, two weeks from now is a commitment?" She hated the tinge of bitterness in her voice. He'd never made her promises, never alluded to more than what they had during their Vegas liaisons. It wasn't fair that she was angry at him for not giving her more, but she couldn't help how she felt.

"That's not enough for me." Straightening, he yanked his T-shirt over his head. Her eyes swept hungrily over his torso, admiring the tight lacing of abdominal muscles that flexed as he moved. He was so virile. Truly breathtaking. Tattoos covered both of his arms from shoulder to elbow in gorgeous half-sleeves. His chest was broad, golden, and bare… except for her name, which crossed the pectoral over his heart. "It was never going to be enough."

Robin sucked in a tremulous breath, stunned by the sight of ink that hadn't been there previously. Her gaze rested on the new tattoo, her vision blurring with tears. "Paul…"

"I do love fucking you." He pulled a fresh condom out of the nightstand drawer and rolled it on. "When I'm not inside you, I'm thinking about it."

Setting his hands on her inner thighs, he pushed into her. She whimpered, her tender pussy tightened by her recent orgasms.

"God, you feel good," he breathed. "I've needed you so much."

His size, so long and thick, was perfect. As if he'd been made for her. Pushing onto her elbows, Robin watched his glistening cock pull free. The heavily veined length was as brutal looking as the rest of him. The sight of it turned her on further. It made her feel powerfully feminine, like a freakin' sex goddess, to incite the raging lust of a man who was so potently masculine and primal in his sexuality.

Robin's tongue traced the curve of her lower lip. "Please," she whispered, feeling empty without him. She'd been feeling empty since she walked out on him, physically and emotionally.

He sank back into her with a low hiss of pleasure. "You're so sexy, baby. So damn perfect and beautiful. I have no fucking idea what you're doing with a guy like me, but I'm grateful. Every damned day."

God help her. She loved him so much.

He tugged the tie at her waist and pushed the two halves of her dress open. He released the center clasp of her bra, freeing her breasts into his waiting palms. Her pussy tightened around him, echoing the gentle rolling of her nipples between his talented fingers.

"I'm so sorry." He was flushed and shiny with sweat, his beautiful hazel eyes as red as hers felt. "So damn fucking sorry that I ever let you think, for even a moment, that you were nothing but a convenient piece of ass to me. I loved you the moment I saw you. I should have told you—"

"I need things from you." She wrapped her hands around his wrists, anchoring herself as the pleasure threatened to sweep her away.

"I know." His hips rocked in a slow and easy tempo. "I need things from you, too."

That caught her. She wanted him to need her. She wanted

to be valuable to him, to serve a purpose in his life. To share his life. "Such as?"

"I need your travel schedule." His lips kicked into a smile when she scowled. "So I can plan my trips to match up with yours. And I need you to move in with me. Your jewelry business is you, right? You can design your pieces anywhere?"

Robin nodded, unable to speak while he was saying everything she'd longed to hear and fucking her so perfectly. The fluid, rhythmic plunges of his cock were driving her half out of her mind. Her entire body was straining with the need to come, her hips lifting to meet his downstrokes. He was so hard and it felt so good to be with him again. To smell the scent of his skin and feel his flesh beneath her hands.

"I'm stuck for now with the brewery in Portland." His words slurred slightly as the pleasure built for him, too. "But if you don't like the city or the house or anything, I'll go where you're happy. I just need time, time I don't want to spend without you."

"Harder," she urged, grabbing his taut perfect ass in her hands. Her neck arched, her head pressing into the bedding as her climax hovered just out of reach. "Fuck me hard."

Gripping her waist, Paul gave her what she needed. His aggressive strokes set her off in a rush.

"I'm right there with you," he groaned, driving powerfully into her. He made that sexy little noise that made her hot, a cross between a grunt and a hum that said more than words how much pleasure she gave him. "Right there... Right. *There.*"

His gaze locked with hers as he came, the heady rush of pleasure shared between them.

"I love you," he grated, shaking with the force of his climax.

She couldn't look away, daring to believe.

Paul got her naked. Robin missed how he accomplished the feat while in her euphoric postclimax haze, but she was grateful for the result. She lay curled against his side, her legs tangled with his. Her head lay on his chest, her fingertips tracing her name imprinted in his skin.

"I was going to fuck you and walk out," she confessed.

"I caught that." He pressed his lips to her forehead. "I wouldn't have let you leave. I would've followed you with my junk hanging out if I had to and hauled you back."

She lifted her head. "Like I'd *ever* let other women get an eyeful of you."

Paul smiled. "I'm all yours, honey. Flaws, baggage, and all."

Her hand stilled and settled over his heart. "You're not ready, Paul. I wish you were."

"The counselor I've been talking to says otherwise."

Robin's heartbeat skipped. "Counselor?"

He nodded. "I'll need to keep seeing him for a while, but I know enough about what losing Curt did to me to have my head on straight again."

Her heart ached for the tragedy he'd suffered. She couldn't imagine what it would feel like to outlive your child.

His fingers linked with hers. "I should have talked to someone a lot sooner, most especially after I started seeing you. It wasn't fair to you that I didn't."

"You can't take all the blame," she said softly. "When we started out, our arrangement was perfect for me, too. No strings, hot sex, and a guy who listened to me ramble on about jewelry. Things were fine until I changed my expectations."

He reached over with his free hand and opened the nightstand drawer. She thought he might be reaching for a condom, and her pulse quickened. Then a dark blue velvet box appeared in her line of vision, and her heart stopped altogether.

Paul set the box on his washboard abs and took a deep breath. "Do you have any idea how hard it is to buy an engagement ring for a jewelry designer who's kicked your ass to the curb?"

Unable to help herself, she reached for the box.

"Wait," he said, staying her. "Going back to the list of things I need from you... I need you to marry me, Robin. The next time we leave this room, I want us to come back to it as man and wife. I promise you'll have the wedding of your dreams, with our friends and family and doves and swans and whatever the hell you want, but I'd really like the vows now—today—and getting married here in Vegas feels like it fits us."

Us. She looked at him with wide eyes, her mind telling her how crazy that was. There were so many courtship steps they were skipping. What they'd had in their year together—not counting the four miserable months apart—was emails, phone calls, six days a month of the hottest sex of her life...

...and a sharp, pure feeling of connection that had hit them both like lightning the moment they'd laid eyes on each other.

"I know it's crazy," he said, reading her mind as he so often did. "But we've been crazy over each other from the start. I'm lovesick over you, baby. I swear you'll never regret taking a chance on me. I'll make you happier than you've ever been in your life."

Swallowing hard, she thumbed open the box.

"Oh, Paul," she breathed, her fingers shaking.

"Do you like it?" His rich, deep voice was laced with a rare note of anxiety. "We can exchange it if you don't. You can pick out whatever you want. Something more traditional maybe—"

"Shut up." The ring was perfect. It was unusual, almost quirky, with a massive diamond—around four carats was her educated guess—surrounded by irregular swirls of multisized rubies.

"When I look at it," he said quietly, "it reminds me of how I feel about you."

She saw that in the ring, too. The unusual design conveyed passionate chaos, and the fact that he registered that quality in the setting cemented her belief that he was the perfect man for her.

Climbing over him, Robin straddled his hips and extended her hand. "Put it on me."

The feel of the cool band sliding over her knuckle was so sublime it caused goose bumps to sweep across her skin. She wanted this so badly, wanted *him*. Her rough-edged brewmaster with his gentle hands and insatiable hunger for her body. The man who listened to her talk about gem clarity and design theory and who patiently explained the difference between lager and ale.

"Yes," she answered him, placing her hand on his chest next to her name over his heart.

Paul framed her ribcage with his hands, his thumbs stroking the lower curve of her breasts. "And what do you need from me?"

"I needed this." She gestured between them. "A commitment from you. I'll also need a room that's mine alone, a workshop with lots of light and space."

"Done."

"And I need you to promise not to change your style for me."

His brows rose. "I have a style?"

"I love you just the way you are. Don't cut your hair or—"

He rolled abruptly, taking the top. "Say that again."

Laughing, Robin looked up into his impossibly handsome face. "Don't cut your hair?"

He snorted. "The part before that."

"Don't change your style?"

Bending his head, Paul caught her nipple between his teeth.

She made a soft noise at the unexpected bite, then arched her back when his tongue soothed the slight sting. When his cheeks hollowed on a drawing pull, she moaned his name and gave him what he wanted.

"I love you, Paul. You're everything to me."

When he lifted his head, the fiercely tender look on his face was one she'd remember for the rest of her life.

Or she could just make him show it to her again. She had a lifetime to work on it.

Salacious Robinson

"HELLO, MRS. ROBINSON."

I can't stop the thrill that courses through me at the sound of the familiar deep voice. But then, I don't want to. I'm horny, and he knows.

"Hi, Jason." I turn away from my husband's tool bench in the garage. The weather is hot; summer in our town always is. Today it's at least one hundred degrees. Suddenly, it feels hotter than that.

My neighbor's son stands shirtless in the driveway; his baggy shorts hang low around trim hips. He's not wearing boxers, and a shiver races through me despite the heat. His cock, which I know to be long and thick, hangs heavily, tenting the cotton khaki of his shorts. I lick my lips.

"How are you today?" he asks, stepping into my personal space.

I look past him. His truck is the only car in the driveway next door. "Fine. My kids are napping. I just put them down."

His full mouth curves seductively at the words he'd wanted to hear. He comes closer, his powerful athlete's body rippling with muscle. I love to watch him move, watch him play. His mother is my friend. I've sat next to her at his college football games. I've sat next to his girlfriend, too.

Jason brushes past me, his shoulder deliberately skimming across my nipples, making me ache for him. He hits the remote on the wall and the door begins to lower, blocking out our neighbors. Before it's halfway down, his shorts are on the floor. By the time the door is closed, he's not the only one naked.

My blood races in my veins. I love the cock he's fisting, I love it fucking me.

His smile is smug. My desperate desire is why he comes to me. He knows how bad I want it, how deprived I am. My need strokes his ego as surely as his cock strokes my cunt.

I jump up onto the edge of the pool table and spread my legs. I'm dripping for him, and when he gets to me, he slides right in. My eyes close, relishing the feel of the hot, hard, huge cock inside me. I lift my heels to the table, opening myself completely. Leaning back on my arms, I slit my eyes to watch him. That's all the stimulation I need, the sight of his youthful body, full of grace and strength, glistening with sweat and lust as he pumps deep into me.

As he holds the edge of the table and thrusts hard and fast, his six-pack abdomen ripples with his exertions. There's no time for foreplay or finesse. There never is, but I don't want either one. I want to be fucked.

I moan; I can't help it. He feels so good. The thick head of his dick stretches, massages, and rubs the inside of me.

"Like that?" he grunts, driving deeper.

"God, yes."

I gasp, arching my hips to take more. The friction is amazing. There's nothing like the feel of being fucked by a big cock. I tell him so and he growls. He loves it when I talk dirty; his girlfriend won't. She's too young, too inhibited. I have no shame.

Sweat dampens his hair and drips down his chest. The delicious scent of hardworking male fills my nostrils. It's so unbelievably hot in my garage with the door closed. Like a sauna. He's breathing heavy, his body working hard. Jason never has any control when he takes me and I make it worse by moaning, by loving his cock as much as I do.

"I'm going to come," he warns. He fucks like a stallion and climaxes like one too—hard, deep, and copiously.

I whimper, wanting it, my nipples so hard they ache, my breasts heavy and shaking with the impact of his hips slapping against mine. His dick swells in anticipation, filling me so full he really has to work to get inside me. The pleasure is incredible.

He floods me, still fucking madly, and I orgasm.

"Yes, yes, yes," I chant. The release of the sexual tension that knots my shoulders and back is so good, I shake. A moment later he stills; his head dropping forward as he catches his breath.

Five minutes later the garage door is opening and a dry, hot breeze blows in, evaporating the perspiration from our skin. The sound of an automobile door shutting nearby alerts us to arrivals.

Jason's father is home and stepping out of his car. I wave. He waves back.

"Thank you for your help, Jason," I call out as he saunters away, his back glistening in the summer sun.

He doesn't glance back. "Anytime, Mrs. Robinson."

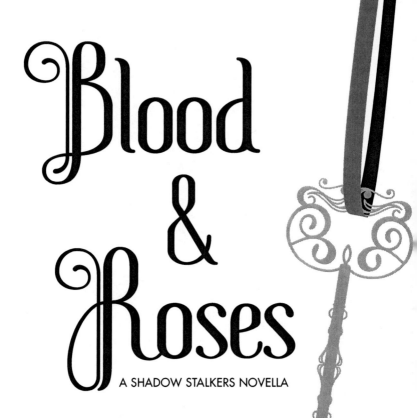

Blood
&
Roses

A SHADOW STALKERS NOVELLA

Chapter One

"JENNIFER PROMISED ME ALL sorts of sexual favors if I buy her one of those." Chad Ward jerked his thumb toward the diner's window, gesturing at a sleek convertible Jaguar that was pulling in across the street. "She got pretty inventive with her suggestions. Inspired me to look one up online."

Jake Monroe's gaze narrowed as he eyed the red sports car, awareness rippling down his spine.

"You have to custom order one like that," Chad went on, returning his attention to topping off Jake's coffee. "I'd do it for Jenn, if I could; but the diner doesn't bring in *that* much dough. Who in hell spends a hundred and fifty grand on a car?"

"Rich, paunchy bald guys who hope to get laid by women young enough to be their daughters." Jake knew someone else who would. Knew her as well as any man could know his woman. Which was why he was certain she wouldn't have come back to Whisper Creek after all these years without bringing trouble with her.

As the driver's side door of the Jag swung open, his attention remained riveted. The ragtop was up, shielding the occupant, but he knew exactly who was going to step out by the flare of heat that raced over his skin. "And someone like *her*."

One long, black trouser-clad leg extended to the asphalt, then the driver unfolded in a graceful rise. Her blouse was black, too, making a stark contrast to the wild red curls pulled back at her nape. She looked cool and restrained, but he knew the woman inside that exterior was anything but. His body tensed and hardened with primal recognition, his breathing deep and slightly quickened.

"Well, well," Chad murmured, straightening. "Can't miss that hair, can you? And she's parked right in front of Tilly's shop. I haven't seen Ana in… Shit. How long's it been now?"

"Almost ten years." *Nine years, five months, and a couple weeks.* It just pissed Jake off that he was *still* counting down the damn days since Anastasia Miller had driven out of his life without looking back.

"Hmm." Chad shook his head. "Wonder if she got what she was after when she left."

Had she? Was it possible she'd found what she was looking for with some other guy in some other place in the world? "Good question."

Ana pulled a satchel out from behind the driver's seat, then shut the door of her expensive toy. She paused, her head turning as if she sensed Jake's gaze on her. She wore big dark sunglasses, effectively shielding her eyes.

Her lips were just like he remembered. Full and pink, and capable of blowing his mind. He'd felt those lips all over his body, still felt them sometimes when he was lying in bed at night, stiff and aching from wanting her.

Rolling her shoulders back, she moved toward the entrance to Tilly's Yarn Shop with a swift, determined stride. She disappeared through the door and not five minutes later, the ladies who gathered there for tea and gossip came hustling out with their knitting bags. The open sign on the door flipped over to read Please Call Again and the shade that covered the inset glass was yanked down.

Jake picked up his coffee, considering. "I'll need the check, Chad."

"Anastasia! My god, baby, I had no idea you'd be coming home."

Ana stared hard at her mother, silently challenging that lie, but Tilly Miller acted as if she didn't notice her daughter's frustration and suspicion.

"Let me see you." Tilly approached with her arms outstretched and pulled Ana close for a hug. "You look like you're heading to a funeral."

"I may yet," Ana said grimly.

"Are you talking about your work?"

"I'm talking about *your* work, Mom. Your life's dream. I'm just here to clean up after you."

Tilly stepped back and smoothed a hand over hair that had once been the same vibrant red as her daughter's, but was now a faded strawberry, sprinkled liberally with white strands. She looked the part of a small-town shopkeeper. Only another world-class thief and grifter would recognize her for what she really was.

"I made a new pot of tea just before you arrived. Why don't you sit and we'll talk? It's been so long since you've been home."

"We don't have time to play this game." Ana crossed her arms, her anger simmering. "Frankie's life is in danger, Mom."

Like their parents, her brother Frank had the same need for the rush, the same fascination for the bright and shiny and illegal. Ana supposed it was in their blood. Inevitable, considering she was named after a famous identity con and Frank was named after an infamous con artist.

"Is it?"

What a question. Her mother was good at pretending to be clueless. "I know he and Eric would've wanted to go into the heist with blanks, but their associate was using live rounds," Ana said tersely. "Whoever he is, he's a wild card."

"You were always so good at dramatizing things, dear." Her mother sank into one of the mismatched chairs arranged in a circle near an unlit woodstove.

Ana had to consciously relax her jaw to speak. "You know you'll never be able to fence those diamonds. You knew it when you set this up. The Crown is too distinctive."

Tilly poured tea as if she hadn't a care in the world. "The Crown of Roses." She sighed. "So rare to find any diamond of that deep pink color, but an entire tiara's worth? Has the piece been stolen?"

"Cut the crap, Mom. Do you think I've forgotten how you talked about the '94 Carlton heist in France? This job in Manhattan was textbook Tilly Miller… until the guard got shot."

Digging into her briefcase, Ana yanked out a tablet and tossed it on an empty chair beside her mom's. "I bought that for you. Look at the newspaper apps on there and read the reports. Did you know that jewelry shop is a Cross Industries property? Gideon Cross has offered a quarter-million dollar reward for information leading to the arrest of the thieves. I've been told that amount will increase to half a million if the guard dies."

Finally, Tilly paled. "Is he that bad off?"

"He had body armor on, but he took two hits: one to the shoulder and another to the thigh. That second hit nicked his femoral artery."

"Dear god…" Her mother sucked in a shaky breath. "You know Frankie would never go along with anything like that. The guard… was it Terence Parker?"

"Yes." Ana gripped the back of an old wicker chair. "I already figured out Terence was your inside man. And it's obvious the shooter wanted him out of the way. A three-way split is much more lucrative. But why not make it a two-way split? Or better yet, take it all. Frank, Eric, Terence, and someone else. Who's the other guy, Mom?"

"I don't know."

"I don't believe you. You had this planned down to the second." Tilly and Bill Miller were known to spend years planning a job that would take only seconds to pull off. Ana was afraid that since her dad had died, her mom had focused on the heist to bury her grief. And she'd dragged Frankie into it with her.

Tilly looked at her with stricken eyes. "There was no fourth guy in the plan. Just Terence, Frankie, and Eric. You know it's safer to keep the number of people involved to the bare minimum."

Ana knew neither Frankie nor Eric would've deviated. Tilly would've trained them better than that. Most likely Terence had brought in someone to guard his interests, someone he'd thought he could trust… and ended up paying for it.

"Jesus, Mom. The shooter is going to turn on Frankie and Eric the first chance he gets, if he hasn't already. I need to get to him before that happens."

Tilly picked up her teacup and saucer, the china rattling as her hands shook. "Are you here for the reward or the gems?"

"You know why I'm here. You knew I'd come, because you knew who the insurer was before you went after the diamonds. That was part of the fun. I'm sure you figured there'd be no harm done—you mastermind your perfect heist, Frank follows in dad's footsteps by pulling it off, your daughter claims five percent of the take in a legitimate finder's fee, and the owner gets their gems back."

"No one was supposed to get hurt," Tilly breathed, looking stricken.

"Someone always gets hurt, Mom. They don't make stealing illegal just to spoil your fun." Sighing, Ana pinched the bridge of her nose. "When were Frankie and Eric supposed to show up here?"

"Not for a week." Tilly met her gaze with unusual somberness. "We knew the insurance company would bring you in on this, and we didn't want any lines being drawn between there and here and you."

"Thanks," Ana said sourly.

"Frank's not even supposed to call until he gets down to Florida. He and Eric planned on stretching the trip out over a few days."

Crossing her arms, Ana snapped, "No matter how clever you are, you went into this knowing I could face prosecution along with you. By not turning you in, I could be seen as an accessory after the fact. And if I took the finder's fee and Frankie's involvement ever got out, I'd have a hell of a time arguing that I wasn't a participant in a multi-million dollar fraud against the insurance company."

"Jake would never let that happen," Tilly argued.

"He isn't God, Mom," Ana muttered, her stomach knotting at the thought of facing her high school sweetheart again. Jake Monroe—a man she'd never gotten over. "I'll have to talk to him. Maybe Eric's contacted him. I'd expect it, considering how protective Jake is."

"Will you be staying in Whisper Creek until this is worked out?"

"I'll be staying tonight, at least. If Terence survives—God willing—I'll be heading back to Manhattan to see him. And if I sniff out any leads on who Terence might've brought in as the fourth, I'll take off to pursue those. How's the Wi-Fi at the house?"

"Still not good. I use the computer here at the shop when I need reliable internet access."

"Then I'll stay at Victoria's Inn."

Picking up her briefcase, Ana exhaled harshly. "Let me know if you hear anything."

"Anastasia." Her mother's voice stopped her when she reached the door. "You'll watch out for Frankie, won't you? He'll be all right?"

"I'll do my best, Mom." But she couldn't make any promises. She couldn't even be sure she wouldn't go down with them.

Reaching for her sunglasses on the top of her head, she stepped outside.

And found a deputy U.S. Marshal waiting next to her car.

Chapter Two

ANA'S BREATH CAUGHT AND her heartbeat accelerated with a mixture of surprise and guilt.

The deputy was a tall and leanly built man with cool blue eyes and a firm mouth. His chiseled face was impassive and his arms casually crossed. His long legs were braced slightly apart, anchoring him to the asphalt as he assessed her from head to toe from beneath the brim of his hat.

"Deputy," she greeted him, regaining her composure.

"Anastasia." His voice was whisky-rough and it spoke her name like a caress. "What brings you back?"

"Pit stop during a work assignment." She shoved her free hand into her pocket to hide how it trembled. Wondering if he had more news than Tilly did, she asked, "Where's Eric?"

Jake's lips pursed. He had a gorgeous mouth. Neither too full or too thin and perfectly sculpted. That mouth knew every inch of her body. She still had dreams about what he could do with it. "He headed down to Florida with your brother."

She nodded and somehow refrained from shifting on her feet. "I never did like Florida. Too much humidity for me."

"How long are you gonna be in town?"

"A few days, at most."

He adjusted his weight, his body moving with sleek fluidity. "So why are we wasting time talking about nothing?"

She stared at him, absorbing everything about the man she'd left behind. He was harder than before. Bigger, too. He'd been twenty-two the last time she saw him. He was fully a man now, his frame filled out. The formidable strength of will he'd exuded as long as she'd known him hadn't changed. "Are we supposed to be doing something else?"

"Getting to the point would be good. You staying with Tilly?"

"No."

"You married?"

She shook her head. "You?"

"No. You'll stay at my place, then."

Heat shimmered through her, her pulse quickening. She hadn't expected him to move so fast. If she was honest, she would admit that she'd been afraid he would brush her off, having long gotten over her. Worse, she'd wondered if he had a woman in his life, someone who had a normal family she could be proud of and he could be a part of.

"How's your internet access?" She was thinking about how much closer she'd be to getting a bead on Eric if she was staying at Jake's house. She would also be closer to Jake himself, the man she loved so much it was like an aching wound in her chest.

"Sweetheart," he drawled, his gaze hot. "You really want to start out that way? I was planning on easing you back into it, but if you're eager to be punished, you just let me know."

Her body responded to the sensual threat with familiar alacrity. Jake had always been able to make her ready for him with just a look, because she knew exactly where that look would lead—to dark pleasure that took her to her limits. "I have to work, Jake. It was a valid question."

"I'm not saying it wasn't. Just that it's insulting to imply that the quality of the Wi-Fi in my house has a damn thing to do with whether or not I'll be nailing you into my mattress tonight."

She winced inwardly. He'd always been raw and blunt when talking about sex, but there was an undercurrent of hurt anger to his words now and it broke her heart. Not that she could show it. Her sympathy wasn't what he wanted or needed, and it wouldn't be fair of her to give it anyway, considering she was the cause of his unhappiness.

"Well—" She cleared her throat. "Glad we cleared that up."

His smile sent goose bumps racing across her skin. "I'm not as far outside of town as Tilly is. My internet is just fine."

"Good. I'll need it."

He reached into his pocket and pulled out a set of keys. "You know how to get there."

Ana took them from him, swallowing hard at the sight of the keychain. It was a round piece of wood, a one-inch thick cross-section of a small branch. She'd made the thing as an assignment in woodworking class. On one side she'd burned the letters *Jake* + *Ana* surrounded by little decorative hearts and asterisks. The other side read *Forever*.

"I've got some business to take care of," he said. "I'll call you at the house to see if you're up for dinner in town or if you'd like me to bring something home with me."

"I could cook."

"Could you now?" He grinned. "I'd like that."

"Sure you would," she said dryly. "You're a man."

Jake pulled a business card out and gave it to her. "That has my office's number and my cell number on it. Call me if you need me for anything."

She held his gaze. "Anything?"

"Been that way for twelve years now, Ana. Despite spending ten of those waiting for you to get your ass back here."

Ana took a deep breath. He was everything she'd always wanted, but could never have. Lawmen and grifters didn't mix. "I'm just passing through, Jake."

"So you said." He touched the brim of his hat. "See you later."

Ana drove her Jag slowly down the tree-lined street, her gaze taking in just how much the area had changed since she'd left a decade ago. At one time—back when Jake's home had belonged to his parents—the house had been one of only a few on a new street. Now the homes lined up one after another, forming the perfect picture of Small-town America.

She parked at the curb in front of the ranch-style house, smiling at the white picket fence that said a lot about the man he was. The yard was immaculately landscaped and a swing hung from the porch rafters. It was just the sort of normal family home she'd always fantasized she would have one day.

Unfortunately, she wasn't normal and neither was her family. Her brain was filled with a variety of larcenous information, which was how she'd come to be an insurance investigator specializing in fine art and jewelry theft—her mind worked like a criminal's.

Keeping Jake had never been an option for her, despite how much they loved each other. His brain had always worked out problems from the opposite side of the law, and he'd always planned on working in law enforcement. She couldn't imagine him being anything other than a cop.

How could she ever ask someone like him to connect his life to those of a band of criminals? The reason she'd come back only proved how right she had been to walk away. What would it do to him, to his career, to their love if she went to jail? She'd known that one day Tilly or Frankie would land into trouble and when that happened, it would impact Jake. She couldn't do that to him. In the end, she'd loved him enough to leave him.

"Yet here you are at his place," she murmured to herself, grabbing her weekend bag from the passenger seat. She slung it over her shoulder and opened the gate, admiring the cobblestone pathway to the front door and knowing Jake must've laid it himself. She imagined him outside on a sunny day, shirtless and sheened with sweat, the muscles of his back and arms flexing as he worked his way across the lush lawn.

She wondered what he'd been thinking of while he was working. Had he imagined a wife waddling over it while pregnant with his child? Or his kids skipping along it on the way in from school? Or a dog bounding over it as neighborhood children played in the yard with his own?

Her hand clenched around the keychain she'd made for him when she was just sixteen.

Been that way for twelve years now, Ana.

Jesus. That was a heartbreaker. And yet she was touched that his love was as true as hers.

She let herself in, dropped her bag on a black leather couch, and took in the surprisingly modern style of the furnishings. He'd gone with pale blue and chrome with black furniture, and the cool palette went remarkably well with the warmth of the gleaming hardwood floors.

If she'd had any sense at all, she would have stayed at the inn. Leaving had shattered her last time. What would she suffer through this time? What would Jake?

Taking a deep breath, Ana pulled the much-loved scent of him deep into her lungs, her entire body tingling with awareness. Jake had been her first lover and her senses were trained to be attuned to his. *He'd* trained them, first with his hands and mouth, and later with restraints and the delicious bite of pain. It was a lifestyle they'd fallen into together, both of them realizing that she had a deep-seated need to surrender to his authority, and in the process, he'd ruined her for other men. Sometimes, when she was lying in bed at night, she wondered if she'd ruined him for other women.

Ana dug out her laptop from her bag and carried it into the dining room. Jake had a square, high table and she kicked off her heels before climbing onto a barstool. As her laptop powered up, she pulled out her cell phone and his business card, and texted him.

Password for your wi-fi?

A moment later, he replied. *An@m1ne69*

She stared at the code and smiled. "Ana-mine-69, huh?"

Wishful thinking or a hint? she texted back.

He answered fast. *An order.*

"Well. Some things never change." Ana flexed her fingers and rolled her shoulders back, focusing her mind on the work ahead.

She was going to dig up information on Terence Parker and she was going to break the law doing it. She pushed aside her guilt, knowing it had to be done. "I hope you pull through, Terence."

Ana had decided to focus on his relatives. She could imagine how it would feel to go into the heist as the lone outsider in a family group—a mother, her son and his best friend. Although Eric wasn't technically related to them, he was practically a brother to Frankie. Terence would understandably want someone similarly close to him on his side.

God… Frankie. Her throat tightened with fear and her eyes stung. Her baby brother had never really had a chance to walk the straight and narrow. And if something happened to Eric, it would destroy Jake.

"One step at a time," she muttered to herself. "Find the fourth."

"You're making the rest of us look bad, Jake."

Jake looked up from the paperwork he was trying to clear so he could take the next day off. Luke Stiles—one of his fellow deputies and a longtime friend—stood in the doorway, grinning. "I heard Ana's back in town and staying at your place."

"Ah, Whisper Creek, where the whispering about other people's business never stops." Leaning back in his chair, Jake gave himself permission to think about the woman who was as much a part of him as his badge. She'd been the most important thing in his life since her family drove into town when she was sixteen. Together they'd helped each other cross the threshold from adolescence to adulthood, and they'd discovered what they needed from the person they loved. A lot of people never figured that out.

And some never found their soul mates.

He still didn't get why they weren't together. He understood that she'd needed to get out of Whisper Creek to spread her wings, but he couldn't figure out why she hadn't let him go with her. He'd cajoled and begged and threatened and teased, making her tell him a hundred times over that she'd never leave him. But in his heart he'd known she would go; he'd seen the truth in her eyes.

She loved him; he knew that and didn't doubt it. There would never be another man for her, not one who knew her as deeply and completely as he did. They'd experienced so much together, raw and searingly intimate encounters that bound them tighter than gold rings and vows.

But as the years passed and she didn't come back to him, he realized something was *keeping* her away and today proved it. The love was still there in her beautiful green eyes. She still wanted him and obeyed him, still craved his hunger for her. If she left again, he'd have his answer—it wasn't him; it was Whisper Creek. And if location was what was keeping them apart, he'd paddle her ass for not saying so.

Luke leaned against the front of Jake's desk. "Is she back for good?"

"Don't know yet."

"Ah… okay. You two coming into town for dinner?"

"She's cooking."

"Really? You should know I was in Home Ec with her for a semester. She couldn't crack an egg."

Jake smiled. "Warning noted."

"You sure about that?" Luke's smile faded. "She did a number on you last time, Jake. I don't want to see you like that ever again."

"I'm not the only one who got hurt. Guess Ana and I can't quit each other."

He waited until Luke left the room, then pulled out his cell to call Eric. His younger brother was supposed to check in twice a day, but he hadn't called since yesterday morning. Which, unfortunately, wasn't totally unexpected.

"Hey, Eric," he said, when he reached voicemail. "You're supposed to be checking in. Yes, I know you're a grown man now, but this isn't about what's good for you, it's about doing something good for me. I worry."

He took a breath, thinking.

"Text me when you get a chance or leave me a message. Shit, send me a picture if you can't be bothered to type or talk. But don't send me a damn mug shot or I'll be kicking your ass all the way to jail."

Chapter Three

ANA FINISHED HER REPORT and emailed it to her contact at the insurance agency. It was difficult showing progress when she didn't want to give up any names. Even using the guard's name was tricky, because he might flip on Frankie or Eric if he felt the heat. So she'd reported that she was researching the backgrounds of all the store's employees, which didn't make her look any more competent that the local cops, but she'd dug up a couple dark spots that would've been viable leads if she didn't already know who was responsible for the crime. The information should be enough to make it look like she was worth her fee... at least for today.

As for her hunch, she'd discovered that Terence had two brothers—one was a tenured professor in Virginia and the other had a sealed record that she'd hacked. Richard Parker had a previous armed robbery conviction when he was fifteen and a variety of petty larceny and drug charges. His record was clean as an adult, but her parents proved that not getting caught didn't mean you were straight.

Shutting down her laptop, Ana slid off the barstool and went to check on dinner. She'd done a quick check of Jake's fridge and pantry earlier and hadn't been surprised to find both well stocked. After debating her options, she'd put a pot roast in the oven and a salad in the crisper. Then she'd opened a bottle of red wine and left it to breathe on the counter. Because she'd prepped in advance, she had time to take a shower before Jake got home.

She grabbed her bag off the couch and headed to the guest bathroom, admiring the tile work in the shower that she knew was another of Jake's projects. When he'd inherited the place from his parents, it hadn't had such upgrades. It had been a cookie-cutter house, one of the first homes built by a developer who'd thought the town would grow much faster than it had. Now it had Jake's stamp over most of it, but the guest bathroom was clearly Eric's domain. The razor on the edge of the sink was a bright lime green and the men's body wash in the shower was the kind marketed to hormonal young men.

Jake had assumed responsibility for his brother at the tender age of nineteen, when the Monroes had been killed by a collision with a drunk driver. Ana had supported him through that rough time and offered him what comfort she could, considering how young she herself was, but he'd been good with Eric from the beginning. Jake was a born leader, firmly anchored by his moral compass and unshakeable confidence.

She'd needed his quiet strength as much as Eric had, having been raised by two of the flightiest people ever to be parents. And even after all these years, Jake was still her touchstone.

Ana scrubbed, shaved, and perfumed herself like a woman bent on seduction, a mindset she hadn't adopted for a very long time. She hadn't packed anything sexy, so her simple cotton baby doll nightgown would have to do.

"Ten years," she murmured to her reflection in the mirror, fluffing out her damp curls with her fingers. "You're bound to be a little rusty."

When she opened the bathroom door, she knew immediately that Jake was home. There was a palpable energy in the air and it flowed over her, awakening her senses. She could hear the shower running in his bedroom and appreciated the time to finish prepping dinner. She smiled when she saw the white roses in a vase on the dining table and when she went to pull out the salad, she found one of Victoria's famous cheesecakes in the fridge.

She was tossing the salad when she heard Jake pad into the kitchen behind her. A moment later, his arms were circling her and his lips were pressed to the side of her neck.

"Hi," he murmured, his voice low and husky.

"Hi back." Her head fell against his shoulder and she allowed herself the temporary luxury of leaning into him. His chest was bare, hard, and warm. "I like the flowers."

"Good." The tip of his tongue touched the lobe of her ear; then he caught it between his teeth. "I walked in the door and the smell of dinner made me hungry. Now I've smelled you and I'm starving."

He wasn't talking about food, she knew. That was proven when his hands slid down the flat plane of her stomach and gripped her thighs just beneath the hem of her baby doll.

"Did you get some work done?" he breathed, bending his knees to press his erection against the swell of her buttocks.

Ana became so aroused the denim of his jeans and the cotton of her baby doll might as well have not been there. She dropped the salad servers into the bowl, shaken by the lust that burned through her. It felt as if she'd been numb for ages and was suddenly reawakened to sensation, overwhelmed by the vibrancy of it after living through miserable loneliness. "Yes, I did. How was your day?"

"I spent the last half of it thinking about you and cursing the paperwork I needed to clear so I could stay home tomorrow."

She sucked in a deep breath. "Oh?"

"Before you leave my bed, Anastasia, you're going to explain to me why we're not together."

"Jake—" Her words cut off as his fingers pushed under the elastic edge of her lace thong. She was slick and hot, primed for him by deprivation and the depth of her love. His fingertip slid between the lips of her sex, stroking through the moisture to tease her clitoris.

"You still want me." He pulled her back against him and rolled his hips, making sure she felt the steely hardness of his erection. "And you know I've never stopped wanting you. We should be in the same bed every night and the same house every day. We both know it."

He stepped back, removing his touch and leaving her bereft. "Can I help with anything?"

Ana shot a narrow-eyed glance at him over her shoulder and found him grinning unrepentantly. He wore a pair of soft, well-worn jeans that hung low on his hips and nothing else. His hair was longer than it had seemed with his hat on. Dark as night and glossy, his hair had always been a lure to her. She loved to run her fingers through it and clench it in her fists as he pleasured her.

"You can set the table," she told him.

He washed his hands at the sink and set to work, not surprising her in the least by having all the necessary components of a dinner setting—cloth napkins, salad and dinner plates, silverware, and placemats. She could imagine him dishing up dinner for Eric every night, ensuring that his brother had as near to a traditional family life as possible.

How ironic that Jake had encouraged Eric to spend time with Frank. He'd thought the Miller family was ideal—the yarn shop owner, the computer guru, and their two kids. Jake believed Frankie would be a good influence on his troubled, grieving brother. He had no idea that her dad had been a hacker, her mom a fence, and Frankie covered everything in between.

It'd broken her heart not to clue him in. And now the heist was weighing heavily on her mind. So many secrets between them. Too many.

They sat down for dinner and Jake sliced the pot roast with quick efficiency.

"How's Eric doing?" she asked him, as she poured the wine.

"Good. Although I wish he'd go to graduate school or join the military. He's a smart kid and he works hard when he's motivated. When he's not, he doesn't apply himself."

"Frankie's got the same problem. Lots of potential, too little drive. I'm afraid he's been a bad influence on your brother."

Jake slid a slice of pot roast off the end of the carving knife and onto her plate. "Are you kidding? Before Frankie came along, Eric was in and out of trouble all the time—shoplifting, vandalism, boosting cars. Frankie changed all that."

"Frankie just taught Eric to be smarter about it, so he didn't get caught."

She sighed at the skeptical look he shot her. Like many cops, Jake couldn't believe anyone could pull the wool over his eyes, especially not his own brother. But there weren't many cops who ran across top-shelf grifters like her parents, and both she and Frankie had learned their lessons well.

He took a drink of his wine and asked, "So you're passing through on a job? You still doing investigative work for insurance companies?"

"Most of the time, yes."

"What's the job you're on now?"

"Chasing down jewels taken during a heist, including a valuable tiara set with pink diamonds."

"Oh?" His blue eyes flared with interest. "Big take?"

"Approximately forty million."

He whistled. "How much do you get for the recovery?"

"Five percent." She watched him do the math.

"Jesus, Ana. Up to two million?" He stared at her. "And you've been doing this a while."

"Long enough. I guess it pays to think like a criminal."

Jake looked down at his plate. They ate quietly for a while, each of them lost in private thoughts. Then he said, "You're a good cook, sweetheart."

"Thank you." She smiled. "I took lessons after I got sick of eating take-out all the time."

"Not having someone to share home-cooked meals with is a lonely life." He took a bite and chewed, watching her thoughtfully. "Is the money why you never came back?"

She focused on cutting her meat. "Not the money, no."

"Were you that unhappy here?"

"Jake." Ana set her fork and knife down and met his gaze. "There are things you don't know about me."

"Bullshit. There's nothing I don't know about you, Anastasia. And nothing you don't know about me."

"Do you think someone's a criminal whether they get caught or not?" She knew what his answer would be already. Jake had fully supported the local authorities when Eric had been caught committing a crime. Eric suffered the same punishments as anyone else in town would.

"Of course."

"Well, then I'm a criminal, Jake. And a good, honest cop like you can't spend his life with a woman who skates the line and occasionally falls over it."

He picked up his wine and sat back then, studying her with those cool cop's eyes. "I have no idea what you're talking about, but let me ask you this: What the hell do you expect me to do if you're the only woman I'll ever want? Be alone? You can't be that cruel, Ana."

"And you can't compromise your principles for me. Eventually, it'll ruin what we have."

"What do we have? Two lonely, miserable lives? I'd love to

fuckin' ruin that." He took a drink and held her gaze over the rim of his glass.

Her breath caught at the fiery look in his eyes.

"And by the way," he went on, "not a news flash that PI's don't toe the line. Cops switch to private investigative work because they find the line confining. I know that. At the end of the day, you're still doing the right thing."

"What if I told you that I don't care if the perps get caught? I just want the take. In fact, there are times when I've deliberately not pulled on a thread because I almost admire them for the guts it took to make the attempt and the brains to get away with it, if they do." She sat back. "I may let these jewel thieves I'm chasing right now slip away, Jake, after I get the gems. What do you think about that? Think you can slide into bed at night with a woman who might be an accessory after the fact?"

His gaze narrowed. "Ana—"

"It doesn't matter, Jake." She hopped off the barstool and grabbed their plates. "I decided years ago that it's a question you're never going to have to answer."

Chapter Four

ANA TOOK THE DISHES to the sink and willed herself to relax. There was no need for them to fight and she was determined that they wouldn't, not when they had so little time together.

"You don't get to make that decision by yourself, Anastasia," Jake drawled dangerously, coming up behind her.

She gripped the edge of the counter, knowing where the warning note in his voice would lead. "You can't change my mind, Jake."

"No. Never was able to do that." His hands wrapped around her wrists. "But I can remind you of what we've both been missing."

Gently, he pulled her hands away from the counter and brought them behind her, pinning them to the small of her back. A moment later she felt the chill of steel as one handcuff clicked shut around her wrist, then another.

An instant calm settled over her.

He turned her around and cupped her face in his hands, his mouth sealing over hers. Ana gasped at the first press of his firm lips, opening herself to the slow, smooth glide of his tongue. He licked deep and slow, savoring her with an easy, unhurried eroticism. She moaned and wriggled against him, impatient and greedy.

His hands moved down to her throat, wrapping lightly around it. The feeling of being collared soothed her further.

"You with me, baby?" he asked softly, the pads of his thumbs stroking over her fluttering pulse.

"Yes."

"The first time is gonna be quick. I've been waiting too long."

Ana nodded, feeling the same way. She was so wet and swollen already, she was certain the slightest pressure on her clit would set her off.

Tenderly, as if she was fragile, he squeezed her breasts through the cotton of her baby doll, hefting them lightly to judge how heavy and tender they'd become. He caught her nipples between his thumb and forefingers, rolling them, tugging with just the perfect amount of pressure. Her eyes closed, her body lost to him.

Jake kissed her again, his tongue gliding over the curve of her lower lip. "I've missed you so damn much, Ana."

"I want to touch you."

"I know." He hooked his fingers beneath her straps and pushed them off her shoulders. "If you're good, I might let you."

"Jake…" She gasped as the scalloped edge of her bodice dragged over her hardened nipples.

"So beautiful," he breathed, stroking his thumbs over the furled tips. Lowering his head, he took one into the drenched heat of his mouth, swirling his tongue around it before his cheeks hallowed on a drawing pull.

She moaned, her head falling back as the sensation of his sucking echoed in the saturated flesh between her legs. The gentle tugging rippled through her, making her shiver in delight. When he paid the same service to her other nipple, her knees weakened and he caught her up, his arms banding around her waist to lift her. Holding her aloft, he ravished her swollen breasts, fluttering his tongue over the tight tips and scraping the edge of his teeth across them.

"Oh god, Jake…"

"Shh," he murmured. "I'll give you what you need, sweetheart. And I'll keep giving it to you until you can't imagine getting by for more than a few hours without my dick inside you."

Jake carried her into the living room and set her down, turning her away from him. He urged her over the armrest of the leather couch with a gentle, but unyielding, grip at her nape. She folded, her buttocks thrust upward to accept the hard drives of his big, beautiful cock.

His hands stroked over her, rubbing down her sides and thighs in soothing circles. Cool air caressed her back as her gown was pushed up beneath the handcuffs. Her fingers flexed with the need to touch him in return, to feel the skin she knew became feverishly hot when he first pushed inside her.

"I love you, Anastasia," Jake said gruffly, bending to press a kiss between her shoulder blades. "You're the best thing that ever happened to me. I won't ever believe that we can't make it work, because we always do when we're together. You can't deny that."

"Jake, please…" The smell and feel of the leather stirred blazing memories from their past, reminding her of the needs only Jake could appease.

His thumbs slid beneath the elastic of her panties and pulled them over her hips and down her legs. His lips followed, skimming over the curve of her buttocks and suckling along the back of her thigh. She began to shake, her body overloaded by need and desire she hadn't felt in far too long. When he sank into a crouch behind her, her breath caught with expectation.

"So pretty," he murmured, his breath hot against the lips of her sex. "So soft and pink."

Leaving her panties around her knees, Jake parted her with his thumbs and paused. She could feel his gaze on her, the heat and hunger almost tangible.

"And I know how sweet you taste, Ana mine."

Ana tensed in anticipation of the first lick, but when it came, she still wasn't prepared. She cried out, her entire body shaking violently.

"Easy, sweetheart," he said hoarsely, anchoring her with his palm pressed flat to the small of her back. "I'll take care of you."

The next stroke of his tongue was skillful, rubbing over the hard knot of her clit with the perfect amount of pressure. She came in a rush, her back bowing as the pleasure seared her senses and racked her over-sensitized body with shudders of delight. In the midst of an orgasm that darkened her vision, Jake's tongue darted inside her, thrusting furiously. The soft velvet of his licking against the tender tissues of her core was too much, yet not nearly enough. Her hips churned into the shallow plunges, her body seeking a deeper, stronger penetration.

"Now, Jake. Now. *Now!*"

He stood in a rush. Ana heard the sound of his zipper lowering; then she felt the silky heat of his rigid erection brush against her. He teased her, gliding the plush head of his cock through the slick lips of her sex.

She arched her spine, her fingers grasping at air, her cheeks flushed and damp from the strain of being bound and unable to reach out to him as she needed. Not just for the physical pleasure of touching him, but to satisfy the demands of her heart.

"I love you," she gasped, unable to hold the words back. "I love you, Jake."

With a low growl, his hips jerked and pushed him into her with one fierce, deep stroke.

"Yes!" Tears filled Ana's eyes and spilled over onto the cushion. She ached for this, the delicious burn of his possession and the sense of connection she'd felt with no one else.

"I want to take you slow." His voice was rough and raspy. "Slow and deep. But I can't… It's been too long."

He hitched against her, shoved the last little bit inside her that crammed her all the way full. "Damn, you're like a fist,

Ana. Squeezing me tight... rippling around me. I'm gonna come hard for you, baby."

Jake withdrew, then slid in to the root. He rolled his hips, screwing deep. The feel of his long, thick cock stroking inside her was perfect—the slight burn as he stretched her, the decadent feel of him rubbing and pushing, the maddening clenching in her core as her body tried to hold him deep...

Gripping her hips, he pumped hard again, an expert stroke that lifted her to the tip of her toes. Ana panted with pleasure, spinning dizzily toward climax.

"Don't stop," she begged, desperate for the friction that would set her off again.

"Never, Ana mine," he purred, lunging quick and hard, shafting her tender pussy. "I'll never stop..."

The erotic sound of flesh slapping mingled with the heated words that spilled from his lips—tender promises and sensual threats, loving praise and coarsely-voiced hunger—all of which made her crazy with lust. She was rocking back into his measured thrusts, moaning at the way they radiated through her, her mind fogged with the intensity of her pleasure.

When Jake bent his knees and hit the perfect spot inside her, Ana unraveled with a muffled scream. She quaked with her release, struggling to breathe as her body seized in the throes of a powerful orgasm. Jake was right there with her, gasping as his body jerked with each scorching spurt of semen. He folded over her, clutching her close, the hard ridges of his abdomen slick with sweat against her palms.

She sagged into the cushions as the tension left her, feeling wrung out and well-loved.

"I need you." Jake's chest heaved against her and when he shifted slightly, Ana realized he was still hard and thick. "I'll never stop needing you."

It took Ana the space of two heartbeats to figure out what had woken her.

Her cell phone was vibrating beneath her pillow.

She pulled it out and squinted against the bright light of the backlit screen. Seeing an East Coast area code, she hit the button to answer the call before it went to voicemail and slipped out of bed. She hurried out of Jake's bedroom and quietly shut the door, then ran to the living room while answering with, "Miller."

"Ana! My god." Frankie gasped with relief. "We're in trouble, Ana. Eric and me… And Mom. Ah, god, Mom…"

"Frankie." Relief flowed through her, making her aware of just how worried she'd been. "Where are you?"

"Newark. Jesus… it all went wrong. Rick went in hot. Fuck— You know how Mom had it planned. Like Cannes."

"I remember." She remembered the famous Carlton heist, just as she remembered that Terence Parker had a brother named Richard. "Is Rick's name Richard Parker?"

"Yes. How did you know?" He barked out a laugh. "What am I saying? Of course you know. He shot his own fucking brother, Ana. Lit him up like… Fuck. Oh fuck… Rick shot his own brother in cold blood."

"Are you safe?"

"Yes, but—"

"Is Eric with you?" She snatched up her duffel bag and dug out a pair of jeans and a top.

"Yes, yes—"

"Do you have the take?"

"Yes. Fuck. Will you listen to me, goddammit! He's got Mom!"

Chapter Five

ANA FROZE, HER HEART thudding violently in her chest. "*What?*"

"Rick knew Mom was the fence. Eric and I ditched him and took the stones, because he's fucking crazy. Shot his own goddamn brother. Who does that, Ana? We ditched him and made off with the take and he got to Mom."

She activated the phone's speaker and set it on the coffee table. "How do you know he's got Mom?"

"He just called and said he had her. Said he'd trade her for the stones. I tried calling the house but I keep getting the voicemail."

"Okay, okay." *Think, Ana. Damn it.* She yanked on a pair of panties. "Where are you supposed to make the trade?"

"He didn't say. He's supposed to call back."

"Listen, I'm here in Whisper Creek. I'll head over to Mom's now and make sure the bastard's not bluffing." She hopped from one foot to the other as she tugged on her jeans, becoming aware of the deep soreness between her legs. "Maybe she's got the ringer off or her sound machine turned up loud. You know how she needs white noise to sleep."

"Ana... He'll kill her. Rick must've planned all along to get rid of everyone who knew anything. He had to have looked her up before we ditched him. There's no reason for him to keep her alive for a trade. We won't know the difference until he's got us face-to-face, then he'll take us out, too."

"Shut up, Frankie." She pulled a sports bra over her head, then grabbed her top. "You're not going to think about anything but keeping your head down and your mind sharp. I'm gonna run by Mom's."

"Okay but—"

"You keep that burner phone on you at all times, you hear me? I want you and Eric to check in every thirty minutes. And find a safe place to hole up and stay there until I tell you otherwise. Don't make a move without me, got it?"

"Yes. I got it. Ana…" Frankie's voice broke. "It's all fucked up. It all fell apart."

"That's usually what happens when you break the law, Frankie. You've just been really damned lucky so far." She shoved her nightgown into her bag. "Be careful. Love you."

Ana was straightening from grabbing her heels off the floor when Jake stepped into the room fully dressed with his gun on his hip and his badge clipped to the waistband of his jeans.

"You can't come with me," she snapped.

"The hell I can't." His gaze bored into hers. "That's my brother out there with yours. Christ, Ana. You're here because you knew they'd pulled off that heist and you didn't say a damn thing to me."

"Because they're not going to jail, Jake!" She shoved her heels in her bag and slung it over her shoulder. "I can take care of this and you can keep your hands clean."

"Is that all you think I worry about?" He stared at her face, then cursed under his breath. "I'd break any law for you. Every law. There's nothing I won't do for you."

"I know." She went to him and put her palm over his heart. "I know you would. I'm just not sure you could live with yourself afterward and I don't want to put you in that position. I love you, Jake. Just the way you are."

Jake lifted her fingers to his mouth. "I have something for you."

"Not now!"

He released her hand and shoved his own into his pocket. A moment later, he was sliding a diamond onto the ring finger of her left hand, a square cushion-cut that caught the light of the moon shining through the gap in the shutters on the windows.

She swallowed hard, afraid to blink. "Jake—"

"I've been holding on to that for years. Now it's your turn." He tugged her bag off her shoulder and dropped it on the couch. "Give me your keys. I want to drive the Jag."

Ana felt damn near giddy. Too much adrenaline, she told herself. Neither of them was thinking straight. It'd never work… unless it did.

But they had to make it through the next few hours first.

"You got a jacket?" he asked.

"In the car. Let's go."

Jake watched as Ana opened the trunk of her car and revealed body armor and a handgun safe. She selected one of three guns she had locked away and slid it into her shoulder holster, then shrugged on a windbreaker and relocked the box. Her movements were calm, practiced, and efficient. Jake marveled at the strong, sexy woman she'd become.

"You okay?" he asked quietly.

"No." Shutting the trunk quietly, she studied the two-story house tucked into the woods. "But I'm really glad you're here. Come on."

In the silver glow of moonlight, the old Victorian with its

round, pointed rooftops and wraparound porch looked like something out of a fairytale—the kind where things went wrong.

Ana kept her cool even after they'd searched the house and confirmed that Tilly had been taken. There were signs of a struggle in the master bedroom, but mercifully no blood.

"Rick Parker could've killed her here, if that was his plan," she said flatly, picking up Tilly's cell phone from the nightstand and searching through it. "Could've made it look like a burglary gone bad. She talked him out of it, maybe gave him information that made her valuable. She conned him. It'll keep her alive for a while. Let's go."

"Hey." He caught her by the shoulders before she moved past him and looked down at her face. Recognizing her fierce determination to keep her emotions at bay, he settled for a soft kiss to her brow.

"Jake—"

"We both needed that. Now we can go."

They went downstairs and were almost out the front door, when Ana stepped on something that crunched beneath her black running shoes. Crouching, she examined the broken glass; then she found its source lying on the floor just inside the door.

"This shouldn't be here," she said, straightening. "Mom has kept this photo on her side of the bed forever."

Jake took it from her, looking at the yellowed image through the cracked glass.

Her mouth curved in a smile. "That photo was taken the day my dad proposed, after they left the bank and took a stroll on the boardwalk. It's a message she knew I would understand. Mom's leading Rick to Atlantic City."

His brows arched. "Isn't that a big leap?"

"Trust me," Ana insisted. "The minute he went along with

whatever story she sold him, it became her show. She's running it. We just need to catch up with them, before he figures that out."

As they drove east on 422, Ana pulled out her laptop and began typing furiously. Jake watched her out of the corner of his eye. Reaching over, he slid his hand beneath her hair and stroked her nape with his fingers.

He was so damn glad to be able to touch her again. To be able to smell her and hear her, to have her nearby to look at. She was keeping him sane instead of frantic with worry over Eric.

She looked at him, her face made stark by her grimness and the shadows of night. "Frankie will take care of Eric. Don't worry."

"It's not just Eric I'm worried about." He tugged gently on her hair.

"I can't think about that. I can't lose it. Not now."

"Okay, so we'll keep your mind off it. Do you travel a lot?"

"Yes, but that's because there was nothing to keep me home. I won't so much now." She returned her attention to her laptop screen. "The good citizens of Whisper Creek will have to get used to seeing me around again."

"Is that where you want to live?"

Her gaze shot to him again. "The last time I checked that's where *you* lived, right?"

"I stayed because it kept me close to your family. I was afraid if I moved away, I might lose touch with you altogether." He shrugged. "Don't look so horrified. There wasn't any place I had a burning desire to get to and Eric needed the stability of staying in one place. But my job can take me anywhere—you know that."

"You'd do that?" she asked quietly.

"I'd do anything for you, Anastasia. You make me a happy man."

Ana was quiet for a few moments, then, "You know how my parents got engaged? They met in Atlantic City. My mom was running an insurance scam and my dad was hustling old stuff. She wanted to get her hands on his antiques and he wanted to get a fraudulent payout. They played each other for a few weeks, then they agreed to meet at a local bank where he was supposed to show the goods for appraisal—he pulled an engagement ring and a bottle of Dom Perignon out of the safe deposit box instead."

"Your dad proposed in a bank?"

"Surrounded by other people's safeguarded valuables—absolutely the perfect venue for my parents. They'd been onto each other almost from the first, but for them the game was their version of flirting and dating. *That's* what my family is like, Jake. And I don't see them ever changing."

"I'm not running scared, Anastasia. If it takes a few decades or a lifetime, you'll eventually figure that out."

Shaking her head, Ana got back to work.

Chapter Six

THE SKY OVER THE turnpike was lightening when Ana answered a check-in call from Frankie.

"Hey," she said quietly, achingly aware of the block of ice in her gut. "I got an email from Detective Samuels in New York—Terence Parker passed away an hour ago."

"Oh, shit. Shit, shit, shit. Terry. Jesus. He was a good guy, you know? He didn't deserve to go out like that."

"Have you heard from Rick?"

"Yeah." Frankie took a deep breath. "And he let me talk to Mom. She sounded okay. Not scared at all. And you were right about Atlantic City—that's where he wants to do the swap. Eric's texting the address to Jake's cell now. I told Rick I'd have to talk to Mom directly before the meet or I wouldn't show up, and I said we wanted to get out of town before nine."

"Good. You're doing real good." She shoved a hand through her hair and said what was weighing heavily on her mind. "Frankie, you and Eric… You need to be working on a Plan B."

Jake cursed. "Ana, damn it!"

She glanced at him and kept talking. "When we turn Rick in, he's going to turn state's evidence to get some leniency on the murder charge."

Frankie's voice was as serious as she'd ever heard it. "We're considering our options, Ana. Don't worry about us. Take care of Mom."

The moment she killed the call, Jake went off. "What the fuck are you thinking?"

"I'm thinking I'd like to salvage as much from this mess as I can. The store is going to get its gems back, Terence's killer is going to be apprehended, and I'm not going to take the finder's fee from the insurance company for obvious reasons. Putting Eric and Frankie in jail isn't going to bring the injured parties any more justice or restitution than that."

She grabbed his phone from his lap and took the address of the meet from his text messages and typed it into the GPS.

He glared at her. "That's all you've got to say?"

"Yes. Think about it, Jake. Think hard. When all's said and done, we'll go from there."

The meet was at a rundown motel in a depressed, forgotten corner of Atlantic City. It seemed worlds away from the boardwalk and tourist mecca. The signs and architecture of the buildings were decades past their prime. Time and the sun had faded what color might have distinguished features before.

Ana wondered if her mother knew this place from its heyday. What had led Rick here? The convenience of exterior walkways and parking directly in front of the room doors? Was that enough to negate the fact that the bank was on the far side of town?

Whatever the reason, she'd valet parked her car at the Mondego Resort for safekeeping before picking up a rental to get to the dive motel. Then she and Jake had split up—he waited in the car down the street, while she holed up in a dingy room that smelled like an ashtray and old sweat. They waited for the call from Frankie that would put everything in motion.

"Room 105," he said the second she answered her cell phone.

"All right," Ana said. "I'm going to head out with the ice bucket. I'll be nearby as you approach the door. Go up alone and make him come outside. Tell him Eric's watching from a safe distance and has the diamonds. If Rick wants to prove his trustworthiness, he'll step out. He'll probably leave Mom in the room for safekeeping. Jake'll drive around back to the bathroom window and see if he can get to her. You with me so far?"

"Yes."

Ana appreciated hearing the quiet strength in her brother's voice. "I'll see you in a minute."

She didn't have to tell him not to look at her too long or too often, or worse, not look at her at all—anything that would point her out as suspicious. Frankie was a pro. Shoving her gun into the waistband of her jeans at the small of her back, Ana yanked her top over it and grabbed the ice bucket. She left the room, gratefully breathing in the fresh air outside.

Texting Jake as she went, Ana walked across the crumbling parking lot of the U-shaped single-story motel. She felt her pulse steady when Frankie knocked on the motel room door— she was never calmer then when a game was in play.

"Jesus, Rick," she heard Frankie say when the door opened. "You look like shit."

"Fucking bastard! You cut me out! Cut Terry out! Where the fuck is Monroe? Where're my fucking diamonds?"

Ana slipped into an alcove that led to a maintenance/housekeeping door and pressed her back up against the wall. Rick was erratic; his breathing was heavy and his voice far too loud. It made Ana nuts to think of her mom having to spend the last few hours with him and as the conversation between Rick and her brother progressed, she grew more and more uneasy.

"Don't fuck with me, Miller, you slimy piece of shit," Rick

snapped. "Do I look like an idiot? *Do I?* I'm not going outside and swapping diamonds where anyone can shoot pictures! Tell Monroe to get his ass over here now!"

"What the hell do I need pictures for? If I had the heat out here, you'd already be done. You've got a kidnapped woman in your room and you're a murderer."

"Bullshit. I never—"

"Terry's dead," Frank said flatly.

The unmistakable *thud* of flesh hitting flesh got Ana's back up. She withdrew her gun.

"Goddammit, Terry—" Frankie stumbled back from the door and into Ana's line of sight. His hand was pressed to his lip, blood trickling between his fingers. Staying where he was, he forced Rick to follow him out into the parking lot.

"*Liar!* You're a fucking liar, Miller." Rick stumbled into daylight with bare feet and rumbled clothes. His blond hair was disheveled and he gestured wildly with his hands. "You've been lying from the beginning. Setting everything up. I told Terry you were going to jack us and you did! Who killed him? You or Monroe?"

"Jesus Christ, you strung-out sonofabitch. *You* fucking shot your brother. What the hell did you expect was going to happen?"

Rick slammed his palms into Frankie's shoulders, sending him stumbling back "What did you do? *What did you do?* I shot him up just enough to make him look innocent. And now he's dead? *Dead?*"

"Read the damn papers, man. Or watch the news. One of your bullets opened a vein. He nearly bled out. Never recovered. He had a heart attack."

Ana stepped away from the wall, taking advantage of the opportunity to intervene between Rick and her mom. She inched toward the open motel room door, her eyes never leaving Rick's back.

She was ready when he spun with a scream and faced her.

"Cop bitch!" he yelled, before charging toward her.

Ana fired low, hitting him in the shin, and watched as he fell to his knee. He reached behind him. She barely ducked the flung blade that stabbed through the stucco wall behind her. Rick lunged past her crouched position and through the open room doorway, tucking and rolling across the threshold, then kicking the door shut.

Turning, she fired at the ancient doorknob and kicked out with her foot. The door held. She fired again just as Rick began to scream inside.

"Where is she? *Where is she?*"

She stopped, holding out her arm when Frankie rushed the door. "Wait. I think Jake's got her."

The rental sedan pulled into the parking lot to their left. Jake was at the wheel. Both Tilly and Eric were in the car with him.

"Oh god," Frank choked out. "Mom."

Ana kept her eye on the room door and the curtained window. "Get in the car and go."

"What about you?"

Rick continued to yell, followed by the firing of a gun and the shattering of glass. "Nooooo! No! No!" More shots rang out, and more wailing. Then it fell eerily quiet.

"Take care of Mom," she told him, pulling her phone out to call nine-one-one. "Leave this to me."

Jake paid the street vendor for his coffee, then turned to face the Crossfire Building again. Foot traffic on the sidewalk swarmed around him, congesting the pavement the same way the cars clogged the street at his back. Car horns blared over the din at regular intervals, yet the residents of Manhattan seemed unaffected by the near frantic pulse of their city.

Tilting his head back, he let his gaze travel up the length of the sapphire-hued spire of glass that pierced the sky along with the hundreds of other towering buildings in the city. The theft of the Crown of Roses was finally coming to a close, and his life with Ana was about to begin. With both of the Parker brothers dead, there was no one who knew the identity of the other two accomplices in the crime, and with all of the items recovered and returned, the cops on both sides of the Hudson River were likely to call the case closed.

The gun Rick had used to end his own life had been a ballistics match to the bullet found in Terence's shoulder, putting that aspect of the crime to rest as well. There was one last thing to do...

Ana came twirling out of the revolving doors of the Crossfire and her searching gaze found him on the corner. Dressed once again in head to toe black, she looked sleek and very sexy. Her mouth curved slightly as she approached him and deftly took the coffee from his hand.

She took a drink and her nose wrinkled. "Ugh. Black. I like a little cream and sugar."

He tapped her on the end of her nose with his fingertip. "I'm sure you like it hot, too, so I waited for you to come out before I ordered you one. How did it go?"

"Good. Gideon Cross agreed to give the reward to the Parker family. That's where it should go."

"He didn't question why you'd give away a half million dollars like you would a five dollar bill?" Not to mention the two million dollar finder's fee for the return of the diamonds...

"No." She smiled. "I'm sure he thoroughly researched my

portfolio before I ever stepped foot into his very impressive office."

Jake's brows rose. "How rich are you?"

"Let's just say I'm very good at my job." Her smile turned into a grin.

"Damn. Got me a sugar mama. How'd I get so lucky?"

Ana licked her lower lip. "Wanna get luckier?"

"Hell, yeah." He caught her hand in his and they set off.

A Dark Kiss of Rapture

of

Rapture

A RENEGADE ANGELS NOVELLA

Glossary

CHANGE—the process a mortal undergoes to become a *vampire*.

FALLEN—the *Watchers* after the fall from grace. They have been stripped of their wings and their souls, leaving them as immortal blood drinkers who cannot procreate.

LYCANS—a subgroup of the *Fallen* who were spared vampirism by agreeing to serve the *Sentinels*. They were transfused with demon blood, which restored their souls but made them mortal. They can shape-shift and procreate.

MINION—a mortal who has been *Changed* into a vampire by one of the *Fallen*. Most mortals do not adjust well and become rabid. Unlike the *Fallen,* they cannot tolerate sunlight.

NAPHIL—singular of *nephalim*.

NEPHALIM—the children of mortal and *Watcher* parents. Their blood drinking contributed to and inspired the vampiric punishment of the *Fallen*.

SENTINELS—an elite special ops unit of the *seraphim,* tasked with enforcing the punishment of the *Watchers.*

SERAPH—singular of *seraphim.*

SERAPHIM—the highest rank of angel in the angelic hierarchy.

VAMPIRES—a term that encompasses both the *Fallen* and their *minions.*

WATCHERS—two hundred *seraphim* angels sent to earth at the beginning of time to observe mortals. They violated the laws by taking mortals as mates and were punished with an eternity on earth as *vampires* with no possibility of forgiveness.

Go tell the Watchers of heaven, who have deserted the lofty sky, and their holy everlasting station, who have been polluted with women, and have done as the sons of men do, by taking to themselves wives, and who have been greatly corrupted on the earth; that on the earth they shall never obtain peace and remission of sin. For they shall not rejoice in their offspring; they shall behold the slaughter of their beloved; shall lament for the destruction of their sons; and shall petition for ever; but shall not obtain mercy and peace.

The Book of Enoch 12:5–7

Chapter One

RAZE'S NIGHT HAD BEEN going pretty well, until the woman he'd just spent four hours fucking stumbled across a naked, disemboweled body on his doorstep. Her scream had shattered the serenity of the predawn, forcing him to knock her out before she drew a crowd. Now, as the sun stretched sleepy tendrils of light over the horizon, he stood over the corpse and struggled to contain his roiling fury.

"Dumped on my goddamn porch like trash." He ran both hands over his shaved head. "Poor bastard."

"Guesstimate of the time your gift arrived?" Vashti asked, her stiletto-heeled boots tapping out an impatient staccato as she paced. Her crimson hair swayed around her shoulder blades, the vividly-hued tresses the only wash of color against her skintight, all-black jumpsuit. She was a comic book aficionado's wet dream, with her lush tits and ass offset by a fallen angel's incomparable beauty. Her appearance was as lethal as the twin katanas she often wore in crisscrossing sheaths on her back, her physical beauty another weapon in the arsenal she used as second-in-command of the entire vampire nation.

"Hell if I know," he bit out. "There was nothing out of place when I got home at midnight. He was found at four."

"You didn't hear anything? Nothing at all?"

Raze scowled. He had a squeaky board on his front porch and everyone knew it. Even if they ruled out the benefit of his vampire hearing, his powerful sense of smell should have picked up on the freshly spilled blood. "No. Christ. If I'd heard any-thing I would have caught the fuckers."

Damned if he'd tell her that it hadn't been possible to hear anything over the woman moaning beneath him and the steady banging of his headboard against the wall as he pounded into her. The smell of hot sex, dripping sweat, and semen-filled latex had saturated the air along with the scent of the blood he'd drunk from her—a lover whose name he couldn't remember now. It shamed him that the broken body on his doorstop had been lost among the sexual excess.

He stared at his name carved into the corpse's left biceps and the cattle-branded monogram he recognized as the mark of a vampire known as Grimm. A growl rumbled up from his chest. Even without the mutilation, the victim was Raze's now. He would stand for the man and the vengeance due him. "I almost wish Grimm was still alive so I could kill him again."

"You've got enough on your plate dealing with his minions," Syre said, entering the room soundlessly.

Despite the hour, the vampire leader looked flawless. Even in casual dark jeans and a plain T-shirt, there was an elegance to him that was regal and commanding. Raze would brave the pits of hell for Syre if he commanded it. They'd come to earth together, fallen together, lost their wings together. Two hundred of them. And there wasn't one of the Fallen who wouldn't give their life for their leader. From the heights of grace as Watchers to the fall that cursed them with vampirism, Syre led them forward with a confidence that inspired them all.

Vash's pacing came to an abrupt halt. "Do we have any idea how many minions we're talking about here? How many have you taken out so far, Raze?"

"A dozen pairs, give or take a few. Adrian was on it, too," he said, referring to the angel who'd severed Syre's wings. Raze had a lot of reasons to resent Adrian, as well as the Sentinel angels who served under him—the Fallen's vampiric punishment being the least of it—but there was no denying that when they were aligned and hunting the same prey, Adrian's involvement was a benefit.

Syre crossed his arms and looked at Vashti, his second-in-command. "Remind me: How long did Grimm evade our attention?"

"Too fucking long. He was in our faces, but I didn't look deep enough. On the surface, his theory had merit. Still does. Or maybe it's wishful thinking. With the number of minions we lose to madness during the Change from fledgling to vampire, I'd like to think there's some way to cut the waste. He wrapped his dogma up with pseudoscience and I bought it."

"He was the one pairing fledglings into couples to ease the transition? I remember discussing it with you. He had enough success in the beginning to justify allowing him to proceed, if I recall."

Raze shot her a chastising glance for being hard on herself. "If you were looking for a ball and chain, and vampirism was one of your requirements in a perfect mate, Grimm was the man to see. He had personality profiles, compatibility charts, et cetera. All of which he used to weed out the whack jobs so he could pair them with nutcases. I knew his doctrine was dangerous, so when I took him out I hunted down all his disciples, too. Whoever is responsible for this, Grimm didn't document them the way he did the others."

"Disciples," Syre murmured. "Interesting word choice."

"It's the right word, trust me. What else would you call the followers of an idiot playacting as a messiah preaching revolt against you?"

Syre ran a hand through his thick black hair, the only sign he gave of any disquiet. "Whoever is responsible, they came directly to you. This is personal."

"You're goddamned right it's personal." He looked at the body again, knowing it wasn't merely a taunt but a message. "Help me turn this guy over."

Syre stepped forward, waving Vash back.

It was a gruesome task. The smell emanating from the open body cavity would torture a human; for a vampire, it was pure hell. They got as far as getting the corpse onto its side. Then the loosened entrails slid out with a soft sucking sound, and they both leaped back and away. Raze had eviscerated his own share of enemies, but this man was a victim, and that made all the difference.

"Do you guys need a hand?" Vash asked, stepping up to them.

"No." Raze had seen the tattoo on the corpse's shoulder blade. Unlike Grimm's brand, the ink was a mark the man had voluntarily applied as a show of loyalty, affection, and team spirit.

"The Cubs," he muttered. "Guess I'm heading to Chicago."

Chapter Two

RAZE HIT THE GROUND running in the Windy City. Within an hour of his plane landing, he'd swept through the building that had once housed Grimm's operation (presently a printing shop) and checked his way through a quarter of the list of Grimm's known haunts. Then, impatient, he took a chance and headed to Wrigley Field.

Although the ballpark was dark and quiet for the night, Raze knew wrong when he came across it and he damn well felt it as he drove by. Parking a few streets away, he slid out from behind the wheel and opened the back door of his rental to grab his blades. He strapped them on with the efficiency of long practice: daggers on each thigh and two katanas crisscrossing his back. Then he darted over on foot, moving so quickly the mortal eye couldn't catch him.

As he approached, he picked up the faint sound of a melodious male voice coming from the field, followed by a chorus of murmurs in reply—sounds too slight for anything but a vampire's hearing to catch. Grimm had been big on staging, too, which made Raze wonder just how close this protégé had been to Grimm and how long he had been working in the shadows.

Rounding the back of the ballpark, Raze climbed up the rear of the bleachers. He pulled his head up over the top, and looked down at the darkened field below. A lone man stood before a group of approximately two hundred robed and kneeling minions. Segmented into pairs with the men in black and the women in red, they formed a perfect pattern of stripes in the center of the field.

Raze listened to a couple lines of bullshit about the supremacy of the vampire nation, then he tuned it out and focused on the leader. The man was tall and lean, dark-haired, and dressed in a three-piece suit. He had a mesmerizing cadence to his speech, a lulling sonorousness that was evident even though Raze had stopped picking out the words.

He debated his next step, knowing this was an elaborate trap for him, one that would be designed with the expectation that he wouldn't come alone. Which was why he'd done exactly that.

But he could still take them by surprise.

Pulling out his phone, he jumped the hoops necessary to reach Adrian.

"Mitchell," the Sentinel leader answered.

"It's Raze. I've got a situation you'll be interested in."

"Where are you?"

"Chicago."

"Yes, that is interesting. So am I."

Raze stilled, his hackles rising at the softness of Adrian's tone. "That's not a coincidence."

"No, it's not. Location?"

He wasn't surprised that the angel was so far from his home base in Anaheim, California. That was Adrian's way. While Syre was cerebral in his leadership, using Raze and Salem to investigate and Vashti as his iron fist, Adrian was the opposite. The Sentinel leader left the administrative duties to others so he could remain a hands-on hunter in the field. A vampire hunter and gaoler—those roles being the sole purpose of his existence.

Raze gave his location, then pointed out, "I wouldn't have called you if I just needed a hand or two. If you're going to send a couple lycans and call it a night, don't bother."

"Don't tell me how to respond to a request for a favor." The lack of inflection in the angel's voice was more disconcerting than an outright threat would have been.

"If you'd let us establish some cabals and covens in the major cities, I wouldn't need to call you at all." The Sentinels used their lycans to keep vampires contained in rural, lower population areas. They said the policy was to protect mortals, but the side effect was the hindering of the Fallen's ability to police their own minions. And every transgression was another mark against them, another smudge barring them from any possibility of redemption.

"How many more rogue minions would there be if vampires were allowed access to such a smorgasbord of food? The spread would become uncontainable. It's already out of control as it is or you wouldn't be calling me."

The line died, leaving Raze cursing at his cell phone. One of these days, he and the angel were going to have it out. But not tonight.

As the couples swayed like hypnotized king cobras, Raze leaped over onto the uppermost bench, then started taking the stairs down, applauding as he went. "Man, you've really got your delivery down. I mean, I could almost buy it … if I was a whacked-out moron."

The man lifted his head and looked at Raze, his eyes glowing in the darkness. "Raze, how nice of you to join us. We've been expecting you. You are, after all, the guest of honor."

Although the distance between them was great, neither of them needed to raise their voices to be heard. "I'd say I was more of a bouncer. One who's going to bounce all your nutty asses into Hell."

"Where are your friends? Surely you didn't come to such an occasion alone?"

"Yeah, it's just me. I tried to round up more of a party, but everyone said it'd be a dud. They were right." Although he kept his descent easy and casual, Raze was hyperaware of new participants to the game as black-clad minions crawled toward him like ants. "Who are you?"

"Don't you remember me?"

"Nope. You don't ring any bells." He could tell being forgotten really chafed and that made him smile. In the back of his mind, he considered the possibility that Adrian might leave him hanging in the wind—the Sentinel hadn't actually agreed to show up. But Raze had no choice but to proceed as if reinforcements were on the way. "Why don't you enlighten me?"

"That's my goal." The man walked closer, his arms extended in dramatic fashion. "The Fallen are so busy wishing to be the angels you once were that you never enjoy being what you are."

Raze pulled one katana out of its sheath, the moonlight glinting off the silver-plated blade. "The only thing I don't like about what I am now is how much time I have to waste hunting dickheads like you."

"Ah … you'd prefer to continue your quest to fuck everything willing to sate your lust. Of all the Fallen, you're one of the most pitiable. At least the others fell for love. You fell only because you can't keep you dick out of warm, wet holes."

Pivoting, Raze sliced the head off the minion who'd attempted to come at him from behind. He took out two more who lunged from the sides, his speed and strength fueled by the bitter truth that had been thrown in his face. Grimm's eternal love bullshit was why Raze had volunteered to hunt him down to begin with. The twisting of love to achieve an even more twisted end stirred violence and fury inside him. He'd watched his fellow Watchers give up their wings for it, and Grimm's doctrine made a mockery of that terrible, heartrending sacrifice.

"See how he slays the bravest of us?" the idiot prophet asked his minions. "His own people. Weakening us from within. We've elected to follow the Fallen, yet they lead us nowhere! We remain in the shadows, hidden from the world, while—"

"Are you going to shut him up," Adrian asked, landing gracefully on a bench and swatting away the incoming surge of minions with an impatient swat of his massive wings, "or is that what you needed me for?"

The vampires on the field had staggered to their feet when Adrian appeared and now they scrambled in every direction. It was a natural, instinctive urge to run from an apex predator, but the Sentinel leader himself inspired a unique awe and fear. Like Syre, Adrian had been blessed by the Creator, gifted with a face and form that was the height of angelic perfection. The thirty-foot expanse of his alabaster wings glimmered in the moonlight, the pure pristine white of the feathers framed by crimson tips, as if he'd trailed the edges through freshly spilled blood. That band of red was a vivid reminder of what he was—a weapon tasked with punishing the Fallen and containing their minions.

"He's mine." Raze raced down the steps and vaulted onto the field at the same moment a dozen lycans in lupine form hit the grass, converging on the panicked mass. He went after the leader, who surprisingly stood his ground and faced off with a pistol in hand.

"I could change your life, Raze."

"Gimme your name."

"Does it matter?"

Raze shrugged and twirled his blade with practiced ease. "Always good to have a name to go with a kill."

The man smiled. "You won't kill me. You need me to tell you if there are more of us, and if so, how many more and where they are. And I won't kill you because I need you, too. If you'd think outside the box, you'd realize that you could be the cornerstone of massive, sweeping advancement. You could have the mate you deserve. You could—"

"You don't know what I deserve."

"Don't make me hurt you, Raze." He looked over Raze's shoulder and his smile widened. "You surprised me by bringing in the Sentinels and their dogs, but we had to get rid of them at some point. Now is as good a time as any."

Using the man's distraction, Raze whipped out the blade strapped to his left thigh and threw it, striking the prophet in the throat. The gun discharged. Pain ripped through Raze along with the bullet that shot clear through his shoulder and out the other side. The wound healed almost instantly, proving the man's words to be true: He didn't want Raze dead or he'd have used a silver-laced bullet.

Behind him, the field erupted with the sounds of gunfire and the yelps of wounded lycans. Raze dropped to the ground. As the robe-clad minions utilized the weapons they'd hidden beneath their robes, he quickly assessed his options. Adrian and a female Sentinel took to the field, their wings deflecting bullets and slashing like blades. Screams rent the air. Bodies were hacked into pieces.

Most minions didn't know what it was like to face a Sentinel. They could never prepare for the lethality of those magnificent wings that sliced like blades and were impervious to all mortal implements of destruction. Unique to each angel, the patterns and colors said much about the angel's soul if you knew how to read them, and their average thirty-foot span meant it was nearly impossible to get close enough to inflict any damage.

Raze took out a minion with his other knife, then crawled to the body of the prophet and took his gun. Lying on his back, he emptied the clip into the converging mass of robe-clad figures, slowing them down so that he could join the fray with his swords. Leaping to his feet, he did just that, cutting a swath through the chaos.

Blood spurted and flowed like a river, soaking the grass and splattering Raze until he dripped with it. It was over in moments, leaving a battlefield upon which two Sentinels stood inviolate, surrounded by snarling lycans and a sea of dead bodies.

Raze pointed the tip of his blade at the two minions he'd managed to spare. "For you two," he murmured, "the fun is just beginning."

Raze made it back to his hotel just before dawn. He showered again, finishing the job he'd started with a hosing down at the field. Restlessness gnawed at him. The hunt wasn't over. What troubled him was that he had no idea what it would take to end it. How many more of Grimm's devotees were out there?

Tugging on a pair of black sweats, he propped up his iPad and placed a call to Vashti.

"Hey," he greeted her, when her face came on-screen.

"Hey yourself." Her gaze narrowed. "You're looking rough. What's up?"

It was hard for a vampire to look rough. He was surprised that she said he did, but he brushed past it and caught her up on the night's events.

"You killed him?" She leaned back into her sofa cushions. It was rare for her to indulge in any downtime, so rare that it took him a moment to pinpoint her location as her home in Raceport. "Just like that?"

"Just like that. After what they did to the man they left on my porch, he got off easy. I made it quick and painless."

Her brow rose. "O-kay … But who's going to give you intel now that the two minions you captured gave up a whole lotta nada?"

"I got his name. Eventually, I'll have his mate." His mouth curved without humor. "Baron has to have one, if only to practice what he preaches."

"Maybe you killed her tonight. Surely she would have been there."

"She wasn't on the field. Trust me, if you'd have seen the way they were dressed and lined up, you'd know that everyone was paired except for him. I agree she was probably there somewhere, but she kept out of sight."

"So how are you going to find Mrs. Baron?"

"I'm e-mailing you his prints." Sitting back, he ran a hand over his shaven head. "It's probably a long shot to hope they registered when they mated, but it won't hurt to check. I'm also sending you a video. They recorded the killing that brought me here. I found it on a jump drive bracelet Baron was wearing. The recording shows a blond woman doing the deed, but I can't be sure that's legit because they sent a doctored version to Adrian that shows me as the killer. That's what brought him to Chicago."

Vash whistled. "They set you up."

"My guess is Adrian was leverage. Baron was under the impression that Syre will do just about anything to stay in Adrian's good graces, including throwing me under the bus."

"You got all that in the few minutes you let him breathe?"

"He wouldn't shut up. One of those assholes who likes to listen to himself talk."

"All right. I'll have Torque look at the prints and video, see what he can dig up. You gonna hang around Chicago for a while?"

He nodded. The data search was in good hands with Torque, Syre's son. No one dug up intel better or faster. The rest would be up to Raze. "I'll wait to hear back from Torque and spend some time on the streets. Maybe they'll come to me."

"Watch your back." Crossing her long legs on the couch, she leaned toward the screen. "And don't trust Adrian. He'll throw you under the bus, too."

Touching a finger to his brow in salute, he acknowledged the warning and signed off.

Chapter Three

WHEN HE WAS ASKED later what drew him to the small jazz club in an upscale part of Chicago, Raze didn't have an answer. The place wasn't his style with its small round tables, live singer, and elegant patrons. But he'd been drawn to it and the sultry voice of the female entertainer that floated into the street on the night breeze. Maybe because it was so different from the hard-edged clubs Torque helmed that gave fledglings a safe place to find blood and sex, and—most importantly—register their name and sire for the records. Raze thought maybe what he needed was a palate cleanser. Something different.

Damn it. He was restless and unsettled. He could barely stand to be in his hotel room. Even with the television on and the Internet at his fingertips, he felt isolated and stifled. He was beginning to wonder if Baron's bullet had been tainted in some way after all. It wasn't like him to … brood. As endless as his life was, he still didn't have time to waste being a pain in his own ass.

He paid the club's cover charge and went inside, discovering a small open space with rust-colored walls adorned with massive impressionist canvases. Pendant lights offered intimate illumination, except for at the bar, where the blue glass shelves were lit with bright white light. The floor was covered in multicolored mosaic tiles and patrons danced freely wherever they found an open space, giving the whole establishment a comfortable bohemian feel.

Sliding onto a barstool, he noted the bartender. The lovely

blonde on point looked like she just might be what he needed, with her sleeves of tattoos, low-slung leather pants, and curvy body. Her hair hung in dreadlocks to her waist and was held back from her delicate face with a black bandana. She glanced at him, looked away, then immediately glanced back. She licked her pierced lower lip and made her interest known with a heated glance.

When she'd finished serving her customer, she came over. "What's your poison?"

"Shiraz."

Her brows rose. "Really? Wouldn't have pegged you for a wine drinker."

"No?"

"No. Jameson, maybe. Or Glenfiddich." She poured expertly and set the glass in front of him. "In the mood for something else?"

His fingertips slid lightly up and down the stem of his glass. "Suggestions?"

"I'm off at midnight."

"I'm free at midnight."

Her mouth curved in a sexy smile and she extended her hand. "Sam."

He stroked her palm. "Raze."

He watched her saunter off, admiring the way black leather hugged her lush ass, then he picked up his glass and stared into it. Still fucking brooding, goddamnit.

He smelled the woman who stole his interest from Sam before he heard her.

"She's not what you want."

The clipped, no-nonsense female voice stirred something inside him, as did her scent. He savored both a moment before he looked at her, appreciating both her directness and the fragrance she wore, which was light and sweetly floral, a perfect accompaniment to the natural female scent of her skin.

Raze glanced aside at the woman who made herself comfortable in the space next to him. She wasn't his type. Too refined and complicated for his tastes, but there was no denying she was beautiful. Willowy body with modest curves. Creamy skin contrasted by dark hair. Vivid green eyes framed by thick, black lashes. She was an altogether stunning package. "She isn't?"

"No." She hooked one nude stiletto heel on the bar's foot rail and set elegant hands on the carved wooden lip of the bar top. No rings, which he found surprising. She was the sort of prime choice female that didn't remain on the market long.

Raze canted his body toward her. High-class, he thought, noting the Rolex on her wrist and the hefty diamond studs shooting multihued fire from her earlobes. In a quick survey, he registered slim gray dress slacks, a sleeveless black silk top, and dark-as-ink curls piled high and balanced on a long, slender neck.

An image of her came to his mind … sprawled naked and prone across a red velvet bedspread, her graceful spine arching as he slid his parted lips along its curve. Decadent. That's what she was, and decadence was what she needed from the man she took to her bed. A long, slow, deep seduction. He didn't have that patience in him tonight. He'd had blood dripping from every inch of his skin just twenty-four hours ago and he had a cold knot in his gut that ached.

Lifting his glass, he wet his lips, absently noting the building heat in his blood. Not his type, but he wanted her. "*I'm* not what *you* want. Not tonight."

She reached for his glass and he gave it up. Blood was the only thing he could ingest, but he'd learned to tolerate a drop or two of red wine.

Her dark green eyes stared into his over the lip of the glass. She swallowed and made his dick hard. "Shiraz."

"Well done," he murmured, his eyes following the perfect arches of her brows and the sculptured beauty of her cheekbones. With a slow and deep breath, Raze realized every other female in the room had faded into insignificance.

"I have good taste." The intimacy of her smile included him in that statement, while the determination in her eyes dismissed his assertion that they weren't meant to be lovers.

He ran a hand over his head and debated what to do. He was no longer interested in Sam the bartender, but he wanted sex and he needed blood. And the only person he wanted either from was the one standing in front of him—the kind of woman a guy didn't take casually. "You could have any guy in this room. Any guy you want."

"Perhaps." She shrugged and settled on the seat beside him. "But I need you. I'm Kim, by the way."

She extended her hand. They shook in greeting and he gave her his name.

"Interesting." Her eyes sparkled. "Suits you."

Raze inclined his head in acknowledgment, maintaining his hold on her for a moment longer than necessary because he got a charge out of it. He'd chosen the name himself after shedding his angelic one. All of the Fallen had recreated themselves and most minions followed suit—a new name for a new life. "Odd place to hunt for a rough ride."

Her lush mouth curved on one side. "You're not rough."

His brows lifted in silent challenge.

"You're not," she insisted with a smile. "You're fierce and in a dark mood, but not rough. And I wasn't trolling for any kind of ride. I came in here for a drink with friends and had every intention of leaving here all by myself."

She pointed across the room to where three of the small tables had been shoved together to make a grouping for a party of a half-dozen people. The men offered toasts to Raze, lifting their beers high. The women giggled and bent their heads together, speaking intimately. Their good-humored nervous response to him almost made him smile.

"Am I a bet, then?" he asked. "What do you win for having the courage to hit on me?"

"Hopefully, a night with you." Kim took another drink, taking the time to absorb the taste of the wine before swallowing. No liquid courage for her. "I was sitting over there, minding my own business, having a reasonably good time. Then I felt a tingle on the back of my neck. I turned around and there you were. I was just going to admire you from afar, but then I saw you were trolling and figured why not me? Plus, I really needed to admire you up close."

"You're out of my league." But he was beginning to think that wouldn't be enough to stop him.

She grinned, which belied her hands-off appearance and made her sweetly approachable. "So earn me. I won't mind the effort, I assure you."

"The effort I expend will likely leave you hobbled in the morning," he said harshly. "You have no idea what I need to get through tonight."

Kim studied him for a long moment, taking a deep breath and then another. Something swept over her delicately beautiful features, something warm that briefly touched the chill in his gut. "I'm not into pain. If that's what you need, then you're right, I'm not your girl. But I don't think that's what you're warning me about. You don't want to hurt me; you just don't want to hold back. And that's what I need, Raze—a man who doesn't hold back. That's what kind of mood *I'm* in."

Now it was his turn to study her. "Why?"

"Does it matter?"

"No." Raze dug in his back pocket for his wallet and laid out a hundred-dollar bill for Sam. "Let's go."

"I have to say good-bye to the team. Got a preference for a hotel? I'll meet you there."

Smart girl, he thought. He wrote his room number on a napkin and slid it over to her. "The Drake."

"You already had a room? I admire your optimism."

"I'm just passing through."

Laughing, she bumped shoulders with him. "I'm just playing with you, rough guy. Besides, twenty minutes in the bar and you've already got two women willing to go to bed with you, I'd say a little optimism is justified."

Christ. He wanted her. His blood was thrumming through his veins, burning with an excitement he hadn't felt in … well, a long-assed time. Impatient expectation wasn't in his nature. Or so he'd thought.

"Should I bring anything?" she asked, meeting his gaze.

"An overnight bag."

She slid off the barstool and grabbed his wine to take it back to her table. "See you in an hour, Raze."

He grabbed her elbow, squeezed gently. "Make it thirty minutes."

Again, she searched his face. Again, she saw something that settled her. "Forty-five. I'll hurry."

"Hurry faster."

"Are you *insane?*"

Kim looked at her best friend and shrugged. "Maybe a little."

"Your dad is a cop," Delia reminded, twisting her martini glass back and forth. "Your brother is a cop. You know better than to go home with strange men you pick up in a bar. He could be a serial killer or a sexual sadist or ... anything!"

"It's because I've grown up with cops that I know what I'm doing with him." She'd watched the way he walked into the bar. The confident stride, the coolly observant eyes that took in everything, the way he carried his powerful body with limber agility. A hunter. She'd bet money he was undercover vice. Just as she'd bet money that something about his job was eating at him now and he wanted to put it away for a night, take some solace from someone who wouldn't be around long enough to remind him he'd lost his edge for a few brief hours.

Looking back over her shoulder, she remembered watching Raze take a seat at the bar, remembered the way he'd looked into his glass as if the answer he was looking for could be found in it. Wasn't she here for the same reason? To seek oblivion in the company of others. So they'd narrow it down to the two of them, and toss in orgasms and physical exhaustion. There were worse ways to spend the night. Like lying in bed alone, drenched in clammy sweat and shaking with fear.

Delia frowned, her dark eyes filled with worry behind her chic electric-blue eyeglass frames. "This sort of reckless behavior isn't like you. You don't want to admit it, but you're still reeling from what happened to Janelle. You're not in the right frame of mind."

Janelle. God. Kim polished off the last of the shiraz. Even though she'd moved into a different apartment in a different building in a different part of town, she couldn't get the memory of coming home to her roommate's murder out of her head. The crazy ex Janelle had been running from for years had finally tracked her down and taken her life, then turned the gun on himself. Kim couldn't close her eyes without seeing it all over again—blood everywhere, splattered over everything, pooling on the floor in a viscous crimson lake. The sharp metallic smell of fresh death had seared her nostrils, indelibly etching a nightmare on her mind.

"I have to go." She dug her business card out of her purse and wrote Raze's name and room number on the back. "If I turn up missing, here's the last place I was."

"Ha! That's not funny, Kim." Delia looked at the others. "Tell her she's out of her mind. Stop her."

Justin looked up as she stood. He shook his head. "Sorry, Dee. She's not changing her mind. She's got the devil in her eye."

"Leave off, Delia," Rosalind said, fanning herself. "That guy was seriously hot. I'm rooting her on. Go, Kim, go. Rock his world. Make him beg."

Delia groaned. "Oh my God, you're all whacked. I'm calling your brother, Kim."

"If it makes you feel better," Kim said dryly, bending down to kiss her friend's cheek. "Go for it. See you guys Monday."

"If you're still alive then!" Delia yelled after her. "You sex-crazy maniac."

Kim was smiling all the way to her car, but when she slid behind the wheel her humor was gone. Replaced by a hotter, more pressing emotion. There was a gorgeous, dangerously seductive man waiting in a hotel room for her. A man who was aching and lonely, just like she was. For tonight, at least, she wouldn't have to take a damn pill to fall asleep.

Chapter Four

THE MINUTE RAZE WALKED into his hotel suite, he felt as if the air had thinned. Being alone was rubbing him the wrong way, which was so opposite from his usual desire for as much solitude as he could wrangle. There were too much stimuli in the world to allow him peace—the pounding of heartbeats, the steady surge of blood in veins, the various scents that betrayed mood and train of thought. He avoided crowds when he could, but now it seemed he was stuck in an odd place where being alone was more miserable than being around others.

Rolling his shoulders back, he pulled the box of condoms out of a shopping bag and set it on the end table by the small loveseat. He left the new bottle of wine on the dinette table and tossed the bag in the trash, wondering what the hell to do with himself.

He ran both hands over his head and down the back of his neck, growling as he struggled with an unusual sense of anxiety. This time lapse from meeting a lover to fucking her was a step he'd been skipping for a few centuries now. He usually laid 'em where he found 'em, and that worked for everyone. If he'd hooked up with the bartender, it likely would have gone down right there at the club, in the back somewhere, quick and dirty. Waiting for Kim was excruciating, because it gave her time to have second thoughts. He wasn't sure what he'd do if she changed her mind. She'd made him want her. Now no one else was going to do.

Raze moved into the bedroom and plugged his iPod into the docking station, his tension easing a little as Hinder drifted out of the speaker. Feeling confined by his clothes, he began pulling them off. His shirt went first, followed by his boots, then his jeans and boxer briefs. He was tossing his clothes over the back of a bedroom chair when he heard the knock out in the living area.

The surge of lust that hit him affected the steadiness of the first step he took. Then it perversely strengthened his stride. His purpose and focus narrowed to his body's need for the woman on the other side of the door. It was a base and elemental craving, purely physical, but a part of him was distantly aware that it was her bold yet easygoing personality that had tipped the scales enough to tempt him to this madness. She was all wrong for him. So wrong. But he knew when he pushed inside her it was going to feel so damn right.

He pulled the door open. His breath hissed on a sharp inhale at the sight of Kim on his doorstep, dressed in a fitted white tank top and worn jeans that hugged her like a lover. She'd let her hair down, freeing the riotous mass of inky curls to tumble around her slender shoulders and halfway down her back. Her feet were bared by jeweled sandals, revealing toenails that were painted black and decorated with white flowers and swirls. Gold hoops hung from her ears, replacing the diamond studs she'd worn before. He was flattered she'd given thought to how she looked for him.

Presently, however, she seemed focused on looking *at* him.

"Wow," she breathed. "Part of my mind is saying I should be freaking out that you're answering the door naked. Another part is thinking: Holy shit, did I get lucky or what? Don't turn out to be crazy, please. I really need this right now."

The raging need inside him quieted. The soft plea in Kim's voice and the momentary shadow of pain in her beautiful eyes altered the dynamic of his approach. He caught her gently by the elbow and tugged her in. When she cleared the door, he released it to shut by itself and he lowered his mouth to hers.

Swallowing her gasp, Raze slipped his arms around her, stroking his hands up her spine and molding her slender body to his. Her duffle bag hit the floor and her hands came up, one holding the back of his head while the other cupped his cheek.

The tender, encompassing nature of the embrace startled him even as it soothed the ragged edges of his volatile mood. He lifted her feet from the floor, tilting his head to get a deeper seal. His tongue stroked into her mouth, finding the taste of cinnamon and her own natural sweetness. He groaned, ravenous for her, but unwilling to devour. He'd thought he needed hard and fast. She'd thought she needed that, too. They'd both been wrong.

She caught his lower lip between her teeth and tugged, her lips soft and wet, her tongue a velvet lash. He wanted those lips and tongue all over his body. Her hands, too. They were strong and sure, confident. Her moan vibrated against him, luring his fangs to descend.

Not ready for that, Raze set her down reluctantly, his gaze locked with hers. She was flushed and beautiful, her eyes clear and open, yet tinged with sadness. As he watched, tears welled and slipped off her bottom lashes.

"Oh, shit," she whispered, releasing him to swipe at her cheeks. "I asked you not to be crazy and then I get weepy over a kiss. I swear I'm not mental."

"It's okay."

"You like picking up teary, emotional women?"

"You picked me up," he corrected with a smile. "And there's usually only one reason a woman like you picks up a guy like me. I'm not sorry to find out differently."

"You thought I objectified you." She ran a sheepish hand

through her glossy hair. "I can't say you're entirely wrong about that."

"I thought that's what I wanted." Impersonal, with expectations that were easy to meet. But it turned out she was right—what he'd needed was her. Giving her the oblivion she wanted was going to keep him busy in ways a quick and dirty fuck would never have done. There was a connection between them, and he realized he needed that far more than he needed an orgasm.

Obviously, Baron's taunts had dug deeper than Raze had given the man credit for. Women didn't connect with him beyond the physical, he didn't give them enough of himself to get that close. It wasn't deliberate on his part; he just didn't work that way. He'd dealt with infatuation and even sexual obsession that women mistook as love, but it was always fleeting. Quickly come and gone. But Kim … she needed what he was capable of giving. It moved him that for once he could fill a need that was more than skin deep.

Her hand on his face slid upward, her fingers tracing the arch of his brow. "I'm glad I found you."

He pressed his lips to her forehead, wondering what she saw in him that put warmth in her eyes. "Let me put your bag in the bedroom. There's some wine on the table. Are you hungry? Want some room service?"

"You don't have to wine and dine me." She smiled. "I'm a sure thing."

Stepping back, he picked up her duffle. "I'm still going to seduce you."

"I won't complain. I'm just letting you off the hook."

With a sweep of his hand, he gestured her deeper into the room and headed into the bedroom. He was about to pull on a pair of sweats when he glanced into the living area and saw Kim undressing. He moved to the threshold, fascinated by the confident, efficient way she took her clothes off. It was no strip-tease she was doing, no narcissistic display of her assets.

Raze leaned into the doorframe and crossed his arms. "I was going to put some pants on."

She glanced over her shoulder at him. "Why? I think we've both seen each other at our most naked just a minute ago."

"Okay, then." Her open honesty was as arousing as her body. "Come here."

She approached him in the same no-nonsense way she'd undressed, bringing the box of condoms with her. He took her in, admiring the sleek lines of her lithe body and the unaffected sway of her trim hips. The contrast between her dark hair and pale skin was a stunning one, framing a figure that had seemed modest while clothed but was perfectly, lushly proportional in the flesh.

"Why am I not nervous?" she asked when she came to a halt in front of him. "What is it about you that makes me so comfortable? I've never even walked around my own house naked."

Raze tilted his head to the side, contemplating that. Most mortals who met him sensed the predator he was. It kept them on edge, which is what so many of his lovers found attractive about him—the hint of danger he exuded by his nature. He was a hunter, they were his prey, and they felt it on a subconscious level. That he put Kim at ease in a way she was with no one else, not even herself, was inexplicable. "I don't know. But I like it."

Her mouth curved. "Me, too."

Uncrossing his arms, he reached out to her, lifting a glossy curl and rubbing it between thumb and forefinger. "You're very beautiful, Kim. You're not the only one who got lucky tonight."

"Thank you."

His fingertips skimmed gently down her arm until they reached her hand. He linked their fingers together and backed into the bedroom, pulling her with him. As aroused as he was by her slender body, he was also conscious of the unexpected intimacy of them being so comfortable together. Almost as if there was a longstanding familiarity between them. A rare affinity he'd never found in his endless life.

When he reached the bed, he sat and tugged her between his legs, then he fell backward onto the mattress, taking her with him. As her body flowed over him, then melted into him, Raze closed his eyes and sighed, releasing the abnormal agitation that had been riding him hard. Her hair slid over his skin and her mouth brushed over his parted lips. His entire body was hyperaware of her, every nerve ending tingling in anticipation of her touch.

I was wrong, he thought. Not hard and fast. Not with her. Slow and deep. Decadent. He could give her that after all.

Wrapping his arms around her, he rolled her beneath him and gave her what they both needed.

Kim wiped her mouth with a napkin. "You've seriously never seen this movie before?"

Raze lay on his side with his head in hand, his gaze moving from the television to where she sat cross-legged on the bed beside him, drowning in his shirt. "Never even heard of it."

"Wow. I love this movie." She stabbed another piece of impossibly tender steak with her fork and lifted it to her mouth, her attention only partially on *The Ghost and the Darkness*. The naked man sprawled across the bed next to her was much more fun to look at. "Patterson went to Africa with a dream and a plan. And then he had to fight to hang on to it. I just love that. Do you like it?"

"I like watching it with you." He smiled and ran a fingertip down the side of her thigh. "I like watching you eat, too."

"I don't know what's the matter with me. I don't usually get hungry after sex, but I'm freakin' starving now." Of course, it wasn't usual for her to have sex for nearly three hours non-stop either. She was pretty sure that if her damn stomach hadn't growled, he'd still be inside her. The thought made goose bumps sweep over her skin.

"Are you cold?" he asked, displaying that amazing perception she'd appreciated all night. It was the nail in her coffin, she knew. There wasn't a woman alive who could resist a man who paid attention to her, who made her feel like she was the only other person in his world.

"No." She pushed aside the longing that kept reminding her it was there, just under the surface, waiting for her to acknowledge it. "I'm feeling piggy eating while you're not."

"Don't. I'll get something when I need it." He squeezed her gently, then let go. "And you'll need the energy."

Invigorated by the promise of more mind-blowing sex, Kim ate faster. Raze turned his oddly beautiful gaze back to the television, and she let her mind sift through the impossibilities of the evening.

Christ, he was beautiful. It was stunning how gorgeous he was. His features were heartrendingly perfect, from the bold slash of his brows to the strong line of his jaw. His eyes were compelling, the irises lit like amber in candlelight. His lips were sinful, not just in their sensual shape but also with what they could do to the female body. His nose was elegant and his cheekbones a work of art. Everything about him was divine. *Like a fallen angel,* she mused fancifully—blessed with looks that drove every rational thought from a woman's head and totally wicked enough to take advantage of that gift.

She almost sighed like a smitten teenager.

And the best part was that the miracle of him was more than skin deep. Despite his devastating attractiveness, she was as comfortable hanging out with Raze as she was with any of her friends. There was no awkwardness, no wariness, nothing to ruin the easy companionship between them. It was in her nature to be cautious. Not only was that trait necessary for the painstaking work she did, but it was also how she'd been raised by a family of cops. You could never look close enough, dig deep enough, or be careful enough.

But Kim could accept that some people just clicked. She had friends whom she'd known would become valuable pieces of her life from the moment she met them. That didn't explain why she wasn't at least partially scandalized by the things she and Raze had done to each other since she arrived. There wasn't a centimeter of her skin that didn't know the stroke of his fingers or the lash of his tongue. He knew parts of her body better than anyone, better than even she did. And his erotic abandon goaded hers.

She'd lost all inhibition. She had done things to him that she'd never imagined doing and she had loved every minute. There was nothing in her head about playing fair or returning favors. She pleasured him because she couldn't help herself. She pleasured him because it made her feel as good as when he pleasured her. He'd shown her that any sexual act could be intimate and mutually pleasurable if you had the right partner. She didn't think there was anything she wouldn't let him do to her or anything he could ask of her that she wouldn't do to him—a man she hadn't known existed just a few short hours ago.

He glanced at her, caught her staring, and smiled. The curve of his gorgeous mouth was wicked, but the heat in his eyes was tender and warm.

Her chest tightened in a way that warned her she was wading

into treacherous waters. Taking a deep breath, Kim set her fork down and wiped her mouth again. "Thank you for dinner."

"Did you enjoy it?"

"Wasn't it obvious?"

"I've heard stale chips can taste delicious after sex," he said wryly.

She laughed and stood, collecting her tray off the bed. "I absolutely enjoyed it. I've enjoyed everything since I arrived."

Taking the dishes back out to the living area, she took a moment to herself, debating whether she should get going now while the getting was good. She considered it long and hard, but the thought of returning to her apartment alone at this time of night made her stomach knot. And the thought of leaving Raze bummed her out so much she knew she couldn't go until it was absolutely necessary. It wasn't like they worked together or had the same friends or even lived in the same city. So what if she moped a little after it was over? He wouldn't be around to see it. He wouldn't be around as a constant reminder of what she couldn't have.

"Hey," Raze called out. "Your phone's vibrating."

She went back to the bedroom, which was softly lit and intimately welcoming. It smelled like him and sex and delicious food. She really didn't want to be anywhere else. Looking around for her bag, she found it on a chair near the closet, several feet away from the bed. "How can you hear the buzzing over the television?"

He shrugged.

Digging her phone out, she looked at the screen and sighed at the sight of her brother's name. She answered without preamble, "It's a little late, isn't it, Kenny?"

"Why the hell aren't you answering your phone?"

"Because I was busy. And it's late."

"Kimberly Laine McAdams. You can't go off with some biker you spoke to for five minutes in a bar and not expect us to be worried sick."

"Oh my God. This isn't Kenny. It's Mom sounding like Kenny."

"That's not fucking funny."

"No, it isn't." She hit the mute button. "Raze. Do you ride a bike?"

He glanced at her with brows raised.

"You know," she elaborated. "Like a Harley."

His grin flashed fierce and sexy as hell. "Heritage Softail."

"Shit." So he was a biker after all. The thought made her hot and needy. Kim took the phone off mute. "I'm a big girl, Kenny."

"Who is still dealing with walking into the murder scene of her best friend!" Ken growled and in her mind's eye she could see him fisting his dark hair with his free hand and clenching his jaw. "You're not the only one who's freaked by what happened to Janelle. I worry about you all the damn time. You need to give me a break, Kim. Stop giving me gray hair. Now what's this guy's name?"

"Why, so you can run him? Do you do a run on all your one-night-stands?"

"You're not the one-night-stand type."

"I am tonight. I'll call you when I get home tomorrow. And tell Delia I'm gonna kick her ass." She hung up, then powered her phone off.

"Everything all right?" Raze adjusted his position so that he was propped against pillows piled against the headboard. Sprawled like that he was a sensual feast.

God. He was just what she'd needed. What she still needed.

She tossed her phone back in her bag and pulled his shirt over her head. "Everything's great. And about to get better."

Chapter Five

RAZE LOOKED AT THE video feed of a blackish rose arrangement perched on Vash's desk and pronounced, "Creepy."

"They're for you." She pushed them aside. "Salem found them on your porch about a half hour ago. No card, but we know who it's from, don't we?"

"Yeah, we do."

"She's his wife, by the way. Of a couple hundred years. Torque traced Baron—previously known as John Schmidt, Baron Seagrave in his mortal life—back to the Regency period, when he married Lady Francesca Harlow."

"Torque's the man."

"Yes, he is. And you're dealing with a woman who just lost the love of her life." Vash's fingers drummed on the table. "Take it from a woman who knows what that feels like: She wants your head on a pike and your nuts roasting on an open fire. She won't let this go until one of you is dead."

"I'm ready and waiting." He glanced out the window at the gradually lightening dawn sky, then over at the closed bedroom door. "But I might be waiting in the wrong place if she's gone to Raceport."

"Torque traced the roses back to a florist in Chicago. If she did her homework at all, she'll know you're hanging around there. But she doesn't know where. She's hoping this'll rattle your cage a little."

"I'll get out more today. Be seen. I don't suppose we'd be lucky enough to have confirmation that the baroness is the woman in the video. A photo match, maybe?"

"Working on it." Vash rocked back in her desk chair. "Listen, I know you like to do your loner thing, but I'd feel better if you had some backup."

"Don't worry about me. I've got this."

"When I find the bastards who killed Charron, an army isn't going to save them. Hell hath no fury like a woman whose mate has been stolen from her. You can't understand. You haven't been there. You don't know what you're up against."

Raze's hands fisted. "I've. Got. This."

"Fine." She tossed up her hands. "Watch your stubborn ass. I can't afford to lose you."

She ended transmission, leaving him feeling pissed off and resentful. He was sick of everyone acting like there was an exclusive club that he was denied membership in.

He moved back into the bedroom and slid between the sheets, careful not to wake Kim, who slept soundly. Lying facedown with her hair fanned across her back and her face turned toward him, she soothed his agitation without even trying. He wasn't used to having someone sleep over like this. Because he didn't need sleep himself, having a lover stay the night just invited questions he couldn't answer.

Regardless, he wouldn't have let Kim go home even if she'd wanted to. He could tell himself it was because it wasn't safe for her to go out by herself at night. After all, the last woman to leave his bed had found a dead body on the doorstep. He could also tell himself it was because he hadn't fed from her yet, but then he'd have to examine why he'd held back. To create just this excuse, maybe?

Reaching out, he pushed her hair gently aside and ran his fingertips up and down the graceful curve of her spine. She was so slender and delicate, yet strong and lithe. Her body had worked tirelessly through the night, taking what he gave her and giving it right back to him. When she'd risen over him and rocked her body onto his, he'd fisted the sheets against the pleasure, his neck arching as she took him to the edge and beyond. It had been a very long time since anything had felt that good.

Raze exhaled harshly, fighting the onslaught of renewed desire. He'd had her enough already. She wasn't a vampire who could heal quick enough to avoid being sore.

"Umm …" she purred. "You have the best hands."

That soft humming noise of pleasure was the death of all his good intentions. He pressed a kiss to her shoulder. "I want you."

"Yes, please."

He laughed, which made her smile and roll to her back, revealing the small breasts he'd played with most of the night. She was revising everything he'd thought he knew about his preferences and desires. He ran the tip of his finger around a pale pink areola. "I love your tits."

"Oh, these things? I've had them forever."

Grinning, he bent over her and took her mouth, slanting his head to get the perfect fit. Kissing was another surprise. He hadn't realized he liked it so much.

He was going to like drinking of her even more.

This time, he wouldn't hold back. The morning was here; their night together was almost over. In a few hours, he'd be out hunting and she'd return to life as she knew it.

Raze slid over her and pushed his arms beneath her. It amazed him that a body so much smaller than his could fit so perfectly. He should have felt like a great, hulking beast on top of her, but he didn't. He should have worried about how he handled her and made an effort to restrain himself, but there were none of those types of concerns or awkwardness between them. It was all so easy. So natural.

Her leg lifted and her foot stroked up and down his calf. Her arms hooked upward beneath his, her hands stroking over the back of his shaved head. He'd never considered his scalp an erogenous zone before, but she made it so. Every inch of his skin was sensitive to her touch, heating and tingling as her fingertips caressed him. She handled him with the care he might have shown her—as if he was delicate and precious.

Her tongue licked across his and he groaned, remembering the feel of it across other places on his body. She gave pleasure with as much abandon as she took it, and he let her. He couldn't help it. Everything she did to him was perfect, circumventing his brain and taking him to that place where he was more animal than man—a creature of sensation and need.

Sliding down, he nuzzled briefly against her throat, then moved lower. He teased her nipples with sweeping brushes of his parted lips and soft, gentle licks. Kim whimpered and tugged his head closer, silently urging him to suckle her, which he would not do. The tender tips were already swollen and he wouldn't hurt her, even if she considered the pleasure worth the pain. Instead he worried the tiny hardened point with the tip of his tongue, fluttering over it like the kiss of a butterfly, before lavishing the same attention to her other breast.

"God that feels good," she gasped, writhing beneath him, her skin heating to the touch. "You could make me come if you quit playing around."

He laughed, something he so rarely did. Squeezing her hip in his hand, he continued his downward progression, his tongue rimming her navel before dipping inside. Her flat belly concaved and a tickled laugh escaped her. The sound delighted him.

With his hand beneath her knee, Raze slid one of her sleek legs over his shoulder, then the other. He cupped her ass and lifted her. His mouth watered; his chest tightened with the anticipation of hearing all the luscious sounds she made while he pleasured her.

At the first long, slow lick, she sighed, her body going lax. "You're so gifted. I'm going to have wet dreams about your mouth for the rest of my life."

His lips curved. He took her with a deep, intimate kiss. Pushing inside her with gentle greed. Listening to her moan as he tongued her slick, tender flesh. Her hips arched, seeking more, and he gave it to her. Lapping through the silken folds like a cat with cream. He circled the tiny knot of her clitoris and stroked over it, relishing the way she writhed and gasped, then begged him to suck. She came with a full-body shiver, gasping his name.

Wiping his mouth on her inner thigh, he shrugged out from under her boneless legs and sat up. He sheathed himself in an unnecessary condom, then nudged her legs wider and sank his hips between them. Fisting his erection, he guided it to her. He paused there, absorbing the heated expectation of the moment. In the hours past, he'd learned how perfect the tight clasp of her body was, how deliciously she held him.

An unexpected but not unwelcome tenderness welled inside him.

His eyes closed as she took the first inch, the pleasure so hot and fierce it misted his skin with sweat. He refrained from thrusting, careful to give her swollen sex the time to accept him. He let her body set the pace, sinking deeper only when she opened for him like an unfurling flower.

"Raze."

Lifting his pleasure-weighted eyelids, he looked down at her, finding her flushed and bright-eyed. Feverish with desire. He cupped her head in his hands, holding her still as he slipped into her to the hilt. He savored the way she trembled around and beneath him, watching her eyes darken as the desire took over. The glance they shared was open and naked, and as intimate as his cock inside her.

"God." Her nails dug deliciously into the muscles of his back. "You're so hard. And big. Jesus, you're so thick and long."

"Umm …" He rolled his hips. "And you're tight as a fist. I pack you full. You couldn't take another centimeter if I had it to give you."

Pushing her heels into the mattress, Kim thrust up at him. "Ride me. I want to come again."

"You'll come until you can't take anymore," he promised, feeling his fangs lengthen within his gums. Lifting his hips, he withdrew and pushed deep again.

"Harder, Raze. Give it to me hard."

Delicate muscles rippled along his length, driving him crazy. Grinding his teeth, he fought the need to fuck her without restraint. He wanted to drag out the moment as long as possible, create memories for both of them of a hungry need so powerful they'd reverberate for years.

"Not yet." He slid in and out, his hips working in a smooth, leisurely tempo. "Slow and easy now. Feel me. Feel what you do to me. How damned hard you make me. As much as I've had you tonight, I still ache for more."

Her head pressed into the pillows, unconsciously arching her neck at the perfect angle for the penetration of his fangs. "Yes. More."

Anchoring her hip with one hand, he clutched her hair in the other, holding her immobile. The pulse in her throat throbbed wildly, her heart pounding as he dominated her completely. His tongue stroked over her madly pumping vein, plumping it. He sucked gently on the skin, bringing it closer to the surface. Her sex tightened around him.

"You feel so good," he groaned, nuzzling the spot beneath her ear. "I could stay right here forever."

"Raze, please … I need—"

The first spasms of her climax rippled along the length of his dick and his control snapped. He struck deep into her vein, his eyes rolling back as the intoxicating flavor of her blood flooded his mouth. The ecstasy of his bite burned through her and she screamed, her body quaking with the force of her orgasm.

He was right there with her, coming as hard as if he hadn't come all night, his body inundated with ecstasy and the power of her blood.

Then the deluge of her memories hit him with the force of a sledgehammer to the face.

Kim lay with her cheek on Raze's shoulder and her arm draped across his hard chest. Her fingers drifted idly up and down the bulge of his biceps. Draped along his side with one leg tucked between his, she listened to the steady beat of his heart and thought about how none of this night had gone as she'd expected it to.

She had set out with the intention of getting drunk, so she could sleep without having to take a sleeping pill. Then she'd seen Raze and figured they'd screw each other into exhaustion. Which they had, but she had pictured more of a rolling, clawing, pounding rut. On the floor maybe. Or the couch if they got that far. She hadn't pictured a bed. She hadn't imagined luxuriating in each other. She certainly hadn't thought about cuddling afterward.

There's something here, she thought. Something that could become important to both of them.

"Kim." His fingers were sifting through her horribly tangled hair. His other hand was splayed over her back.

"Hmm?" She snuggled closer. Everything about the way he touched her made her feel good. Hell, he'd sucked on her neck and she'd had the orgasm of her life. None of the hickies she'd gotten in high school had ever revved her engine, let alone blown the top of her head off.

"Would you tell me why you cried when you first got here?"

She stiffened, unprepared for the question.

"Shh." He pressed his lips to her crown. "You don't have to."

"No. It's okay." After a shaky breath, she told him, stumbling over the words a little because she hadn't talked about it since the police questioned her. Saying the words brought the painful and horrifying pictures in her mind to life, making her relive the agony of finding her home a bloodbath and her dearest friend lying in the gore like a rag doll. The tears came with the words until she was sobbing violently.

Raze rolled carefully, covering her with his body in a hot, hard blanket of powerful male. He tucked her under him, sheltering her, his cheek pressed to hers and his arms caging her shoulders. The quiet strength of him sank into her, shoring her up. Anchoring her. She didn't have to be strong for him. She didn't have to hide her pain to make it easier for him. She didn't need to shield her grief behind a smile so he'd think everything was all right.

He didn't say anything, which was such a gift. She wondered if he knew that or if it was just his way. His was an old soul. She'd sensed that from the moment their eyes had met.

Eventually, Kim quieted, her heart feeling so much lighter that she might've shed a tear over it, if she'd had any tears left.

"There's a lot of shit in this world," he said, kissing her softly. "I'm sorry you had to experience any of it."

Cupping his cheeks, she lifted his head and looked into his eyes. "You experience a lot of it, don't you?"

"Yeah." He rolled to his back and heaved out a sigh. "I have to wade through some of it today. Can I see you tonight?"

Delight fluttered through her tummy. "Would you like to come to my place? I can make dinner."

He looked at her with those amber eyes and smiled wryly. "I have some unusual dietary restrictions. How about movies instead? I'll bring over one of my favorites and you pick out another one of yours. I'll feed you while we watch the shows."

"Okay."

"Okay? Really? That's good?"

She bent over and nudged his nose with her own, hiding a smile over his startled wonder. One could almost think he'd never planned a date before. "It's great. You're great."

He answered that with an exuberant kiss.

Chapter Six

RAZE HAD BEEN WANDERING around the city for half the day when he picked up a tail. He took a circuitous route to be sure and when he was, he pulled out his cell phone and called Vashti. "Problem."

"Hopefully I've got a solution."

"It's two o'clock in the afternoon and I've got a minion sniffing after me."

There was silence, then a whistle. "Well, that's interesting."

"It's scary as fuck and you know it." Only the Fallen could take sunlight; minions were mortally photosensitive. The only exceptions were minions who'd recently drunk Fallen blood, which afforded them temporary immunity that would last seventy-two hours at most. "We have a full accounting of the Fallen?"

"I'll double-check, but I can't think of anyone in that area aside from you."

"Let me know what you hear. In the meantime, I'm going to have a little chat with my shadow and see what I can shake loose." He killed the call and shoved his phone in his pocket.

A group of teenagers exited a store in front of him, clogging up the sidewalk and providing the distraction he needed. Darting behind them, he entered the store and shot out the rear delivery entrance. He found himself in a small alley lined with trash and dumpsters and framed above by fire escapes. Leaping the two-story distance to the first escape ledge, Raze settled in to wait, knowing his tail would eventually follow his scent.

Ten minutes later, a tiny brunette stepped out of the shop into the alley. He took a deep breath and smelled vampire. Crouching, he prepared to jump when it struck him that she wouldn't be alone. She would be half of a pair.

He hopped down and blocked the swing of her fist, then shielded his groin when she attempted to take him down with a knee to the nuts. She pressed on, raining blows and kicks, which he deflected with greater speed, his forearms parrying jabs so quickly that to a mortal eye he would've seemed to be no more than a blur. He waited for the perfect opening and took it, stunning her with a blow to the neck and catching her in a headlock. Spinning her around, he caged her with her back to his chest.

He yanked her head to the side and bit deep. Her memories flooded into him along with her blood, giving him all the answers he needed ... except for where to find Francesca. The baroness had gone under, contacting her minions via phone or e-mail. His fangs retracted and he was licking the tiny wounds closed when her mate rushed into the alley.

"Behave, Lake," Raze warned her softly, puzzled by some of what he'd read in her mind. "Or I'll tell him about your little piece of ass on the side."

She stilled, breathing roughly.

Her partner, Forest—how sickeningly sweet was the deliberate pairing of *those* names?—froze at the sight of his woman helpless in Raze's arms. "Hurt her and die."

Raze grinned, but noted the shine of feral madness in the minion's eyes. He'd seen inside Lake's mind and knew what these two did on their dates—blood and pain were their aphrodisiacs. "I won't hurt her ... yet. But I've got her scent and I've drunk her blood. I could find her in the Times Square crowd on New Year's Eve. Think about that."

Forest's hands clenched and unclenched rhythmically. "What do you want?"

"Take a message back to the baroness. Tell her to quit dicking around and face me. I have places to go, rogues to kill. I can't hang around Chicago indefinitely."

"You'd fight a woman? A lady. One of your own kind." Forest began to shift restlessly, licking his lips. His eyes were lit with a sick hunger. It seemed Forest found it arousing to watch his woman manhandled.

It was a terrible fact that the majority of minions lost their minds after the Change. Mortals weren't designed to live without their souls and the Change took that from them. If it were up to the Fallen—who were the source of the dark gift—only carefully selected mortals would be Changed, but vampirism was like a secret shared only with trusted friends, who in turn shared it only with their most trusted friends, and so on. The spread had long ago become uncontrollable as the unstable minions began to Change others indiscriminately. It was Adrian's job to mitigate the fallout, an endless mission that pitted the Sentinels against the Fallen in a contentious battle of wills.

"The baroness is no lady," Raze shot back. "I've watched a video of her slicing an innocent man open—alive—while humming a merry tune. She can do that, she can fight me. So give her my message: I'm not wasting my time hunting someone who hides behind their minions. She's got forty-eight hours to take me on or I'm passing her off to Adrian."

"I'll tell her." Forest smiled with eager malice.

Raze shoved the vampress forward into her mate. "I'll be seeing you two again."

Hopping back onto the fire escape, he climbed to the roof and set off from there.

"No way." Delia planted herself on one of Kim's kitchen island barstools and shook her head emphatically. "Guys that look like Biker Boy are personality deficient. That's the trade-off for the hotness—they're self-absorbed jerks."

Kim smiled and continued putting groceries away. "You're right. Absolutely. Except for Raze."

"There has to be something wrong with him."

"Yeah … He doesn't live in Chicago."

"He snores."

"Nope." Although she realized she'd never been awake while he was sleeping. "Actually, I'm not sure."

"So that's a maybe. He's an early ejaculator."

Kim laughed until her eyes got teary. "Oh my God … No. Definitely no."

"Being good in bed is a challenge to him. He's a womanizer who views sex like a sport—all technique and no heart."

"He's not the least bit detached. In fact, part of what I loved about sleeping with him was how into it he got. Like having sex with me was toe-curlingly, eye-rollingly good. As for being a womanizer … Yes. Probably. He was going to screw somebody last night. I was just lucky enough that it ended up being me."

"So, there's another con—a pretty big one—right there. Does he talk about himself constantly?"

"He doesn't talk about himself at all."

Delia's sloe eyes narrowed behind her glasses. "Maybe he's married."

"Married to his job. Trust me, I know the type. I lived with two cops."

"Self-centered? You had to spell things out for him to get yours."

"He knew what I needed before I did. He noticed my goose bumps for chrissakes." Kim shut the fridge door and returned to the island, curling her hands around the bullnosed edge. "It's going to sound corny, but it's like he's totally in tune with me. He knew when I was hot or cold. He knew where to touch me, how to touch me, how long to touch me … Jesus, I cried all over him about Janelle and he didn't freak out. He didn't tell me everything was all right or ask me to stop crying. He didn't go into another room or make noises about it being time for me to go."

"Damn it." Delia pouted. "That's so not fair. I blew him off and you reeled in Mr. Awesome Sauce."

"I'd apologize, but I wouldn't be sincere."

Delia smiled. "I'm glad he's not a serial killer."

"Me, too." Although he just might slay her when all was said and done. She'd been thinking about him all day, thinking about things she wanted to do with him, places she wanted to take him. Like her favorite pizza shop. And the Field Museum, where he could see the real lions from *The Ghost and the Darkness*.

"You've got bags under your eyes, Kimmy girl, but you look all happy and glow-y. I'm really glad about that."

"I haven't felt this good in a long time," she admitted, tidying up the countertop because she wanted Raze to like her place and feel comfortable in it. "A part of me thinks that's stupid. I'm a mature, successful, professional woman. I shouldn't have such a crazy mood boost over a guy I've known less than twenty-four hours. But that's the way it is. I needed him and he was there."

Delia tucked a strand of her chin-length hair behind her ear. "What will you do if you still need him after he's gone?"

"I don't know. I guess that'll be up to him and whether he'd like to keep in touch or not."

"When does he leave?"

Kim glanced at the digital clock on her stovetop. "Too soon, whenever it is. I have to get ready. He's going to be here in an hour and a half."

"You could convince him to keep in touch with you." Sliding off the stool, Delia straightened the skirt of her flirty blue dress.

"I don't think anyone can convince Raze of anything once he's made up his mind." Kim's chest tightened at the thought of having even a tiny hold on Raze.

"Think about it. You're not his type. He walked into that bar looking for a back-alley screw or something like it. Then you walked up and rocked his world, just like Roz said you would. He let you into his personal space, fed you, took care of you. You've got him already, Kimmy. You can keep him, if you want to."

"If that's true, why did you give me the third degree and say all that stuff about something being wrong with him?"

Delia grinned, and pinched her thumb and forefinger together. "Maybe I'm just a teeny bit jealous. But mostly I wanted to make sure you were thinking things through and not getting blindsided by a gorgeous, dangerous-looking man who's a god in bed."

"You suck. Thank you for caring."

Coming around the island, Delia lifted to her tiptoes and pressed a kiss to Kim's cheek. "Have fun tonight. Call me tomorrow and give me all the deets."

"Are you going out tonight?"

"Oh, absolutely. You've inspired me to find my own Mr. Awesome. He's got to be out there somewhere. Hopefully tomorrow I'll have some juicy news to share with you. Wish me luck."

"All the luck in the world," Kim assured her as she walked her to the door. "Thanks for hanging out and shopping with me today."

"I loved it. We should do it more often. Gives me an excuse to augment my own lingerie collection. Bye!"

Shutting the door, Kim engaged the locks and leaned back against the paneled wood, examining her living room as if she'd never seen it before. Her new place was smaller than the one she'd shared with Janelle. She had started over from scratch, replacing everything, including the frames on her pictures. While her previous home had been a riot of color, her new place was softly neutral with occasional dashes of blue. She couldn't bear to have red anywhere.

Imagining Raze in her private space, a place she'd yet to invite a romantic interest over to see, was deeply personal. She could say in all honesty that she couldn't imagine inviting any other guy over to invade it, aside from her coworkers. She really hoped he felt comfortable while he was here. She wanted him relaxed and at ease, open. She wanted him as naked emotionally as he'd been last night. She craved that intimacy as much as she craved his hard, muscular body.

Thinking of the stuff she'd bought on her shopping trip with Delia, Kim smiled.

"I'm not done rocking your world, Mr. Awesome," she murmured, setting off down the hallway to get ready.

"Forest and Lake got the Fallen blood via a courier delivery this morning," Raze said into the screen of his iPad. "An unmarked blood bag they shared between them."

Vash frowned into the camera. "That's a problem."

"I e-mailed the info I got from Lake's memory of the package and receipt. Let's hope Torque can track it down to its source."

"Are we looking for a mole here? A minion smuggling out Fallen blood?"

Because the Fallen couldn't be everywhere at once, it was necessary to fortify minions to pick up the slack. All of the Fallen routinely stored blood for that purpose. "We need to look more closely at that video of the murder. Not just at who's in it, but where. That body was fresh. She killed him nearby and someone sheltered her while she did it. They also knew me well enough to gauge the best time to dump the body. Maybe that's why she wasn't at the meeting at Wrigley Field."

"She should've gotten back to Chicago before you."

"Not if she was waiting on Fallen blood to take back with her."

Vash growled. "Fuckin' A."

"Yeah …" He glanced at the clock. "I have to go."

"Why? Clue me in. Do you need backup?"

"It wouldn't hurt. We've definitely got some cleaning up to do in this city. But that's not why I've got to run. I have to get ready for a date."

Her brows rose. "Is that what you're calling your suck-and-fucks nowadays? Dates?"

"Shut up. The last I heard, dinner and movies constituted a date."

"Jesus." She slumped back into her chair. "Maybe whatever Grimm's crew has got is contagious and you caught it when you bit Puddle."

"Lake. I'm signing off now, Vash. 'Night."

Raze was out of his chair and moving into the bedroom a heartbeat later. He was dying to get to Kim and he'd have to wander all over Chicago first to be sure he didn't drag a tail with him. If he'd been thinking straight that morning, he would've had her come to him again. Nice and anonymous. If someone was watching the hotel, she'd just look like a guest herself with her bag and direct beeline to a room as if she was a registered guest.

But she wanted him at her place and he wasn't going to disappoint her or make her think he just wanted to get laid by changing the plans now. Last night, she'd made sure to have her own transportation and to meet at a public place when she hooked up with a stranger. To go from that level of wariness to the trust of inviting him over to her private space was important, and he didn't want to fuck it up. He'd just have to be real careful. No problem.

For the first time in a very long time, Raze was looking forward to a beginning rather than an ending, which was the inevitable result of hunting.

As he headed into the shower, he was whistling, anticipation a heady warmth in his veins.

Chapter Seven

WHEN THE DOORBELL RANG, Kim felt her stomach flip. Putting a hand to her belly, she took a deep breath, then ran to the door. She looked through the peephole and even through the distortion from the rounded magnifying glass, she felt that same punch of need that had hit when he'd first walked into the jazz club and her life.

She pulled the door open. "Hi."

He crowded her in and kicked the door closed, his mouth on hers before the latch clicked shut. She'd never seen a person move so fast, it stole her breath. Then his passion kept her from regaining it. His lips slanted across hers, his tongue sliding deep and making her shiver. As he bent her backward, she clung to his broad shoulders, feeling the warmth and strength of him through the cotton of his black T-shirt. Behind her back, the white roses he'd brought her tangled with her hair, but she didn't care.

"Hi back," he growled, nuzzling his nose against hers. "Christ, I missed you all day."

Kim grinned, her dazed eyes noting the way his irises seemed to glow from within. "It's crazy, I know, but it was the same for me."

He released her and thrust the flowers at her. "Here."

She bit the inside of her cheek to hold back a laugh. He looked so sheepishly embarrassed as he awkwardly held out the bouquet. Hoping to put him at ease, she teased, "Roses! How lovely. You totally earned a blow job for these. Thank you."

"Seriously?" Raze's brows shot up. "Well, that explains a lot."

"Such as why so many men make the gesture?"

"Yeah." He scowled. "But it doesn't explain why no one told me the trade-off until now."

She headed into the kitchen to grab a vase. "Probably because you don't need any props to get women; they fall all over you without them. Of course, now that you know, you can check out it for yourself and see what happens."

She jumped as his arms came around her from behind and he nibbled the side of her neck. "You may need to stock up on vases," he purred.

Laying the bouquet on the countertop, Kim turned in his arms and caught him around the waist. "No bribes necessary. I like getting you off that way. I suspect I'm acquiring an oral fixation on you."

His hands pushed into her hair, massaging her scalp. He looked down into her face. "What's wrong with you?"

"Excuse me?"

"There's got to be something. No one's this perfect. Throw me a bone, will you."

The reminder of her conversation with Delia tickled her and her smile deepened.

"I had a nose job." She touched the bridge. "There was a bump here and I had it shaved down. I can't dance. I have no rhythm whatsoever. Can't sing either. Roz says I sound like cats fucking."

Raze erupted into laughter.

She grinned back at him.

He leaned his cheek against the top of her head. "I'm a guy with issues. You could do so much better."

"Maybe I will, when you try the flower thing with someone else."

"Fair enough." Gripping her ass, he hauled her up against him. "How was your day?"

"I went shopping. And bought you a surprise."

"Oh? Lemme see."

"Not yet. And you? Work go all right?"

He nodded and visibly clammed up. "Yeah."

Running her hand over his head, she smiled. "Don't worry. I won't ask."

"Why not?"

"Both my dad and brother are cops. I know the drill. When you can talk about it—when you *want* to talk about it—I'm here. And ... I knew something about your job was eating at you yesterday. I understand not wanting to talk about it."

"You peg me for law enforcement?"

"Am I wrong?" she challenged.

Cupping her face, he kissed her. "No. Not really."

She let him back away and resumed putting the flowers in a vase. "Make yourself at home."

"That's easy to do. Your place is as beautiful as you are." His voice faded as he moved into the living room.

Kim leaned heavily into the counter, breathing carefully in and out. He was such a force of nature and her hunger for him was outside the scope of her experience. She'd never had relationship issues, never had any problem with commitment or affection or sexual attraction. But this ... It was like being hit with a Mack truck every time. "Did you forget to bring a movie?"

"No." He looked across the open floor plan at her and pulled a DVD case from the waistband of his jeans at the small of his back. "I'll show you mine, if you show me yours."

"Umm ... sounds fun." She carried the flower arrangement into the living room and set it on an end table. "Whatcha got?"

"Unforgiven."

"Huh? Who's in it?"

"Clint Eastwood. Morgan Freeman. Gene Hackman." He handed her the case.

"Oh." Her mouth curved ruefully.

"What?"

"There's something else wrong with me: I'm not a fan of westerns."

His eyes were warm with amusement. "Give it thirty minutes. If you're not enjoying it, I'll entertain you another way."

"I can go for that." *Yum.* She licked her lips.

"And yours?" He crossed his arms and looked sexy as hell. "What are you putting on the table?"

"*Gabriel.* Have you seen it?"

Raze's mouth opened, hung that way for a moment, then closed again. His lips twitched. "Angels?"

She deflated. "You've seen it."

"Probably not the same story," he said wryly. "What's it about?"

"Fallen angels who kick some serious— What's so funny?"

He tried to wipe the smile off his mouth with his hand. "Do they turn into vampires?"

"Who? The angels? No. It's not a comedy, you know. It's dark and gritty."

"Gotcha." But he was clearly still very amused.

"Then again …" She thought about it. "That might actually be a cool story. Maybe some werewolves, too? Like *Underworld* with angels? Could be interesting."

Laughing, he picked her up and spun her around. His delight spurred her own and she found herself laughing with him.

"You're crazy, Raze. You know that?"

"About you." He took her mouth in a breathless kiss.

Kim ended up liking *Unforgiven,* as Raze had known she would. He couldn't explain how he knew, it was just there. It was as if she had a rhythm to her, a unique tempo that resonated perfectly inside him. And he'd liked *Gabriel,* as she'd suspected he would.

Synergy, he thought, tightening his arms around her. He lay stretched out on her sofa, barefooted and comfortable. She was sprawled between his legs, her back to his chest, her arms crossed over his. Every breath he took smelled of her, that unique fragrance that was partly a soft floral perfume and mostly her natural essence.

He'd never experienced anything even remotely similar to this casual intimacy. Associations for him had always been necessities—he worked with his teams, he fucked the willing, and he relaxed alone. All of the Fallen had lost their souls when they'd lost their wings, one couldn't exist without the other. But the rest of the Fallen had loved before they fell and he'd wondered if perhaps the ability to know love was something he could've only learned when he'd been whole. Perhaps he had missed his chance.

Clearly, he'd been wrong to think that way. He'd never understood the saying *My heart's not in it.* Why did your heart need to be in anything? Do what you need to do. But now he knew. He'd enjoyed his work, sex, and his solitude, but his heart had never been in any of it. Until, perhaps, now.

Raze pressed a kiss to her temple, marveling at how drastically his life and outlook had changed in a mere day. "You know," he murmured, "now we can say we've known each other days, as in plural."

Her head moved on his chest as her gaze slid from the

television to the digital clock on her cable box. "It feels like so much longer than that."

She sat up despite his protests and shifting, moving to straddle him. He watched her, riveted by her elegant sensuality. She was way, way out of his league, but somehow he was making her happy. She caught the pull of her zipper, one that ran from cleavage to waist on the simple but pretty strappy emerald dress she wore.

"Ready for your surprise?" she asked, with sparkling eyes.

"Hmm … A surprise." He gripped her thighs beneath the hem and squeezed. "You're all I need."

"And I'm what you'll get." The dress parted and she drew it over her head.

Jesus. He went hard all over. Her delicate breasts were cupped by mere scraps of green satin framed by black lace. The wisp covering the sweet flesh between her thighs was nothing more than a tease. The whole sparkled with crystals and contrasted beautifully with her creamy skin, dark hair, and peridot eyes. He lost his breath for a moment, along with his brain.

"A surprise," he murmured. "And a gift. God. Kim. You shred me."

Her greedy hands slid up beneath his shirt and her mouth sealed over his. She took him. And gripping her hair, he gave.

They spent Sunday morning being deliciously lazy, rolling around in bed and talking about their work. Raze could say little about the particulars of what he did, but he told her he traveled a lot and worked in teams occasionally. He told her about Vash and Syre, Torque and Salem, smudging details as necessary to get the gist across. It was easier than he would have thought to talk so much. Kim made it easy by listening attentively and refraining from asking questions he couldn't answer. In return he strove to be as honest as possible under the circumstances. Eventually, he'd tell her everything. After he discussed it with Syre and Vashti.

Kim talked about her job as a medical laboratory scientist and he listened raptly, amazed that of all the people he could've found this depth of connection with, he'd found one who spent her days looking at blood. She was, in her own way, as drawn to the vital substance as he was. What were the odds?

She was a trust fund baby, which allowed her to do what she loved for a living. Most of her friends were also her coworkers and Janelle had been her best friend since grade school. As he'd expected, Kim had been engaged once, shortly after graduating from college, but she'd broken it off when she realized she wasn't ready to settle down.

Shortly after ten, she went into the kitchen to grab breakfast and he returned a call from Vashti that he'd missed while indulging in Kim.

"Vash." He kept the video off and held the phone to his ear. "News?"

"The team of six I sent arrived this morning and they're already sweeping through what's left of your list of known Grimm haunts. They have orders to gather what intel they can and pass it along to you. You're primary, so stay available."

"Of course."

She snorted. "You could've been hunting last night."

"Yes. And probably should've been. But it's my time now, Vashti. After all these years, it's finally my time. I'm not wasting it hunting down a crazy bitch who won't be found until she's ready." He heard the doorbell ring and pulled on his jeans. "I rattled her cage yesterday. She'll be crawling out soon, because she'll want to deal with this on her turf and I've threatened to leave. I bet she makes a move by tomorrow, and I'll be out today making myself as easy a target as possible."

"I've e-mailed the cell numbers of your team. Touch bases with them and—"

Raze killed the call when Kim entered the room with a dozen Black Beauty roses. There was laughter in her eyes and a mischievous smile on her lips.

"I guess this is a hint," she teased. "I'm glad you approve of my oral skills, since I certainly enjoy—"

Shoving his phone into his jeans' pocket, he brushed past her on his way to the front door. "Did those just arrive?"

"Yes. Raze, are you—"

"Lock the door behind me. Don't open it for anyone except me." He was gone in a flash, taking the stairs at the end of the hall, his heart racing with a sick panic. He raced down the single flight of steps to the first floor and skidded into the lobby of the apartment complex in his bare feet. The lone elevator car was empty and the doors sat open, but when he turned his head, he saw the logo on the back of the delivery person disappearing out the revolving glass door.

A female. Blond hair tucked up under her ball cap.

Bloodlust hazed his vision. Her ladyship hadn't expected him to be there when she went after Kim and she was arrogant enough to forgo the quick kill. She wanted to play, like she had with the Cubs fan.

He pursued, uncaring of his bare feet and chest. She was climbing into the back of an unmarked van when her driver—Lake—saw him. The vampress hit the gas, and Francesca leaped into the interior. Raze dove into the open doorway, tackling the baroness as the van jerked back into the flow of traffic to the blaring of horns and squealing tires.

She fought, her claws raking into his flesh, her fangs bared as she hissed like a wild creature. A gun went off, the bullet whistling by his head. Raze crushed her to his chest and rolled, using her body as a shield against the shooter in the passenger seat. Her ribs cracked in the vise of his grip.

Her scream pierced his ears. As Lake skidded around a corner, they nearly fell out of the open van door. Gaining his knees, Raze threw Francesca backward into the passenger, startling the man into firing. The bullet lodged in her back, her eyes widening with agony. Horrified by what he'd done, the man dropped his gun and it slid on the metal floorboard into Raze's waiting hand. He took out the minion with a shot to the head and grabbed Francesca by the wrist, yanking her into him so he could pierce her throat with his fangs.

As her blood pumped down his throat, he caught everything she knew—every plan she'd made, every minion she'd told about those plans. He learned the identity of the traitor who'd been providing her with Fallen blood and he knew how to find the names of those he needed to hunt. Not so many, but that wasn't what disturbed him.

He released her before the silver poisoning from the bullet tainted the blood he drank. She slumped to the floor. Lake screamed and hit the brakes, sending him crashing back into the bench seat. She shoved the transmission into park and threw the door open.

"Take a step," he warned, straightening, "and I'll kill you slow instead of fast."

She paused, sobbing, standing in the apex of the open door and the body of the vehicle.

Raze gestured her back into the van with a jerk of the pistol. When she returned to the driver's seat, he directed her to drive to Baron's safe house.

Chapter Eight

FRANCESCA, LADY SEAGRAVE, EYED the big vampire who prowled around the refuge she and Baron had created together and felt the hatred sizzling in her blood along with the silver that burned like acid. He was lost in the recording he listened to on her wireless headphones, his face a mask that revealed none of his thoughts. But he had to hear what she'd heard through the bugs she'd placed in his hotel room. The tenderness and affection that had developed between him and his mortal lover were evident in every word they spoke to each other, every breathless cry and pleasured moan.

It was going to wound him terribly when he lost her, perhaps even break him, considering how long he'd gone without anyone being necessary to him.

The crash of something breakable shattering on the floor sent a jolt through her. There were others in her home; two men Raze had called to assist him. They were presently rifling through her things, watching the videos she'd made of certain memorable kills. They watched and listened with such horror, as if it was a surprise that a vampire should hunt prey. That's what was fundamentally wrong with those in power of the vampire nation—they acted like animal rights activists who advocated vegetarianism, an impossible stance when ruling those who could be nothing but carnivores.

Mortals were food and sport. It was a joke that vampires should hide their existence and scrape for scraps to eat when there was so much to be had. The Sentinels were powerful, yes, but Syre had never once made an attempt to break out of their rigid boundaries. Who knew what they could accomplish? She and Baron envisioned a world in which vampires ruled as they should. She hadn't Changed to live like this. What was the point of having so much power if you never wielded it?

Raze yanked the headset off his ears and shot daggers into her with his gaze.

Her mouth curved. "It's my right to take her from you. Baron gave her to you as surely as if he'd introduced you. You wouldn't have been in Chicago to meet her if not for us."

"Were you planning on going through my entire black book?" he shot back. "Taking out every person I've fucked?"

"Oh no," she crooned, nursing her vicious fury like a babe at her breast. "She's special to you. Not like the others. Otherwise, you wouldn't have been at her place this morning. You would've taken what you wanted and left before sunrise. I miscalculated how quickly and deeply you fell for her, but it doesn't matter. She'll die, whether or not it's my hand that kills her. You have so many enemies, Raze. She won't last a minute in the grand scheme of things."

Francesca had to give him credit, his face and body language gave nothing away. But she knew the impact of her words. Tossing her head back, she laughed.

"You're a crazy bitch," he said grimly. "I'm just wondering if you were always psychotic or if the Change warped your brain."

"I Changed for him. We Changed for each other, so we'd always be together and you've taken him from me. And for what? You're as much of a Sentinel pet as the lycans. Now *you'll* lose something irreplaceable. You've finally found what you've been missing and it's about to be ripped from you. I hope you'll see what's done to her. I hope you watch while she's cut and torn and broken. I hope her screams stay in your head—"

There was a split second in which she registered the gun in his hand. And then there was nothing.

Raze studied the baroness's slumped head with icy detachment. She remained upright courtesy of the ingeniously heinous chair he'd found in her home—a chair with silver-plated spiked manacles at the wrists and throat, and a bottom and back with blades that protruded or retracted via a handle on the backside.

Turning away, he looked around the warehouse loft and considered what she'd left behind. There was an entire bookcase of recorded atrocities stored in jeweled cases. It was a collection that could never fall into a Sentinel or lycan's hands, or questions would be raised that had no good answers. Some of what he'd seen would haunt him for years to come, minions who'd succumbed so completely to bloodlust that they were little more than ravening beasts. Raze wasn't certain there was anything—even the Creator's command that the Fallen live endlessly with their vampiric curse—that could prevent a war if Adrian believed vampires were a threat requiring complete eradication.

After all, Adrian had broken other commandments without punishment.

"This place is a house of horrors," Crash muttered behind him, tossing the disks into a crate to be destroyed. "And they were proud of it. They could've kept all this shit in a cloud or on a hard drive, but they wanted the visual of how many kills they had under their belt."

Raze's phone vibrated in his pocket and he pulled it out. "Raze."

"How extensive is the infestation in Chicago?" Adrian asked without preamble.

His back stiffened. "I'm taking care of it."

"If you think that's going to be enough to put me off, you haven't learned anything about me in the last several eons." The smoothly modulated tone of the Sentinel's voice only made his words more disturbing. "Discovering a few hundred armed minions in a heavily populated metropolis is a big fucking problem. Tell Syre if he can't get a handle on his ranks, I'll take the necessary steps to manage it myself."

"Why don't—"

"You and the six minions who arrived today have forty-eight hours to wrap it up and clear out."

The line died, leaving Raze cursing at an angel who couldn't hear him.

There were times when he thought there was no way to clean up the mess the Fallen had made, times when he thought even damage control was out of their reach. There were tens of thousands of vampires policed by less than four hundred combined Fallen and Sentinels plus a few thousand lycans. The odds were against them in every way.

He'd felt helpless before, but now he had something he couldn't bear to lose. He would hunt down the ones whose names he found here in Baron's safe house, but that wouldn't make Kim any safer. As long as they were connected in any way, she would be a target.

Back in his hotel room, Raze looked into the video feed of Vash's office on his brand-new iPad and caught her up. "I got the list of Baron's followers off his laptop and most of the team is out hunting them now. They had me tailed from the moment I arrived at the airport. While I was killing Baron at the ballpark, the baroness was here in my room planting bugs."

"So now we know why she wasn't there that night."

"Right. That's what I couldn't get: Why the hell did they draw my attention? If they hadn't dumped that body on my porch, we wouldn't be on to them now. Reviving Grimm's doctrine was a ruse. They used it to round up enough minions to put on that show at Wrigley Field, but their real agenda was to get those bugs on me for future intel gathering. We found them in every room of my suite and on my iPad. They planted tracking devices on my bags. They knew every move I made and would have continued to know, if she hadn't fucked up and gone after Kim this morning. The baroness hadn't planned on my being there."

Vash pushed her hair back from her face and looked grim. "I hate to say it, but your Kim is going to be a problem for you, unless you're planning on Changing her and taking the risk that she won't lose herself in the process. You've made a lot of enemies over the years."

Everything inside him recoiled at the thought of losing Kim in any way, by his actions or someone else's. "That hasn't escaped me. But I wasn't their only target. They had rudimentary plans to lure you and Salem out, too."

"Well, fuckin' A." Her amber eyes were hard and cold. "They're lucky they went with you first. They wouldn't have liked dealing with me."

"I thought the same thing," he said wryly. "In a related matter, Adrian called me today. He's ordered me and the team out of Chicago by Tuesday. To say he's not happy about armed minions in the city would be an understatement."

"Fuck him and the high horse he rides," she snapped.

He smiled. "You're just pissed because he's got us by the balls with this one."

"Whatever. The fucker shouldn't always be right." She took a deep breath. "Listen, I don't want to distract you from what you're doing, especially while you've got Adrian breathing down your neck, but … Nikki's gone missing."

Raze froze. Torque's wife. "What do you mean by 'missing'?"

"She was supposed to pick up Torque in Shreveport last night, but she never made it."

"You'll need me." It wasn't a question.

"Yeah. But take care of what's on your plate there first. We need to put a lid on that mess and I need your head in the game when you get back here."

"Keep me posted."

"Of course."

He signed off and stood, methodically packing up his things. There wasn't much.

"The room is yours," he told Crash. "I'll call you when I get out in the field. I have something to take care of."

Crash waved absently, his attention riveted to the data on Baron's laptop.

Raze had barely knocked on Kim's door when it was yanked open and she threw herself into his arms.

"Is everything all right?" she asked, pressing her face into his chest.

With one arm around her waist, he lifted her feet from the floor and carried her into the apartment, closing them inside by leaning back against the door. "For now."

What a lie, he thought. Everything was far from all right. No matter what he decided, it was going to be painful for both of them.

She searched his face for answers. "Talk to me."

He dropped his bag on the ground and wrapped his arms around her, engulfing her in the strength and heat of his body. "I brought my crap to your door, Kim. And then I came back anyway."

"Damn right you came back." She had the same look of determination on her face that she'd had when she picked him up in the club. "I would've hunted you down if you hadn't."

"You wouldn't find me." And God, it killed him to think of her trying to. Because he understood the drive, the need and hunger to be near each other. It's what brought him back to her even when he knew the best thing for both of them would be for him to walk away completely.

"Try me," she challenged grimly. "If you want to go because you don't feel anything for me, that's fine. I won't make it difficult for you. But as long as I think you're taking the same ride I am, I'm not letting you get off easy."

He pressed his cheek to hers, swamped with wanting her, with wanting *this*—the sense of being right where he should be. He carried her to the couch and sat, arranging her so that she straddled him. She draped her arms over his shoulders and leaned back, affording him the opportunity to drink in the sight of her. She wore blue jeans and a loose V-neck T-shirt, looking soft and sexy and beautiful.

"Am I in danger?" she asked. "Is that what the roses were about? Is that what you're kicking yourself over?"

"Not immediate." Raze's fingers shifted into her hair, pushing it back from her face. "But as long as I'm with you, it's always going to be hovering in the background. You don't need any more traumas, Kim. You've had more than your share already."

"I come from a family of cops. I'll be okay." She cupped the back of his head, making sure his gaze stayed locked with hers. "It's good you came back, Raze. Whatever else you may think, whatever else is going on, it's important that you came back. It was the right thing to do."

He hugged her again, running his hands up her spine to mold her into him. "I've got work to do today and I didn't ask you first, but I gave up my room and brought my stuff here."

"Good."

"You say that now, but you don't know what I am and I can't tell you until I'm given permission to."

"You tried warning me off the night I met you, remember? And it didn't work, even when you were just a seriously prime piece of beefcake." Kim squeezed him hard. "It's not going to work now that I'm invested."

"You don't know what I do. You'll need to know. I'll need to tell you when I can, but I have to leave soon. No later than Tuesday. And I don't know when I'll be back. It could be weeks. Months."

"Just so long as you come back. Promise me that. That's where we'll begin. We have the phone and Internet. We can see each other via videoconference. It won't be the same as touching you, but at least we're not giving up."

His head fell back onto the sofa cushion, his eyes trained on the ceiling but not seeing it. "I'm going to be honest and tell you what's running through my head. Dropping this now would be the best thing for both of us. We've had a couple days together. A week from now it won't seem as intense. A few months down the road, it'll be a fond memory. That's the easy way to go."

"You're absolutely right." She took a deep breath. "I was thinking the same thing while you were gone. I was rehearsing what I'd say to you, how to put across that I'd had a great time, but the weekend was enough for me. There's something here, we both know that, but it's just a spark right now. With a little time and a little distance, it'll burn out."

He exhaled harshly. "Yeah."

"But then I realized I'm not okay with that." She was staring at him when he lifted his head to look at her. "Because I don't know if I'll find that spark again. I don't if it would be the same if I did find it later. What if this is it? What if you're the best thing that ever happened to me? Am I going to spend the rest of my life wondering what could have happened if I'd been strong enough to try? I don't want to live with those questions haunting me."

"I'm pretty sure I'm the worst thing that's ever happened to you," he muttered. "Let's clear that up now."

"And I'm pretty sure you could turn into a werewolf during full moons and I wouldn't care."

"What?"

"Or maybe a troll on Wednesdays? Maybe you're a vampire, and that's why I haven't seen you eat."

"Christ." He couldn't help it; his lips twitched with the urge to laugh. Which was just part of her magic. He was a different person with her. And he liked being that guy. Liked being *her* guy.

"Ha!" Kim's eyes sparkled with mischief. "I spend most days examining bodily fluids, which a lot of people think is gross. We all have our blemishes. And we're not talking about marriage here. We're talking about taking a chance. Making a few phone calls. Sending a few e-mails."

She nuzzled his nose with hers, a playful gesture that no one else would dare to make with him. His lungs seized with a terrible yearning. Tilting his head, he kissed her, drinking her in. Her lips were soft and sweet beneath his; her returning kiss was deep and slow. Savoring.

"What do ya say, rough guy?" she murmured against his mouth. "Wanna take a chance on me?"

"Yes." Raze took her mouth again. "Yes. Fuck. But I have to go now. I have to work."

"But you'll be back."

He ran his fingers through her hair and nodded. "I'll be back."

Iron Hard

A CLOCKWORK CRAVINGS NOVELLA

Chapter One

London, 1820

"YOU ARE ATTACHED TO them."

Annabelle Waters took one last, lingering look at the mechanized lovebirds in their velvet-lined delivery box, then closed the lid. "I'm attached to all my creations."

"Let me rephrase," her brother said. "You are *especially* attached to these."

She met her twin's blue-eyed stare. "Have you any notion of how difficult it was to calibrate the resonance frequencies so that if one should fail the other will also?"

"They are your best work yet," Thomas agreed. "But that isn't why you favor them so, and we both know it."

Annie looked at the empty bird cage in the corner of her workroom, then shifted her attention to the clock on the mantle. With a sigh, she pulled the safety goggles off the top of her head and ruffled her short cap of dark curls. "I have to make myself presentable."

"Allow me to deliver this one."

"The baron asked that I personally demonstrate how they work. Considering the obscene sum we charged him, it is the least I can do."

"Annie—"

"I promise to speak of you," she rushed on, knowing what he desired, "if the opportunity presents itself. But the subject must be delicately approached. His lordship's future patronage and endorsement could change our fortunes in profound ways."

"I know. But you've no notion of what it is like at his shipyard," he complained. "I have waited in that line for nearly a year and am no closer to gaining employment than I was when I began. Every man in England wishes to apprentice under his banner."

She knew that; it was impossible not to know. Baron de la Warren had returned from the war a hero, a sky captain lauded for his brilliant strategies and swashbuckling boldness. He was credited with the destruction of Boney's dirigible fleet and romanticized for his patched eye, which gave him the appearance of a pirate of old. Peacetime had done nothing to lessen his appeal. He was, in fact, more popular now. His import empire offered well-paying work and apprenticeship to many destitute yet able-bodied young men, like her brother. Annie had been startled when his lordship had commissioned the lovebirds, wondering at the private man who lived beneath the public personage. What manner of warrior thought of such a lover's gift? She was more than a little eager to see for herself.

The long case clock in hall began to chime with the hour. Annie proceeded with her egress. "I will find an excuse to mention you. Perhaps I can convince his lordship to visit under the guise of viewing some of my other creations. He could find nothing untoward about meeting you here, and once he does, he'll certainly engage you. How could he not? You're just the sort of intelligent, ambitious young man he cultivates in his employ."

"It's not working," he grumbled after her. "Your flattery."

"Yes, it is." She slowed at the sound of creaking floorboards and heavy footsteps.

The soothing whirring of gears preceded the appearance of

their butler as he rounded the balustrade in the visitors' foyer. He slowed his steady forward momentum when he saw her, his striated glass lenses turning to adjust his polarized vision.

"Please have the coach brought around, Alfred."

He acknowledged her request with an imminently regal dip of his head.

"Thank you," she said, unable to refrain from smiling.

The servant was one of her most prized creations, albeit one lacking the painful sentimentality of the lovebirds. As much as she longed to keep them, she also could not wait to be parted from them. They awakened memories she'd learned to suppress through an intense focus on her work.

It had been five years since Waterloo. *Five years.*

He wasn't coming back.

Annie secured her hat to her head with an ivory pin and collected the boxed birds with gloved hands. Alfred pulled the front door open, allowing the low-lying fog to roll in over the cracked marble floors with the sinuousness of a lover. She left the house, skipping over the shattered second step to reach the street, which was deserted aside from her steam coach.

What had once been a fashionable neighborhood for the wealthy was now home to a pile of rubble. When Prinny had urged the willing and able to stake claims on salvageable abandoned properties, she and Thomas had chosen a row house that stood as a lone sentinel on a ravaged street. It was quiet here. She was spared the distraction of belching delivery wagons and the repetitious *tick tick tick* of insectile vendor cart legs picking their way over pockmarked cobblestones.

Lifting her skirts, Annie climbed onto the box seat and settled herself. She pulled her driving goggles over her eyes, then gripped the wheel as she let the break, holding on tightly as the coach lurched forward.

In short order, she left the city behind. Baron de la Warren lived on the outskirts, away from the smoke and fog that shrouded London. When she finally arrived at the massive iron gates that kept the fawning world at bay, she rang the bell. The locking mechanism had been built as a work of art, with copper meshing gears and tin ornamentation. She watched admiringly as the chains slid smoothly over well-oiled sprockets, causing the gates to swing inward and grant her entrance.

Within high brick perimeter walls, the baron's property was massive. A dirigible landing pad was situated on the left side of the brick manse and a large carriage house was visible in the distance on the right. Sleek hounds followed her progress up the lane, their iron plates flexing with the ease of snakeskin.

Once she reached the circular front drive, Annie reined in her delight and focused on the meeting ahead. Clearly his lordship held an appreciation for mechanization and she had no qualms in saying that she was the best engineer in London.

Squaring her shoulders, Annie caught the brass ring held in the jaws of a massive lion's head doorknocker and rapped it sharply. She was initially surprised when a human butler opened the door, but that passed swiftly. The baron could afford the luxury of live servants and their wages. She, on the other hand, had created Alfred from scrap parts.

The butler took her hat, gloves, and pelisse before showing her into a shadowed study.

As he bowed and moved to turn away, she said, "I will require more light, please."

The striking of a match preceded the flaring of illumination from one of the room's corners. Her head turned swiftly, her breath catching as a man stepped forward. She scarcely paid any mind to the door clicking shut behind the retreating servant.

"Will this do?" he asked in a low, rumbling voice. He turned up the flame in the gas lamp he carried and joined her at the desk where she'd deposited the birds.

She stared, riveted by the savage beauty of his face and the intensity with which he regarded her. His dark hair was long, hanging to his shoulders in a thick, glossy mane. A wide band of pure white strands embellished his left temple, framing a silver eye. Even as she watched, the metallic iris turned, the lens adjusting to accommodate the brighter light. A scar ran diagonally from his temple, across the eyelid and over his upper lip, explaining how he'd lost the eye he had been born with. The blemish did nothing to mitigate his comeliness. While it altered her perception of the symmetry of his features, it was in a manner she found highly appealing, as she did the air of danger surrounding him.

The provocation she felt was far from fear.

Breathing shallowly, her gaze raked over his face, admiring his dark winged brows, brilliant green iris, and the impossibly sensual shape of his mouth. His jaw was square and bold, his cheekbones high and expertly sculpted. He was far too masculine to be pretty, but he was certainly magnificent, and younger than the strip of white hair and his world-weary gaze would suggest. The drawings of him in the gazettes had never done him justice.

"Miss Waters," he greeted her, extending his gloved hand. "I cannot tell you what a pleasure it is to receive you."

"My lord. The pleasure is mine." She curtsied and placed her fingers within his palm, shivering as he clasped her. There was a sincerity in his commonplace greeting that startled her. Then something else unexpected—the unforgiving strength of metal curling around her fingers—stole her attention. "Your hand…?"

"My arm," he corrected.

An entire arm. Mechanized. Excitement coursed through her.

He watched her with searing intensity. "Would you like to see it?"

"Yes. Please."

Releasing her, he stepped back and shrugged out of his beautifully tailored velvet jacket. He tugged off his gloves; first the one on his mechanical hand, then its mate covering his physical one. She was amazed by the dexterity of his copper fingers as he freed the button at his cuff and rolled his sleeve up.

Her lungs seized at the wondrous sight. She took a step forward without her volition, her gaze riveted to the softly whirring copper and steel gears. They had been fashioned into the shape of an arm and so precisely meshed that she doubted even air could slip between the cogs. Encased in what appeared to be thin glass, it was worthy of museum exhibition.

"How extensive is the replacement?" she asked, fighting the urge to run her hands over it.

"To the shoulder."

Her tongue darted out to lick her suddenly dry lips.

His green eye flashed with heat and his mouth—that wicked, wonderful mouth—curved in a rakish smile. "I would gladly show you the whole, but I'd have to undress further. Do you object?"

"No." She quivered with anticipation. "Please."

The baron loosened his cravat. She was so mesmerized by the expert craftsmanship of his artificial appendage, she scarcely registered that he was disrobing. Until the tight lacing of his abdomen was bared. Followed by the rippling expanse of his powerful chest.

"Oh, my…" Her arousal spiked. Her blood was hot for him, her body softening to accommodate the hardness of his. Unseemly thoughts filled her mind. Naughty thoughts. Highly sexual.

He was scarred on his chest as well. As with his face, the puckered bullet hole and multiple knife slashes only made him more delicious. Annie's lips parted on lightly panting breaths, her breasts swelling within her bodice.

She flushed and tore her gaze away from the seductive expanse of flame-lit muscle and golden skin. It shocked her to realize how much effort was required to focus on his finely wrought arm instead. In truth, it had been far too long since flesh and blood had held more appeal than steel and grease. She found herself at a loss over which arm was more skillfully cast—the one afforded him by the grace of God or the one crafted by an earthly engineer.

"Exquisite." Annie referred to the entirety of him, not merely the manmade pieces.

Judging by his sudden low growl, the baron knew it.

Sharp tension spiked between them, a heightened awareness that swept across her skin in a pricking wave. An aching need built between her legs, a reminder that she had suppressed her desires for years. Or, more accurately, it had been that length of time since a man had proven capable of rousing them. After the loss of Gaspard, she'd wondered if grief had made her immune to masculine charms. But the baron was proving her wrong. Her gratitude for that was as potent as her attraction.

Turning away abruptly, she faced the desk and lifted the lid on the delivery box with unsteady hands. The lovebirds glimmered in the firelight, their tin feathers flexing as they moved closer to each other. "I hope these are satisfactory, my lord."

He came up behind her, his greater height enabling him to

look over her shoulder. He stood so close she could smell him: warm, virile male with the faintest touch of clove and bergamot.

"My god," he said gruffly, reaching around her to slide his hand beneath a bird and lift it out. "I have never seen the like."

Annie's stomach quivered with delight at his praise. The way the baron hefted the small creature—curling his palm around it and testing its weight—incited scorching thoughts of his hand on her breasts, cupping them from his position behind her, admiring her form with equal warmth.

"Do not remove them too far from one another," she warned. Her voice softened with the memory of another pair of birds, a gift from a man she'd once thought to spend her life with. "They cannot be parted, if you don't wish them broken."

"Broken." His warm breath blew across the shell of her ear. "Is that not true of us all? Once we find the other half of ourselves, we are never again whole without them."

"Yes." Her gaze remained riveted on his hand, the warm live flesh carefully holding her delicate creation. "Will they be a gift? For your other half, perhaps?"

"They are for you, Annabelle," he said softly. "To replace the ones you lost."

"My lord?" Her chest lifted and fell in an elevated rhythm. She wondered if he knew how the soft hum of his turning gears affected her. The low sound coursed over her senses in a constant tingling stream.

"Gaspard Vangess served under me. He spoke of you. As beautifully as you create things with your hands, he created you in words." There was the veriest hint of his lips against her ear. "Before I saw you in truth, I dreamed of you. Wanted you."

With shaking hands, she took the bird from him and set it carefully back in the box. Its partner cooed and shifted closer.

"Have I frightened you?" he asked hoarsely. "I meant to woo

you carefully. That remains my intent. I apologize that I wasn't prepared for your effect on me. The moment you entered the room, I was ensnared. But I won't press you beyond your allowance."

"I'm not frightened." She exhaled in a rush. "He is gone, then?"

"Yes."

"I knew it. Felt it." But she also felt a quiet, painful relief to know her first love's fate for a certainty. Not knowing had become the most painful aspect of all.

"His last words were of you. He secured my promise to replace the birds he'd once given you, the ones you lost during the London invasion. He went to war to make the world a safe place for you to have precious and fragile things, and he wanted to see that goal met and come full circle. I chose to present you with a gift that won't die. I cannot replace Vangess, but I can give you something of him that will never leave you."

A tear slipped free, along with an aching weight she hadn't realized she was carrying. "My poor, sweet Gaspard."

The baron stood at military rest behind her, a stoic yet soothing presence. "My heart aches for your loss."

"Thank you." Annie watched the small parrots nuzzle against each other. She was powerfully aware of her desire to do the same with the man behind her. A man with whom she felt an undeniable affinity and appreciation. "I am no longer the girl he told you about."

"No. That girl was his. Annie, he called you. But I think Bella better suits the lush and courageous woman you've become."

And the woman she'd become was suddenly unencumbered. And so very lonely. She watched the lovebirds and envied their bond. "For a time, I was broken."

He touched the top button of her jacket where it lay against her nape. "And now?"

"Now… I am whole but empty." And mantled by a man

who stirred her blood while desiring her in return. An unexpected yet welcome miracle.

"What you would have of me? You have only to ask."

Her head fell forward, her eyes drifting closed. "I want you to touch me, my lord. I want to be the Bella you see when you look at me. I want to be filled again."

Chapter Two

THE BARON NUZZLED AGAINST Annie's upswept hair. The first of her coat's buttons was urged free of its hole. The rest swiftly followed, coaxed into surrender—as she was herself— by the baron's agile and dexterous mechanical hand. When he pushed the garment forward, over her shoulders and down her arms, she reveled in the rush of air that cooled her fevered skin.

"I must tell you," she whispered. "My brother, Thomas, aspires to work for you."

"I will train him myself."

The largesse of his quick offer and the joy it would bring to Thomas softened her heart. "That isn't why I want you."

"I wouldn't care if it was."

Annie glanced over her shoulder, her heartbeat faltering at his beauty. "Why not?"

He brushed the backs of his fingers across her cheek. "Clearly a man with my embellishments would benefit considerably by an association with an engineer of your skill, but that does not mitigate the fact that it's the living parts of me that need you most. Requiring each other for more than sex is a blessing, Bella, not a curse."

She lifted her arms over her head, wrapping them around his neck and pulling his mouth down to hers. His kiss curled her toes. Lush and deep, he took her mouth with a fierce possessiveness. He ate at her, licking and suckling in a manner that had her writhing against him, seeking the kind of closeness that required bared skin.

The remainder of her clothes were swiftly shed—her shirt and skirt, pantalettes and stockings. When he freed the stays of her corset with a hiss of compressed air, she sighed along with the sound, her inhibitions stripped away with her attire. Not that she'd had all that many by the time he touched her. The baron had been seducing her from the moment he commissioned the lovebirds. The journey to this point, both mental and actual, had only lured her deeper under his spell.

"Annabelle." He cupped her breasts through her chemise, lifting their moderate weight and kneading gently, just as she'd imagined mere moments before. He rolled her nipples between thumb and forefinger, and her head fell back against his shoulder, her lips parting on rapid breaths. Both of his hands were warm, his touch both reverent and rapacious. Her nerve endings woke from their extended dormancy, prickling with near-painful intensity. She grew slick and hot between her legs, her sex throbbing with greedy hunger.

Her fingers slid through the long, thick strands of his hair to reach his nape. She stroked him there, shivering when he groaned. Her hips began to rock in small circles, deliberately massaging his cock with her derriere. "My lord…"

The baron nipped her ear with his teeth and clutched her possessively between her thighs. "Raphael," he corrected. "I want to hear you say it."

His lips moved across her nape, caressing, goading without words. Her heartbeat stuttered.

"*Raphael.*" Clutching fistfuls of courage along with her chemise, Annie pulled the garment's hem to her waist, the material sliding between his gentle grip and her tender flesh.

He parted the lips of her sex with scissoring fingers. "I'm going to put my mouth here and lick you. Make you come."

Annie sagged against him, slicking his artificial hand with the liquid proof of her desire.

The use of that hand told her that he knew her. Understood her. There were few who collected her appreciation for mechanization. Even Thomas wondered at her fascination with well-oiled and effortlessly moving parts. He didn't comprehend the thrill she felt, the rush of excitement and pleasure. She wasn't certain she understood it, but there was no denying her attraction to the baron. All of him. The parts pulsing and breathing with life, and the metallic ones having those very effects on her.

"I want my mouth on you, too," she confessed. She would start at his lips and work her way down his arm, sucking each copper finger before performing the same service to his cock.

"It will be." Raphael caught her by the waist and lifted her, eliciting a soft cry of surprise. He carried her to the damask-covered settee and arranged her on her back, sinking to his knees on the floor beside her. Gooseflesh raced across her skin. One of her legs was lifted and draped over his muscular shoulder, then his head lowered to the glistening flesh between her thighs.

The first teasing lick made her arch upward with heated lust. Sweat misted skin that felt too tight and hot. "I am too fast with you," she gasped.

"Am I not equally so with you?"

"You are a man."

"I promise to make you happy about that."

Annie laughed, then caught her breath, her stomach concaving as he covered her with his mouth. *Yes.*

Her moan echoed through the cavernous room, her fingers pushing into the silky curtain of his hair. He tongued her gently, the pointed tip stroking feather light over her distended clitoris. Pleasure coiled like a compressed spring. Too swiftly. "Raphael. Please."

"Not yet." Lips curving against her, he angled his head and speared his tongue into her quivering sex.

Beyond shyness or shame, she tightened her leg over his shoulder, tugging him closer. Raphael obliged with a growl, fucking her aching flesh with quick fierce stabs. She rocked into his working mouth, circling her hips without thought or reason. Effortlessly, he lifted her, balancing her with one hand as he pushed two unyielding copper fingers inside her.

Fingers that *vibrated*.

Annie jerked in startled delight. The slightly ribbed texture of the flexing joint meshing sent tremors through her limbs. She sobbed as the vibration increased, beading her nipples into painfully hard points. He began to thrust, his fingers pumping through her spasming tissues with tender purpose. Determined. Expert. Knowing just the spot to rub with those wickedly pulsating fingertips. All the while he sucked her clitoris, tugging and worrying the sensitive point with frenzied flicks of his tongue.

She gasped his name as she shuddered into an orgasm so powerful it blackened her vision. Violent trembling wracked her body and she clung to the edge of the settee, seeking an anchor as reality fell away.

The baron lowered her gently to the cushion, his wet mouth nuzzling against her inner thigh before he withdrew from her and pushed to his feet with powerful grace. He undressed swiftly and unabashedly, his abdomen lacing tightly as he dispensed with his boots, a task impossible for most men without the aid of a valet. Flushed with lust, lips wet and swollen from the attention he'd paid to her, the baron's gaze slid over her like a tangible caress: soft, yet resolute; his mind clearly occupied with all the ways he wanted her and how he would have her.

It was a novel and highly exciting perusal for her. Gaspard

had been nearly as untried as she had been, their love having grown from adolescence. Raphael was mature and delectably well-practiced.

He set one knee on the cushion between her sprawled legs and stabilized himself with one hand around the wooden lip of the seatback. "What are you thinking?"

She realized then how exposed she was, how immodest and unguarded. "What have you done to me?"

He cupped her cheek with his free hand. "No more than you have done to me. This arm you admire is not the one given to me on the battlefield. Such craftsmanship could not be found in that hell. The grafting of the first, crude replacement was excruciating. Death would have been a kindness and there were days when I prayed for it. Gaspard Vangess—awash in needless guilt that I had shielded him from the blast that took my arm—would sit with me and distract me with tales of you. He regaled me with stories of a rambunctious girl with freckles on her nose and mischief in her blue eyes. Mindless with agony and laudanum, my mind took possession of the memories he shared. For a time in my delirium, you were mine and I loved you beyond all reason. It was for you that I recovered, only to realize you were a dream that belonged to another man, a promising airman who was killed a fortnight before I returned to the fleet."

"Raphael—" She cupped his hip in her palm.

His breath hissed out. He mounted her, his patience seemingly at an end. The thick head of his cock tucked into the slick and swollen entrance to her body. She held her breath, waiting.

"Please," she whispered. At his first slow push, her head fell back.

"Christ." His luxurious hair brushed her cheek. "Your cunt is tight and hot. So wet. Perfect."

Catching her leg behind the knee, he anchored it on his hip, opening her wider. He withdrew slightly, then returned in a practiced roll of his hips.

Her nails dug into his clenching buttocks. "Faster," she urged in a voice so hoarse she scarcely knew it.

He laughed, and the arrogant maleness inherent in the sound spurred her further. She threw her hips upward, taking more of him.

"Vixen." Raphael kissed her even as he pinned her to the settee with a firm but gentle grip on her hip. "I won't allow you to rush me."

Her fingers kneaded restlessly into the hard muscles of his back. "You cannot command me as you would your crew."

"No?"

"You said you would fill me, not tease me to madness!"

All levity fled his breathtakingly handsome features. He pulled back, then pushed deeper, exhaling in a rush when she tightened greedily around him. He was hot to the touch, his skin slick with sweat, his muscles rigid. But he would not be spurred into rutting atop her as she wished. "I want something from you in return, Bella."

Wrapping both legs around him, she tried to draw him closer. "What more can I give you?"

"This," he purred, working his thick cock inexorably deeper. "Your passion, your need. I want to be the one you hunger for, the one who shares your bed. The only one, from this day 'til my last."

Even in the extremity of her lust, her mind raced with the impossibility of their mutual infatuation. And yet… something more profound was between them as well.

"You know," he went on, altering the angle of her hips to slide farther into her, "as I've known, that we are what the other needs or you would not be arching beneath me now."

Dear god, she wanted the baron with a primitive hunger. She wanted him as she knew him to be: Bold. Dauntless. A force of tremendous will. What an adventure it would be to become the mistress of such a man… "Yes, I know."

He stilled, staring down at her with those gloriously dissimilar eyes; one as brilliant as an emerald, the other like polished silver. "But I cannot be a kept man."

She blinked up at him. "Beg your pardon?"

His mouth curved with wicked amusement. "Young men emulate me. I have a reputation to uphold. You must make an honest man of me."

"Raphael." Her chest tightened painfully. With hope. With fear. With lingering grief. "I—"

With an exaggerated sigh, he straightened his arms and began to withdraw. When she realized he intended to cease their bedsport completely, she narrowed her gaze. Two could play.

Tightening her legs around him, she caught his shoulders and wrenched to the side, rolling them both to the floor.

The drop was short, mere inches. He landed on his back. *Laughing.* Jaw set with determination, she reached between them to position the cock that was as impressive as the man himself, then sheathed him in her body with a swift plunge of her hips.

A soft cry escaped her. His mirth fled with a serrated groan. She set her hands palms down on his chest and gave a tentative swivel of her hips, easing the pressing fullness of his deep penetration.

"I'm conquered," he said hoarsely. "My surrender is unconditional and absolute."

"But I've yet to state my terms."

"I concede to them all."

Her brow arched even as she rose up on her knees, stroking

her eager sex with the length of his throbbing erection. The sensation was exquisite, as was he, this legendary man who awakened a stirring emotion she'd thought forever lost to her. "Where is the strategy in that, Captain?"

Raphael caught her hips and surged upward, filling her. "One must lay claim to a territory before one can cultivate it."

Clutching his wrists for balance, Annie began to move in earnest. Her spine arched with heated pleasure as he worked with her, lifting his lean hips to meet her downward drives. Beneath the onslaught of sensation, her body moved as a thing separate from her mind, the need to ride his pumping cock too potent for moderation. An approaching orgasm drummed through her blood, coaxing wrenching cries from her with every desperate thrust.

He pushed the low table aside with a powerful sweep of his arm, then rolled her beneath him. Fisting the thick Aubusson rug in his mechanical hand, he anchored her by the shoulder and pounded his lust into her with heavy, rhythmic lunges. Her legs fell open, inviting him deeper, her neck arching with the brutal rush of desire.

"Bella," he growled, an instant before he jerked inside her. The first hard pulse of semen made her gasp, spurring the climax that joined with his. She tightened around his spending cock, milking his seed with rippling spasms. He groaned with every clinging grasp, circling his hips to hit the end of her.

Her arms encircled him as he lowered his chest to hers, his back slick with sweat and his muscles quivering like a stallion run hard and long. Her eyes closed on a shuddering sigh. She contemplated possessing such a lavishly splendid creature as the baron and being possessed by him in return. The endeavor, when committed to so early in their association, was not without tremendous risk. But the rewards… Already she felt like a butter-fly newly emerged from its cocoon.

He pulled her tighter against him and breathed her name. Turning her head, Annabelle claimed him with a kiss.

Catching Caroline

Dear Reader,

This story was written before I sold my first book. In other words, it's not up to the same standards as my present-day writing. When the rights reverted to me, I considered editing *Catching Caroline* again. Then I realized there was really no way to edit this story; I would have to rewrite it. Caroline is uniquely unlike my usual heroines. Changing her would require changing the whole tale, and changing the whole tale would destroy it. This story is written differently from how I would write it today, but that's okay.

I hope you enjoy it!

— Sylvia

Prologue

"WICKED MEN ARE A weakness of mine."

"Good heavens, Julienne." Lady Caroline Seton smothered a laugh as she entered the Dempsey ballroom. "You are incorrigible."

Julienne La Coeur arched a brow. "You have no notion of how fortunate you are to be unhindered by the rules of Society. You may do and say whatever you wish. You can associate with the rakes you prefer and marry whomever you like. I, however…" She paused and shot a glance at her aunt behind her. Lowering her voice, she continued, "Am destined to do whatever I'm told."

Caroline offered a quick commiserating smile as she waited at the top of the staircase for the majordomo to announce their party. Her gaze drifted across the occupants below, taking in the various gowns and the number of guests in attendance. At one time she had attended such events with her own family, but they had passed on to their reward long ago and she had learned to manage on her own. Her comfortably sized trust funds and lack of familial ties afforded her a freedom other women of her station, women like Julienne, did not enjoy. Unfortunately, it was also very lonely.

With her thoughts elsewhere, Caroline might have passed over impressively broad shoulders and hair as dark as night had the tiny hairs on her nape not stood at attention and her jaw not begun to ache in a wholly unfamiliar way.

She stilled, her attention riveted on the tall man whose powerful torso tapered to a narrow waist and lean hips. His black hair gleamed under the golden glow of the chandeliers, the ends curled lovingly around the top of his starched cravat. The evening attire of stark black and white appeared to have been made with him in mind, showing off the austere beauty of his features to perfection, a beauty enhanced by the statuesque blonde who clung to his arm.

Caroline stared at the man shamelessly, knowing that even if the animal inside her had not felt the singular attraction, she would have wanted him anyway.

With his full lips and intense gaze, he was gorgeous, his face so perfect as to outshine any classical painting or statue of her recollection. She'd never witnessed a more resplendently masculine being in her life. There was something about him, a dangerous edge, a predatory alertness she found utterly mesmerizing. Just looking at him made her nipples hard, her body soft, and caused moisture to pool between her thighs, readying her for his possession.

Just one look and she was nearly undone.

"Jack Shaw."

Caroline glanced aside at Julienne. "Beg your pardon?"

"The man you are presently drooling over is Jack Shaw, an American. Obscenely wealthy I've been told, due to his shipping interests."

"He's…stunning," Caroline murmured, acknowledging even as she spoke what an understatement that was.

"Yes," Julienne agreed. "With a fabulously wicked reputation. How I envy you your choice of men such as him."

Wicked. Caroline shivered with desire. She knew he would

be, just from the sight of him. As if he could feel the longing and need in her regard, he looked up and caught her gaze, revealing the molten silver color of his irises.

The connection was devastating. Caroline was unable to halt her instinctive reaction. Her own blood flooded her mouth before she realized her fangs had descended.

It took everything she had to prevent leaping from the staircase and biting deep into his neck. The desire to pierce his skin, to drink him in, was so overwhelming she didn't trust herself to be around him. In the century she'd been vampire, she'd never experienced such a soul-deep pull to another being.

Startled, confused, and deeply afraid she would do something she'd regret forever, Caroline covered her mouth and spun blindly away. She ran past gaping guests in the crowded foyer and fled to the safety of the night beyond.

"You're coming with me, Caroline. Whether you like it or not."

Caroline watched Julienne pace across the Aubusson rug in her parlor and released a deep breath. Arguing with Julienne La Coeur about anything was a chore. Her friend was too stubborn by half.

"I told you, Jules. I'm not feeling well." Settling more comfortably into her seat, Caroline attempted to look ill.

"Nonsense," Julienne scoffed, coming to a halt directly before her. "You look the picture of health as always. Besides you've been convalescing for a week, plenty of time to recover from what ailed you when you ran out of the Dempsey affair."

Shaking her head, Caroline knew she couldn't continue to hide in her residence forever, but the fear she would chance upon Jack Shaw again was strong enough to make the idea appealing. He'd come calling twice already, bearing lovely bouquets of flowers, and both times he had been turned away. Any notion she might have held that she'd gone unnoticed was completely dispelled. He knew her name. Worse yet, he wanted to court her. The thought sent her into a mild panic. Even if she could control the animal within her, she was not free to accept his attentions as long as she was promised to another.

Julienne sighed. "You are attending the Moreland ball with me. I won't take no for an answer." She dropped to a crouch beside the settee. "Please, Caroline," she begged. "These events are positively dreadful when you're not around. Aunt Eugenia fusses all evening."

"Why is the Moreland ball so important to you?"

Blushing, Julienne admitted, "Lucien Remington is rumored to have been invited."

"Good grief. Talk about wicked men, Jules."

"Ummm…isn't he? So you see, you must come with me and distract my aunt so I can ogle Remington at my leisure."

Staring into her friend's hopeful features, Caroline couldn't find the heart to refuse. "Oh, very well then," she gave in with a laugh. If she was very careful and very fortunate, she might be able to survive the evening without crossing paths with Jack. "But I'm taking my leave early. So ogle with haste."

Jack traversed the lamp lit garden trails with his customary noise-less tread, his heart rate quickening as he followed the woman who had occupied his mind ceaselessly for the last sennight. He turned a corner on the gravel walk and paused, staring at the dark-haired beauty who stood drenched in moonlight. Dressed in ice blue satin with pearls in her hair, Lady Caroline Seton was a vision he almost doubted was real.

His gaze drank in every detail of her—the creamy swell of her breasts above the pearl encrusted bodice…the graceful curve of her spine…the delicate arch of her throat that begged for the brush of his lips…

"Breathtaking," he breathed, awed by the sight of her.

She turned to face him.

Slender, with shoulder length raven curls surrounding a face of such beauty he was robbed of his breath, Caroline caused a sharp stab of recognition deep within him.

"Mr. Shaw," she whispered, taking a stumbling step backward. She'd seen him in the ballroom, he was certain of it, but she'd quickly turned and headed in the opposite direction. He'd had a devil of a time finding her after that.

Smiling, he sketched a low bow. "Lady Caroline. It is a pleasure to finally make your acquaintance." He straightened and then stepped closer.

Caroline backed away, but seemed unaware of the hedge at her back that would soon halt her retreat. Jack saw no reason to point it out.

To the untrained eye, she might seem frightened, but the heat in her gaze betrayed her. She stared at him with a burning intensity so hot it sparked a fiery awareness.

She looked beyond his shoulder, her fingers twisting restlessly in her skirt.

"We are alone," he said softly, taking another step. "I won't harm you. I simply wish to speak with you."

That wasn't entirely true. He'd wanted to meet her, yes, and talk with her. But if they suited, as he suspected they would, he also wanted to claim her.

"Wh-what is it you wish to discuss with me, Mr. Shaw?"

"Jack," he corrected, stepping closer still.

She smelled like vanilla and spice, a scent that was at once familiar and unknown, a scent that urged him to bridge the gap between them until nothing separated his body from hers.

Caroline swallowed and Jack's entire body hardened. Her gaze was ravenous, filled with a hunger that ignited a similar need within himself. No woman in his life had ever looked at him as she did.

"Mr. Shaw, it's best that you stay away from me."

His mouth curved. "You could ask anything of me, sweet, and I would do my best to grant your desire. To stay away, however, is not something I'm capable of doing."

"You don't understand—"

"Are you still unwell?" he asked gruffly, frowning with concern.

"No." The low tone of her voice made his blood heat in his veins. Eyes wide, Caroline took another backward step only to be brought up short by the hedge.

Jack tugged off his glove and reached out to her, brushing a finger along the edge of her bodice. His breathing deepened at the feel of her satiny skin. "Your heart races as fast as mine."

"Please…"

He stared into her eyes and saw the longing there, a longing he reciprocated. "If you have a care for me at all, love, you would ease my torment."

"Jack…you must go. Forget I exist."

"Tell me I'm not what you want, Caroline, and I will walk away. Otherwise, I intend to kiss you."

She started to speak, her eyes wide and pleading, but in the end she said nothing.

With unsteady hands he reached for her, lowering his mouth to hers. Her taste, sweet and ripe, flooded his senses, and Jack groaned, clutching her more tightly to him. He had not been mistaken. The fit of her body against his was perfect. She was perfect.

Caroline melted into his embrace, returning his kiss with welcome fervor. Her lips parted and her tongue slid along his, licking and tasting the deepest recesses of his mouth. Jack shuddered, his entire body aching as her gloved fingers curled around his nape, holding him to her.

And then suddenly he was alone, his arms empty.

Bewildered, Jack spun about, searching the garden around him. He found no trace of the woman he'd just held.

Like a dream or misty apparition, Caroline was gone.

Chapter One

Two years later

CAROLINE CLOSED HER EYES and took a deep breath. Standing on the foredeck of the merchant vessel *The Dreamer*, the misty salt air bit at her skin and caused her to clutch her shawl more firmly around her. She'd left the warmth and comfort of her cabin to find a reprieve from thoughts of Jack, but it was impossible. Beneath the smell of the ocean she could still detect his evocative masculine scent, a scent that heated her blood and made forgetting him impossible.

He owned this ship, as well as a dozen others, and his presence lingered here, taunting her with the promise of what she wanted most, but could never have.

Under more ideal circumstances Caroline would have found berth on another vessel, but time had been of the essence. Jack had returned to America months earlier than she had anticipated.

She'd heard word of his return at almost the exact moment she'd sensed him. Rushing to her lodgings, she'd gathered up her belongings and boarded the first ship back to England. It was her misfortune that the earliest departing vessel had been one of Jack's, because her haste had cost her dearly.

These last days at sea had been torture. Jack's essence had seeped into every pore of the ship. He haunted her dreams, would give her no peace. Every night as she attempted to sleep he visited her, begging in his velvety voice for her to return to him. *Come back to me, Caroline*, he urged. *Come back*. The heat of his nocturnal caresses and the ravishment of his kisses drove her to madness.

Opening weary eyes, Caroline gazed out over the water. Swirls of mist partially obscured the cloudy sky, the silvery gray color reminding her so much of Jack's eyes.

From the moment she'd first seen him in the Fontaine ballroom, she'd been lost. The passionate kiss a week later had destroyed her. Even now she could feel the heat of his expert lips against hers, and the remembrance of his taste made her mouth water.

She wanted him so desperately she knew she would never be able to control the animal within her. It would bleed him dry; she would not be able to stop it. She had to stay away, far away. A man as beautiful and magnetic as Jack Shaw did not deserve to die in such a heinous manner. He radiated life and vitality, and she would flee to the ends of the earth before she drained him of the very things that had caused her to fall in love with him. A love that had been doomed long before she met him.

And so she ran. From France to Italy to America, she'd barely catch her breath before Jack would arrive, the expansion of his shipping interests causing him to visit all of the places she fled to.

This last missed encounter had come too close. Caroline could only hope his overseas business was resolved and he would remain in America. She was tired, lonely, and hungry for him. Misery was sapping her strength and resolve. If Jack came near her again, she wasn't certain she had the will to resist him.

And he would pay for her weakness with his precious life.

It was nearly two o'clock in the morning when Jack Shaw strode down the gangplank of his ship in London. Thick fog swirled around his boots as he left the dock and vaulted into his waiting carriage. He looked at his man of affairs who sat across from him. "She's in residence? You're certain?"

"Yes, Mr. Shaw. Lady Caroline is here. I saw her myself, just to be sure."

Jack breathed a sigh of relief and relaxed into the squabs. He'd deliberately timed his docking, aware that if he arrived during the day word would spread of his arrival and Caroline would hear of it. For the sake of his ego, he'd denied for years that she was running from him, but after this last occasion in Virginia he could no longer delude himself.

Lady Caroline Seton didn't want anything to do with him.

At the age of five and twenty Caroline was considered a spinster by choice. Highly sought after for her beauty and unaccountable wealth, she rejected all suitors. She was an enigma in every respect, a beautiful and vivacious young woman who had taken the *Beau Monde* by storm. Her origins were unknown, her courtesy title derived from a tenuous tie to a title now held in abeyance. Jack appreciated her mysterious appeal for a variety of reasons, not the least of which was the pleasant notoriety that allowed him to find her wherever she was.

Unfortunately, he'd caught only fleeting and rare glimpses of her over the last two years. Yet every time he saw her Caroline attracted him on some deep, primitive level he'd never experienced before. She traveled with no abigail or companion to lighten her journeys and he respected her strength of will and intrepidness. No other female of his acquaintance would travel the world alone, flaunting convention and unafraid of censure. He appreciated her individuality and admired her for it.

"You've gone to a great deal of trouble to locate Lady Caroline," his man of affairs murmured.

Jack's chest expanded on a deep breath. Caroline was the only woman he had ever pursued.

He hungered for her, desired her on a level that went far beyond the physical. She felt their unusual connection as well, or she wouldn't be avoiding him. But running was futile. There was truly no choice for either of them. After that night in the Moreland garden their fate had been sealed. Soon she would see that.

"I missed her in Virginia by only an hour," he brooded, remembering the nearly unbearable frustration he'd felt when he learned she'd fled to London on one of his own ships. But he had come for her. She would not be getting away again. This time he would soothe her concerns.

This time he would be catching Caroline.

The carriage rolled to a halt and Jack alighted. He paused on the street and gazed up at the home where his love slept. Three storied and Georgian in design, it was situated in a part of town that was not quite fashionable. The street was quiet and dark. It was a location that suited Caroline—mysterious and on the fringes of society.

"Here is the key, Mr. Shaw."

Jack turned and held out his ungloved hand, his fingers curling around the metal that would grant him his deepest desire.

His carriage moved away, the clopping hooves of his team of four and the rolling of the wheels echoing eerily around him. Climbing the front steps of Caroline's townhouse, Jack gained entry with the key he'd ordered made from a wax impression.

Once inside he moved unerringly through the darkened

house, following her scent and traversing the galleries without light until he found her.

Testing the door to her bedchamber, he was relieved to find the portal unlocked and he entered, sliding the bolt home behind him.

The room was shadowed in almost complete darkness. The fire in the grate was banked and barely gave off light, but he had no difficulty seeing. It was a small room, but perhaps that was merely the impression he received from the massive bed that dominated the space. Before the fire waited two wingback chairs. A book and blanket rested upon the arm of one; a cozy picture that warmed him as surely as the coals.

As if she sensed his presence, Caroline stirred restlessly. "Jack," she breathed in a sleep- throaty murmur that made his skin mist with sweat and his cock swell.

Stepping away from the door, he moved toward her, the tight knot of longing he'd felt these last years loosening with her proximity. He lit the taper on the nightstand and paused at the fierce reaction of his body to the sight of her in the bed. In the golden glow of the candle Caroline was ravishing.

Her soft, creamy skin was flawless. Against the white linen pillow, the gleaming curls of her hair were spread with wanton abandon. His fists clenched against the powerful urge to run his fingers through them, to cup her head in his hands and hold her still for his ravishment. Her full lips were parted with the deep, rhythmic breaths of slumber, which lifted her chest and outlined her ripe breasts against her night rail.

He smiled. Within moments those breasts would be bare and pressed to his chest, that sweetly parted mouth would be panting and crying out his name as he made love to her like he'd wanted to do for years.

It was time for her to see him as well, to remember and

feel the powerful attraction between them, an attraction so overwhelming that time, distance, and unfamiliarity had not affected it.

Taking a seat on the edge of the bed, Jack brushed the back of his hand across her cheek. She nuzzled into the caress, but slept on. His smile widened. Using the sheer power of his will, he called to her, *Caroline, come back to me.*

Caroline sat up, and discovered Jack Shaw once again invading her dreams. Dressed simply in sweater, breeches and boots, his casual attire bred a familiarity far removed from the glittering ballrooms and Society events from which she knew him and dreamed of him. His hair was slightly longer than she normally pictured it, the dark ebony strands falling across his proud forehead and curling at his nape.

But some things were constant. The sharp silver of his irises glowed with sexual intent and his full, firm lips were curved in the wicked smile that made her heart race.

She took a deep breath, resigned to her torment. He was so achingly gorgeous she had no defenses against him, and the tenderness of his gaze shattered what was left of her heart. Pushing her curls away from her face, she asked mournfully, "Why must you torture me?"

He blinked as if she'd startled him. "What are you talking about, sweetheart?"

"You know very well what I'm asking you. Why can't you allow me even one night of restful slumber? I think of you ceaselessly during my waking hours, why must my sleep suffer as well?"

Already her body ached far worse than usual. Her skin was

tight and hot, her breasts heavy and tender. She licked her lips, desperate for a taste of him, and watched his eyes flare with desire at the movement.

Jack rubbed the line of his jaw thoughtfully before answering. "If you would cease to run from me, your dreams would be less troubled."

Caroline shook her head. "You know I cannot do that."

"Why?"

"You know why," she snapped. "We have this conversation nightly. Why must we discuss it again?"

"Because we must, love," he said patiently.

"I will hurt you, Jack. I've told you before. I will hurt you terribly and I couldn't bear to do that."

He reached for her hands, then appeared to think better of it and withdrew. "Hurt comes in many forms. It hurts that you run from me."

Rising from the bed, Jack began to pace, the powerful muscles of his thighs flexing beneath the tight breeches, making her mouth water. She was reminded of how vital it was that she resist her desires, but she longed for him to understand.

"As long as I stay away from you, you'll remain safe. I love you enough to do what is best, despite how it pains me."

He stilled mid-stride, his smoky gaze locking with hers. "Beg your pardon?"

His sudden shock chilled Caroline to the bone. Every night she confessed her love to him. Never had he responded in such a fashion. She slipped out the opposite side of the bed, putting the large piece of furniture between them. He cursed as he watched her reaction.

"Caroline—"

"You are not a dream!" she accused.

Jack rounded the bed.

"Stop!" She held up her hand to ward him off. "Remain where you are."

"Allow me to explain."

"No!" She shook her head vehemently. "You must go. Now."

He raised a sardonic brow. "You just confessed to loving me. I'm certainly not going to leave."

Caroline damned herself for not paying heed to the throbbing that permeated her entire being. But she slept hard, like the dead. Even now she struggled into full wakefulness. "How did you gain admittance to my home?"

"I have a key."

Her eyes widened. "How did you...? No. Never mind. Don't explain. Leave it on the nightstand and go."

Suddenly, he stood directly before her, having moved so quickly as to be undetectable. "Jack—" she began, but he silenced her with his mouth.

Just like that night in the Moreland garden, every nerve ending in her body reacted instantly to Jack's kiss. Heat scorched through her veins and melted her resistance. He urged her closer, and then closer still, until her breasts were crushed against his powerful chest and his cock burned through their clothing to heat the skin of her stomach.

His hands, work roughened and callused, came up to cup her face, his thumbs brushing across her cheeks and prodding her mouth to open. Caroline complied helplessly and he groaned, his head tilting to the side to deepen the contact.

Jack's taste was intoxicating, rich and heady, and his scent... She wanted to drown in it.

Virile and masculine, it was uniquely his and it called to her. Everything about him called to her.

Her mouth moved feverishly beneath his, her tongue sliding past his lips, drawing the taste of him deep inside her. Clutching fistfuls of his sweater just to remain standing, Caroline lost all ability to move or think, her animal springing to the fore with a surge of triumph. And then, just as quickly as he'd grabbed her, Jack released her.

"Damnation," he muttered, his hand going to his mouth. When he pulled it away it was bloody.

She had pierced him with her fangs.

Caroline stumbled backwards, horrified. "Oh, God, Jack. I'm so sorry. I couldn't help it…" Backing into the corner, she fought the beast inside her, a beast that had tasted a blood so rich it was desperate to drain the being that contained it. Panicked, she began to cry. "Go, Jack. Please. I'll hurt you if you stay."

He came toward her inexorably, undaunted by her distress or her pleas. She sank to the floor, tears flowing down her face.

"Love, don't cry," he soothed. "I can't bear it."

"Go away." She tucked her knees up to her body and wrapped herself around them. "Please…"

"Shhh… 'Tis nothing, a small nick that will heal soon enough."

Her tortured gaze lifted to his and he smiled, a heart-stopping, gorgeous grin.

A grin that revealed a sparkling pair of fangs.

"You didn't know," Jack breathed, noting the obvious shock on Caroline's face.

She began to tremble all over. "All this time…"

He staggered as everything became clear. "Is that what these last years have been about? Is that why you've been running from me?"

"Oh, God, Jack…"

He pulled Caroline to her feet and into his arms, his heart swelling with emotion and relief.

He'd begun to wonder if he were mad, chasing a woman who didn't want him across three continents. Now he was grateful he'd continued the pursuit. Her motivation had been love, just as his had been.

Wrapping a slender arm around his waist, Caroline pressed a kiss to his jaw, the sweetness of the gesture making him cherish her all the more. Her scent, that warm combination of vanilla and exotic spice, intoxicated him. The press of her body... the softness of her curves... the long, slender fingers that cupped his nape and ran through his hair... All of it was beyond what he remembered. He'd had centuries' worth of women. None had burned him with their touch as Caroline did.

Her mouth, moist and hot, traveled across his throat, her tongue laving at his skin, tasting him and warning him of what was to come. Jack hissed as her fangs sunk into his neck, piercing with practiced skill and flooding his entire being with a sexual pleasure so intense he almost spilled his seed. He gripped her hips and ground his cock against her, the desire that overwhelmed him almost bringing him to his knees.

He'd never been bitten before. As a pureblood he had been born the way he was, not turned.

It was a novel and completely rapturous sensation to give to her in this way, the soft suction of her mouth spurring his ardor until his cock ached with the need to be inside her. Bending his head, Jack nuzzled the neckline of her night rail away and with a growl of possession bit into her.

Instantly a connection snapped into place between them. It was the kind of affinity he'd heard of before, most notably from his parents, but after centuries of existence Jack had thought he would never find such a love for himself. Yet by some miracle he had. Caroline belonged to him now and he belonged to her. The thought filled him with such joy he could hardly contain it.

Caroline purred with contentment as she drank from him and Jack understood completely. Her blood was pure and sweet like a thick wine of excellent vintage. His entire body turned hard and aroused as the strength of her essence poured down his throat, filling him with her heat just as he longed to fill her with his. He'd waited so long and spent so much of the last two years searching for her that holding her now simply wasn't enough.

When her nails scratched his back through his sweater and her body writhed against his, he sent out his Calling, probing deep into her mind until he saw her Hunger. It held her in its grip, urging her to feed and claim him, to become one with him, devour him. And through the need he witnessed her fear that she would hurt him and he felt the love she held for him. A love that had grown unbidden, but was precious to her nevertheless. It was precious to him as well.

Caroline was confused by the depth of her need for him. She didn't understand it, mistaking the need to join with the need to consume. He tried to calm her, tried to explain, but the heat of her desire was such that he couldn't get through.

Jack tore at the placket of his trousers, freeing his erection. Tugging up her night rail, he gripped her bare waist and lifted her. With a few strides he pinned her to the wall, his cock seeking her heat. She clutched him tightly to her, moaning against his throat, giving him the permission he hadn't asked for, but had needed anyway.

Clenching his buttocks, he thrust into her, deep and hard. Her pleasured cry vibrated against his neck. His answering groan tore straight from his loins, the burning tight grip of her body nearly more than he could bear.

Releasing her throat, Jack cursed, his entire body shaking

with the need to finish this, to ravish her, to fill her with his seed. Her flesh was silk under his hands, her scent permeated the air around him, seeping into his very pores, branding him as surely as he would be branding her.

"Don't move," he growled, as she tried to crawl into his skin. The need to go slowly, to pleasure her, was foremost in his mind. He had an eternity to fuck her in whatever manner he desired. This time would be for her.

He gasped as her cunt tightened around him. Slipping out of her damp, clinging depths, Jack thrust forward again, gritting his teeth as the need to come nearly overwhelmed him. Heat wrapped around his spine, swelling his cock and drenching his skin with sweat. Pleasure inundated him in waves, each crest more powerful than the last. Her desire flooded his mind, making his own that much more difficult to contain.

Caroline whimpered and released his throat. "Jack…"

Her breath gusted across his ear and his cock jerked inside her, his arousal so acute it was painful. His large hands cradled the delicate curve her spine, drawing her closer, hugging her to him. He was afraid to move, afraid to hurt her with the force of his passion.

"My love." His arms shook as he nudged deeper into her, hoping to relieve the tightness of his sac and nearly sinking to his knees instead.

Caroline's fingers entwined in Jack's silky hair and then tugged as her body shivered around the throbbing shaft that stretched her deliciously. "You have to move, Jack," she whispered against his skin. He was huge, wondrously huge, filling her completely and she wanted more than just this fullness. She wanted move-ment, friction—a hard, deep fucking that would end this biting craving she'd felt for years. "You have to move now!"

Thrusting his hips hard against her, he held her to the wall, impaled on his cock, as his hand left her buttocks and moved between them. "If I move, this will all be over before either of us is ready."

"I don't care," she cried. "I do."

His thumbs brushed across the lips of her sex, then dipped inside. Finding the hard point of her pleasure, he rubbed softly, massaging the cream-drenched skin that was taut with the effort to accommodate him. "Come for me, love." His tongue swirled along the shell of her ear and then dipped inside. "Milk me," he whispered, his voice dripping with sin.

Spurred by his words, Caroline dug her nails in his shoulders and held on as rapture, sharp and searing, shattered her, shivering through her in rippling spasms.

With a harsh groan of relief, Jack released his desire. She wrapped her legs around his hips, using the curve of his buttocks as leverage, rising and falling with his thrusts, taking as much of his cock as she could.

He was killing her with pleasure, taking her as if he couldn't get deep enough, couldn't stroke her fast enough. She sobbed, struggling against him.

"Yes, sweet," he rasped, pumping into her with astonishing speed. "Scream my name, come for me again." He thrust hard and then ground against her, sending sparks of sensation from her core to the tips of her toes. His thrusting grew more frenzied, his cock thickening magnificently until she was certain she was losing her mind.

Crying out his name, she came again, her body gripping him rhythmically until he followed her with a haunting moan, flooding her with his seed. Panting, shuddering, he buried his face in the curve of her shoulder as he emptied himself inside her.

When he finished, he pressed a reverent kiss to her skin. "Caroline," he murmured as he carried her to the bed. "All these years…centuries I've waited." He lay her down gently, his semi-erect cock slipping from her sated body.

"How old are you?" she asked, snuggling into the pillows.

"Too old for you." He brushed the curls back from her face, his own visage tender and flushed with passion in the candle-light. "But I hope you'll have me, nevertheless."

Straightening, he yanked his sweater over his head, revealing a torso rippling with strength.

Unlike the indolent aristocrats she associated with, Jack was strong and fit, a hunter forever in his prime.

Caroline sighed at the sight of him. "How did you come to have a key to my home? And why? You just recently returned to America."

"I went to America in pursuit of you. Just as I went to Italy and France and a dozen other locations." Sitting on the edge of the mattress, Jack tugged off his boots. Unable to help it, she reached out and caressed the flexing muscles of his back. As her fingers brushed across the top of his shoulder, he turned his head and kissed her fingertips.

"Truly?" Her heart skipped and then raced, resuming the same feverish pace she'd experienced just moments before in his arms.

He tossed her a careless smile over his shoulder. "Truly. I've been chasing you for years, my lovely Caroline. I acquired the key through nefarious means because I knew of no other way to reach you, and I don't regret it. From this night on, we'll weather the years together."

Her heart aching, Caroline curled back into the pillows. Now that she knew the depth of Jack's affection it would be even more difficult to leave. The smell of him, the taste of him, the skin she'd felt beneath her hands would haunt her forever.

Tonight was all she had. Selfishly she clung to it, determined to enjoy what little happiness fate would allow her before the dawn rose and forced her to go.

Arching his back from the bed, Jack awoke to pleasure so intense it hurt. "Bloody hell," he gasped, his eyes flying open to find his love straddling his hips, his cock held tightly within her creamy depths.

Caroline smiled down at him, her fingertips drifting across his chest and swirling around the flat points of his nipples. Riotous, disheveled curls surrounded her face, which he saw as clearly in the darkness as if the room were lit with a hundred candles.

"God you are so beautiful," he breathed, lifting his hands to cup her breasts, his thumbs returning the favor she had just paid to him. She moved on him, lifting with her lithe thighs and then sinking to claim his cock again. His fangs descended as the Hunger took over.

Jack dropped his head back on the pillow and allowed Caroline to have her way with him. Through heavy-lidded eyes he watched her fucking him, watched the lust and love that drifted across her porcelain features, watched the pleasure she took in his body, and reveled in the fact he could give it to her.

There was so much he had to teach her about their kind, so much he could sense she didn't yet know, but they had an eternity for such sharing. At the moment he considered nothing but this joining. His hands dropped to her thighs, his thumb brushing across the mark that adorned her hip.

How he loved her! Loved how she hungered for him, hungered enough that the hours he'd just spent pleasuring her senseless had not been enough to sate her. Jack imagined all the endless mornings ahead of them, his body hardening further at the thought of waking again to this delight. Caroline whimpered at his added girth and rode his cock faster, her firm, high breasts bouncing with her motions.

His orgasm followed hers, draining him until he sank into the mattress, exhausted. Caroline sprawled across his chest, her sweat slicked skin bonding with his. "I love you," she sighed, snuggling closer. "Never forget that."

"Ah, sweet." He crushed her to him, wishing he could explain how he felt, but knowing there were no words to express the deep need she appeased. "How could I? I expect you to remind my in just this way for the rest of eternity."

But when he woke just after dawn, he was alone again, just as he had been that fateful night in the Moreland garden. He closed his eyes and searched for her, but the echoing reply he'd basked in all night was gone. He sat up and the sheets rustled behind him. Turning, he spotted the missive on her pillow...

I cannot ask you to wait for me, however I pray that you do. There is something I must resolve, but I cannot say how long it will take me. Once I am free, I will come for you.

Yours forever, my love,
C

The warm languor in Jack's veins turned to icy fear as he read. And then the fear buckled under the weight of his grim resignation.

Caroline had run again.

Chapter Two

CAROLINE STARED OUT THE porthole window and brushed the tears from her face. An eternity without Jack was a prospect so devastatingly bleak she could scarcely think through the pain of it. It couldn't be borne. She wouldn't allow it. Somehow she would find a way to have him.

"Milady?"

She glanced over her shoulder at the young seaman who waited beyond the open door of her cabin.

"Do you have any trunks to be brought aboard?"

Her throat clenched tight with misery, Caroline could only shake her head and look away, her vision blurred by the tears that welled ceaselessly. There had been no opportunity to pack, not with Jack sleeping just a few feet away from her wardrobe. She'd have to acquire new clothes when she arrived in France. It was there she decided she would begin her search.

"Very well then," he said cheerfully. "We'll be casting off soon."

"This ship is not leaving the dock."

The carefully controlled voice behind her sounded nothing like the one that had murmured so sweetly to her just hours ago, but Caroline knew it was one and the same. She spun about and stared at the apparition that dominated the slender doorway. Jack stood there, his breathtakingly handsome face so harshly set she took a step backward in fear.

His silver gaze burned into her and never left her face as he ordered the young sailor to leave them. Entering the tiny cabin, Jack kicked the door closed and thumbed the lock.

"Wh-what are you doing?" she asked, her voice faltering.

"There will be no more running, Caroline."

"You don't understand—"

"No!" he barked. "You are the one who fails to comprehend. I am weary of chasing you, Caroline, but I won't stop. Not ever. I will hunt you down, I will run you to ground. There is no place where you can hide from me."

Frightened at his vehemence, Caroline twisted her fingers in the skirts of her traveling suit. "There is something I must finish before we can be together."

"The hell you say."

"I was told to wait for another," she blurted, hoping desperately that he would forgive her once he knew. "The woman who changed me did so with a purpose. She said something about time and love—"

"Love will find a way against time itself."

Caroline gaped. "How did you know?"

"'Tis is an old vampire proverb. One of the many things I planned to share with you."

Fresh tears fell as she explained further. "The woman felt I would be a perfect spouse for her son. She said love might take time, but it would find me. *He* would find me. One day he will come for me, Jack. But I intend to find him first. I will tell him of my love for you, how I cannot imagine my life without you. I will never belong to another man. Never!"

"Caroline—"

The words tumbled out of her mouth in her haste to tell all. "She placed a mark on me. She said he would know me by it. He will believe me, Jack, and I will make certain he understands that there can never be anything between us."

Studying Jack's face, Caroline saw that her words did not soften him. Instead his ire appeared to grow before her eyes.

"And you didn't feel that you could share this with me?" he asked sharply. "You couldn't tell me this, discuss this with me and allow me to help you? What of the love you professed to me, Caroline? Where is the faith that my love for you would see you through any challenge you faced?"

Stung, she retorted, "What good will it serve for you to see another man's claim to me?"

His jaw clenched as he thrust out his hand displaying his signet ring. "This claim?"

She gasped at the crest that mirrored the mark on her hip. Her eyes lifted to his. "You knew?"

"My mouth and hands caressed every inch of your skin. Did you think there was any part of you that escaped my notice?"

"You said nothing!"

He gave a sardonic laugh. "I had other more pressing matters to attend to last night. With an eternity ahead of us, I saw no need for haste."

"That woman…was your mother?" Caroline shook her head, her heart aching. Her hand gestured between them. "So this feeling…this *love*…has been arranged?"

"No one can force love to grow betwixt two people, not even a master vampire like my mother."

She frowned. "But you came for me. Why?"

"From the moment your lips touched mine in the Moreland garden I knew what you could become to me. It was that potential that drove me these last two years, nothing else."

"Why didn't I know?"

"She left you the choice, Caroline. In the end the decision is yours to make. Whether or not I am the man you want is a conclusion you must draw for yourself. Nothing binds you to me.

The mark she gave you was simply to guard you from those of our kind who prey upon the unprotected. That crest shows that you were chosen by an ancient family, that you are important to someone and would be missed."

Shocked, she looked away, afraid to believe that she could indeed have him, even as hope welled up within her. "My love binds me to you," she whispered, chancing another glance at him. "I cannot survive without you in my life. I've been miserable without you."

Jack took a deep breath, the silver of his irises molten with a hurt that she had caused. "How could you have left me so easily?"

"Oh, Jack… Leaving you was many things, but easy is not one of them. I thought it was the only way. How could I come to you fettered by the chains of another?" She held out her hands and walked toward him. "I would have searched the world over, left no stone unturned—"

Gruff voiced, he cut her off. "This habit of yours to run must be broken."

"I would not have left if you'd told me you were the one," she pointed out with an arched brow. "Your silence led me to false conclusions."

"I won't tolerate it again," he said, his voice softening but deadly earnest.

"I won't run." Her arms encircled his taut frame. "I shall never leave your side. You'll never be rid of me."

He crushed her to him and rested his cheek atop her head. "I want to throttle you for leaving that damned letter."

"I'm so sorry. Please, you must believe that. If I didn't love you it wouldn't have mattered.

For a brief affair, I wouldn't have bothered. But to have you forever I had to be free."

"You can have me now. In that bed behind you."

Caroline tilted her head back to look at him. "*Here?*" she asked, incredulous. He growled and she felt a tremulous excitement grow within her.

"Here." Jack stalked forward, forcing her to retreat toward the tiny bed. "You're going to prove everything you just said to me."

"The ship…?"

"Won't be going anywhere."

"My gown…?"

His wicked smile made her shiver. "Lift it."

The backs of her knees connected with the mattress and she fell on her back, her hands yanking and pulling franticly at the many layers of her skirts.

Jack's expression of pure possessiveness made her heart race. When he tore open the placket of his breeches and his cock sprang free, hard and long and impressively thick, she flooded with moisture and licked her fangs.

He spread her legs wide and began to slip inside her, taking his time, making her feel every inch. Lacing his fingers with hers, he pinned her arms above her head. "Never again," he warned.

With a gasp, she arched upward. "Never."

"You'll marry me as soon as we can arrange it."

"Yes…"

He began a luxurious rhythm, slow and sensual, an erotic dance of hardness into softness, and it swept through her in a gentle wave. Holding both of her hands with one of his, he reached for her knee and anchored it to his hip, opening her further so he could drive his cock deeper.

He fucked with such skill, such breathtaking expertise, and she loved him so much she cried with it. The loneliness she'd felt for so many years was gone, replaced by Jack's strong, steadfast presence in her heart and mind. The connection was deep, one that awed and amazed her. Closing her eyes, she touched him back, and felt his love surround her in tender embrace.

"God, Jack. You feel so good…"

He groaned and quickened his pace, the soft sucking sound of their lovemaking making her ache with the need to come.

"Please…" she begged.

"You'll wait for it," he growled. "After what you did to me this morning, you'll wait."

"I love you."

Jack pressed his lips to hers as he shuddered at her words. "Damn you."

She cried out his name as he brought her to orgasm with a powerful thrust. She felt his cock jerk inside her as he came, hot pulsing bursts of semen that pushed her over the edge until she shivered beneath him in another, more powerful release.

The gentle rocking of the ship brought Caroline out of the deep drugging pleasure to a gradual awareness of their surroundings. She laughed at the feel of linen beneath her cheek, a not so subtle reminder that they were both still fully clothed. "Jack. Tell me this isn't one of my dreams."

"If it is, my love, don't wake up yet. I've only just begun."

Snaring
the
Huntress

Dear Reader,

This story was written many years ago. In other words, it's not up to the same standards as my present-day writing. When the rights reverted to me, I considered editing *Snaring the Huntress* again, but I'm a different writer now and would likely write a different story, which would destroy this one.

So I present *Snaring the Huntress* to you in the exact same form in which it was first published. I hope you enjoy it!

—Sylvia

Chapter One

AS SHE HAD EVERY night for the last week, Star woke up without an orgasm.

Running her hands through her sweat-dampened hair, she growled in frustration. There was something fundamentally wrong with having a totally hot sex dream that didn't end with her getting off.

"Dreaming of him again?"

The soft feminine voice echoed through the metal confines of Star's ship.

Tossing aside her coverlet, she hopped out of bed, too worked-up to go back to sleep. "Yes, damn it. The bastard. If I didn't want to fuck him so bad, I'd kick his ass."

"You do realize you are speaking of a figment of your imagination?"

"Yeah, I know, Two-Thousand. I'm losing it from lack of sleep." Naked, she padded barefoot down the hallway until she reached the bridge. "The craziest part is I still have no idea what he looks like. He's just this yummy deep voice in the darkness. I swear that voice makes me so hot." And his hands—those warm, tender hands. They knew just where to touch her, stroke her, caress her.

She shivered.

"Why do you wake up?"

"Because he leaves!" Star complained. "Right before we fuck, he leaves."

Dropping into the captain's chair, she checked out the navigational readings. "How are we doing time wise?"

"Excellent. You will be on top of your fugitive soon."

"Good. I could really blow off some steam right about now."

"Will you kill him when you capture him?"

Star sighed at the question, and turned her gaze away from the cockpit window and its view of the galaxy beyond. "Probably."

"You answered with very little hesitation."

Shrugging, Star kicked her feet upward to rest on the console. She'd purchased the newest model Starwing with the bonus earned from her last capture. "Why feed him rations all the way back to Primus when they'll just kill him when we get there? I'm a hunter of criminals, not a restaurant. Besides, he'll be a handful. I don't want to deal with him."

"While I agree that is practical, do you not worry that perhaps the Supreme Court Justices passed sentence too quickly?"

"You know," Star grumbled, "for a computer, you do a lot of hypothetical thinking."

"All correctional CPUs are programmed to second-guess decisions. It helps keep judges on their toes."

"Yeah, yeah. You know the rules, Two-Thousand, and so did he. Jacians can't be on the loose when their heat is on them. They can't control their sexual urges, and if they're not locked up with their pre-assigneds, they'll rape or go irreversibly crazy. It's just that simple."

"For you, maybe." If her computer could have sighed, it would have. "What if he was not attracted to his pre-assigned partner?"

Leaning forward, Star snatched up her nail file and began to shorten her claws. The damn things grew like weeds. "When a Jacian is in heat, even a deck plate is attractive."

"Regardless, how would you like being locked in a room with someone you would not want to have sexual intercourse with?"

Star rolled her eyes and shot a quick glance at the console readout. They were five clicks away from Rashier 6. Intel had reported that the Jacian had last been seen there. If his med file was correct, he'd be entering his heat now, which effectively trapped him on the planet. His body couldn't do anything for the next week besides fuck. "You're missing the point. He's so desperate for it right now, he'd want to have sex with you."

"Funny, Star."

"Actually, it's not. Poor bastard. At this moment, his brain is so sexually focused that piloting a ship is impossible, and using mass transport would get him arrested."

I almost know how he feels, she thought grimly, her blood still thrumming from her earlier dream.

Except she wasn't breaking Interstellar Council Law, and he was. Some of her cases were a little tougher than others, like this one. She really did feel sorry for the guy, but she was a judge and her job was to follow the letter of the law. Black and white. Right or wrong. There wasn't any place for her to give leeway because she sympathized with him having shitty genetics. And she was the only judge who was of the Hunter species. Her ability to hand down fair verdicts was heavily scrutinized, and left her no room for error. While another judge might have been able to appeal for a reduced sentence, she could not. That was why she was so surprised the Jacian government had asked her to personally handle this capture. It was almost like they wanted their rogue ambassador dead.

"Maybe his pre-assigned had qualms."

"Whatever, Two-Thousand. Now you're being ridiculous. You know his pre-assigned was hot for it." Jacians were a telepathic species renowned for their exotic beauty. Pale green skin mottled with softer and darker shades of green. Thick, silky hair in various colors. Eyes in a rainbow of jeweled tones. And their inexhaustible sexual appetite, which they augmented by reading their partner's fantasies and then making them come true. All traits that made them highly sought after as mates.

"Have you been with one? Sexually?"

"Nope." Star stood and stretched, lifting her arms over her head and pushing out the bony spines that coursed the length of her back before retracting them again. "I like sex as much as anyone, maybe more than most, but days on end with the same guy would kill me. Even if you are fucking most of the time, there has to be some time when you're not. You gotta sleep and eat, right? And once men start opening their mouths, it gets tedious fast."

"You are kidding."

Laughing, Star checked the programmed coordinates, and started the mental preparations for the hunt. She liked to be ready for anything. It's why she was the best. Because of her skill, she was counting on this being an easy capture. The Jacian was holed up somewhere, either with a woman or going mad with need for one. He didn't stand a chance.

"Of course I'm kidding, Two-Thousand. I love men. Everything about them. That's what sucks about this assignment. Jacians don't usually go rogue. In fact, this is the first case I've heard of in my lifetime. A shame to have to waste a prime Jacian male like this, but he had a trial and was duly sentenced. Wanted dead or alive. Those are our orders."

"I am curious as to whether you agree with the popular opinion about their beauty."

"I don't know, I've never seen one." Star opened the weapons bunker and withdrew her favorite blade. She didn't need it. Physically, she was equipped with the claws and teeth to kill anything. But using a knife or blaster kept her prey alive. "I've always been too busy collecting the judicial credits I need to make it to the Supreme Court bench."

"I have pictures of him," Two-Thousand coaxed.

"No, thanks." Moving back down the hallway to her quarters, Star caught up the silvery blond tresses that flowed down her back, and tied them in a knot at her nape. It was time to get ready for the hunt. "Jacians are pretty distinctive. I just have to find the one with the raging hard-on."

"But they have varying hair and eye colors."

"I'll keep my eyes trained below the waist. No problem."

"How about a first name?"

"Ambassador Teron is good enough." She sighed. Softness was a luxury she couldn't afford. "You're a computer, you don't understand."

"What do I not understand?"

"It makes it harder to terminate prey if they actually become individuals."

"Ouch."

"Yeah," Star muttered. "That's what he'll be saying when I catch up with him."

They'd sent the Huntress after him.

If he weren't in so much pain, Roark would be flattered. As it was, he was merely relieved his plan had worked so well. Of course, this meant the Supreme Court wanted him terminated. The Interstellar Council never sent a Hunter after anything they didn't want dead. But if everything worked out as he hoped, it would all be worth it. Death was a small price to pay for the realization of his true desire. A desire *he* chose, not one that was forced on him by genetics.

Roark leaned his head against the wall and closed his eyes, a wracking shudder coursing the length of his long frame. At this point, he rather wished for death. He'd begun the heat cycle yesterday, and his veins burned with the unrelieved hormones in his blood. Every muscle was straining, his breathing was labored, and sweat poured from his skin. If he'd started fucking at the onset, he'd be languorous and playful now. But he wanted what he wanted, and he would get her. He was not a man who took well to being denied.

But damn it! He wished she'd hurry.

He'd chosen lodging just outside of town, and did the best he could to hide, while not hiding too well. She was a Huntress. If she tracked him too easily it would arouse her suspicions. But now he wished he'd just stayed out in the open, so she would have found him already. He needed relief, a few hours straight of it, so he could think clearly and handle her properly.

He heard the door latch disengage, and sighed with relief.

Finally, after years of waiting and lusting, Star had arrived.

Star entered the darkened cottage with a deliberately noisy step, tossing off her cloak with a shrug of her shoulders. If there was a woman inside being kept against her will, Star wanted her to know that help was at hand. But as she sniffed the air, she relaxed. There hadn't been any sex going on in this rental in awhile. Her prey, however, smelled delicious. A dark, spicy scent filled the room, and she breathed it in, finding it both arousing and familiar.

Shaking off the distraction, Star forced her attention back to the task at hand. The innkeeper assured her that a Jacian male had checked in yesterday, and according to the security vid, he hadn't left. So where was he?

He'd kept the lights out, but that was more to his disadvantage than hers. She was a Huntress. Her people could see in the dark, smell from great distance, and move with amazing rapidity. In fact, they were known so much for their physical attributes that most other species had forgotten how smart they were. A fatal mistake in most cases.

Star blinked, putting into place the thin optical membrane that made night vision possible, affording her an unhindered view of the room. A bed, still made, took up the center, with two small tables on either side of it. To the right, a door led to the bathroom. To the left was a desk, beside which stood a cooling and heating unit. From the smell of it, the ambassador hadn't eaten since he'd arrived.

Great, he was horny *and* hungry.

She snorted derisively. What a shitty case. But then she always ended up with the most undesirable assignments. She was the first of the Hunter species to attain the bench, and because of that she had to work twice as hard, and hand down twice as many verdicts, just to get the same respect and the same number of judicial credits. Two of her classmates had already moved up to the Supreme Court, despite having far less experience than she. They'd both failed and had been retired quickly.

Sure, Hunters could track and kill anything, but they could also be gentle, fair, and wise— basically, they had brains to back up their brawn. And it was her life's goal to show that fact to the universe. Her species was depending on her to prove the Council wrong.

"I hope you didn't dim the lights for me," she murmured, the hilt of her small dagger gripped firmly, but not tightly.

"I certainly didn't do it for me," came the low, velvety voice she knew from her dreams. It swirled around her, originating from nowhere and yet permeating everywhere. "I would much rather see you. You do hunt naked, like the rest of your species, don't you?"

Star paused mid-step, her pulse quickening at the sound of that deep growl of sensual promise. She shook off the tingle that coursed over her skin. "Who are you?" she breathed, every nerve ending flaring to life. "*Where* are you?"

The room was empty.

"That depends. I'm either your prey or your lover. You have to decide which."

She checked the bathroom. Nothing. "I don't know you."

"Don't you, Star? I've held you in my arms, caressed you, licked every inch of your skin. You have a scar on your left hip. A battle wound. I like to kiss it. Suckle it, like your nipples…"

"Shut up." Her spines shot out, a sign of arousal and fear. She was the predator here, but she didn't feel that way. "Get out of my head."

"Can I get in somewhere else?" he purred. "I'm rather desperate at the moment. You took longer than I expected."

For a moment, she swore she could feel the heat of him behind her. She tilted her head back, and looked up at the ceiling a moment too late. The Jacian dropped down from a harness, and caught her up. He ran to the wall, and pinned her hard against it. The blade in her hand skittered away, but still she moved to grab him, finding instead that her spines had sunk into the wall and held her securely.

"Oh shit," she groaned, as he cupped one breast in a familiar grasp. If she stayed aroused, she'd be stuck for awhile. "I'm so screwed."

"Not yet," he breathed, his tongue flicking across her nipple. "But you're about to be."

Chapter Two

ROARK OPENED HIS MOUTH and surrounded the peak of Star's perfect breast. He was almost dizzy from the smell of her, the feel of her, the taste of her skin. Dreams could not accurately convey all of this. She could only see herself through her own eyes, not through the eyes of a man who lusted for her, so their shared dreams could not give him this pleasure. Nothing in the universe could give him this pleasure.

His tongue stroked softly, abrading the tight nipple. He shuddered, the burning in his veins nearly excruciating. He knew he had to arouse her swiftly. The first fuck would be quick, he'd waited too long, but he had to make it good for her or she'd arrest him as soon as he was finished.

"So that's what you look like," she said, her voice breathless. "You're gorgeous. But I'm still going to kick your ass when you're done."

He wanted to look his fill of her, but couldn't risk turning the lights on now. One glance at her lush beauty, and he'd be fucking himself to orgasm and leaving her behind.

But later, once the edge was off, he intended to see her in all her glory. All that silver blonde hair and pale skin. And those big blue eyes, lighter in shade than his sapphire ones. She looked like a celestial angel—until those razor-sharp claws came out and she bared those pointy canines.

"You know who I am." He flooded her mind with images of them together, echoes of the passion they'd shared in her dreams. His hand drifted between her legs, finding the soft, smooth skin and the slickness of her desire. She gave a soft cry, a sound he loved and had heard so many times. It was enough. Lifting one of her lithe, long legs, he spread her open. Then he stepped between her thighs, and took his cock in hand.

"Wow." Star's hands touched his stomach, and then brushed across his cock. "At least it was worth waiting for."

"Sorry," he said, sounding anything but. "You had to be primed before you got here, or I'd be in the brig now instead of in you."

He rubbed the head of his shaft against her, coating himself with her cream. Pausing a moment as his frame shook violently, Roark waited for the heat wave to pass before pressing into her.

"You better not leave this time." She was panting and shifting restlessly against him, her legs locked around his waist as if to trap him to her. "Or I'll kill you for sure."

In answer, he rolled his hips and surged into her.

"Oh hell," she gasped. "I don't even know your name." And then she came. Hard rippling spasms gripped his cock, stealing his breath and stilling his heart.

"Damn," he growled, his thighs shaking with his need. "You're so small…tight as a fist." He worked his cock into her with powerful thrusts, grunting with every deep plunge.

Definitely worth dying for.

His head fell back and he howled his release, two days of misery shooting out of him and flooding into her. Clutching her suspended body tightly, he stroked himself with her cunt until he was drained.

For now. The next heat wave would hit within moments.

He rested his damp forehead against Star's, fighting for control, their labored breaths mingling. "Hi," he managed. "I'm Roark."

"Hi, Roark. Nice to finally fuck you."

Star shook her head. This was *soooooo* wrong. A judge was not supposed to have sex with the criminals. "This doesn't change anything, you know."

"Yeah, I know." He turned his head and began to lick the sweat that misted her skin.

Deep inside her, he throbbed, his erection unabated. It felt so good, it took every bit of control she had not to grind herself onto that massive cock.

He was beautiful, the ambassador. *Roark.* She couldn't see colors with her night vision, but she could see everything else. The spots that mottled his silky skin made a wondrous pattern. His hair was dark and straight, hanging almost to his hips. His mouth, with its sculpted lips, was a work of art, and she moaned as he turned his head and pressed it to hers.

"Just give me a week, Star." He licked her lips. "Then I'll go with you without a fight."

"You *can't* fight me," she said dryly, her hands brushing across the tops of his broad

shoulders. He was very big. Tall, and well-muscled. Very yummy, but still… "I'd tear you apart." "But then you'd miss having all you want of this." He pumped his cock through their cream.

She shivered. "You're a cunt tease, you know that? A fucking week I've been squirming over you!"

Roark laughed, and it was a warm sound, so vibrant and full of life. His hand cupped her nape and he nuzzled his nose against hers. "It wasn't easy for me either, you know. I've waited almost two years to come into my heat."

"What does that have to do with anything?"

"It was the only way I could reach you. The time during our heat is when a Jacian's telepathic powers are strongest. I could not have dreamed with you at any other time, and without dreams we would not be together. You are too focused on your work. If it were possible, I would have had you sooner, and without risk to my life, but this was the only way."

She took a few moments to absorb what he'd said. What the hell was she going to do?

Whatever detachment she'd felt when she walked in the door was gone. Her prey wasn't some nameless, faceless body. He was a man. A man who had been loving her nightly for a week. A man who, even in the grip of a tormenting heat, had taken the time to please her as well.

"I can't go through my heat without you, Star." He slid his hands down her arms and then laced his fingers with hers. "You'll have to kill me if you won't stay. I'll go mad trapped like a wild animal in your brig." He thrust as deep as he could go. "I'd rather die if I can't have you."

You'll have to kill me. How the hell was she supposed to do that now? He was inside her.

"Why?" To risk all this…for her…she didn't even know him.

He reached up and touched her hair. "May I?" Star nodded, and he pulled the tresses free of their knot. "I've spent a great deal of time in the courts on Primus. This," he shifted her hair through his fingers, "caught my eye. I followed you. I watched you work, I saw the compassion you strive so hard to hide. I like your toughness as well as your softness, and I love that the advancement of your species is so important to you. As an ambassador, I can relate to and respect that."

"I've never seen you," she scoffed.

"I wear a black cloak and hood."

Her eyes widened.

"Ah…I see you've noticed me. I have to cover myself. My appearance is…distracting."

Star snorted. "That's an understatement." Frowning, she asked, "Do all Jacians look like you?"

"We share the same level of similarity as any other species." Roark lifted her hair to his nose, and took a deep breath.

"So, no," she answered, startled by her reaction to his tenderness. "You're exceptionally hot. Women fall at your feet and beg you to fuck them."

His mouth curved in a smile that made her heart leap. "Would you have done that? No? Well then, my looks offer no advantage I would be interested in. Hence the robe."

Slipping his hands around her shoulders, Roark pressed his body fully to hers. She felt the tremor that moved him, felt the sudden swelling of his cock inside her. Her breasts grew heavy, her blood heating and slowing with her arousal. He smelled divine—a potent allure for her heightened senses. His skin was soft and sleek over beautifully defined muscles. Her hands touched his back, slid down his spine, kneaded his flesh.

"Kiss me, Star," he begged softly in the deep, dark voice that moved her. "Like you did in our dreams."

She shouldn't. But his mouth waited just inches from hers, the mouth that had pressed kisses to every inch of her skin. Licking her lips, she tilted her head and gave him what he wanted, her tongue sliding along his, drinking in his taste. He groaned and then began to move, his cock slipping from her inch by inch and then gliding back inside, the thick head stroking every tender spot.

"Oh man," she breathed, shuddering just like he did, the feel of his deep, steady plunges making her writhe in his embrace. His long, silky hair swayed all around him, caressing her legs where she held on for dear life. She'd wanted this for a week, and yet the hunger he fed was far older than that.

"Is it good for you?" he purred, knowing damn well it was. He bent his knees and shifted his angle, massaging her so deeply her eyes watered. "How's this?" He pulled out to the very tip of his cock, and then rolled his hips, screwing back inside.

Her plaintive moan was all the answer she could manage.

His skin grew hot to the touch, his muscles trembling beneath her hands. He was holding back for her. Again. "Go ahead, Roark." Star licked the shell of his ear, then bit the lobe. His cock jerked. "Take what you need."

"Star…"

"I want it," she whispered.

As if her words freed him from invisible restraints, his entire body hardened, then like a coil held too tightly, he sprang into action. He withdrew his cock and then slammed his hips to hers, the wall behind her protesting with a creak. Again he slipped out, again he thrust, his rhythm increasing with every lunge until he was pounding into her, giving her the long, deep plunges she'd begged for in their dreams.

Pinned as she was, she could only take what he gave her. She struggled for leverage, for control, but found none. Roark bit her shoulder and then growled, "Want to come?"

"Yes! Damn you."

He ground his pelvis against her clit and watched her orgasm, his gaze so hot it burned her skin. She rippled around him, milking him, clenching tight to hold him deep. She curled her body around his while he cried out and spurted his pleasure inside her. The feel of his power reduced to such desperation was amazing. That he'd wanted to share this only with her was more so.

As he finished, he held her tightly, but his grip was tempered with unmistakable tenderness. Her body was dense with muscle and unbreakable bones, but Roark made her feel cherished and delicate. Far beyond the sex, this heated after-embrace was achingly intimate—his sweat mixed with hers, his tongue licking at the bite mark, her hands tangled in his hair.

She could never terminate him.

So now…what to do with him?

"If we—" She cleared her dry throat. "If I agree that we stay here fucking for a week, do I have to hang off the wall the whole time? What happens when I have to pee?"

Laughing, Roark drew his head back and kissed the tip of her nose. "That's something I didn't know about you, your sense of humor. I like it." He stepped back, his heavy cock slipping wetly from her. Star pouted at the loss, and he groaned, but there was no help for it. She'd never retract her spines if he didn't let her calm down a bit.

"Lights," he called out, and she blinked to see him in the new brightness.

"Oh jeez." She swiped her fingers over her mouth to check for drool. In full color, he took her breath away. Inky black tresses set off eyes the color of sapphires—a deep, dark translucent blue.

Then she registered how those eyes looked at her, and she swallowed hard.

He walked a slow semi-circle, his body moving with a fluid, powerful grace. Every muscle was clearly delineated, bunching and flexing as he strode with quiet command and made his thorough perusal. He reached out, his fingers brushing the sides of her breasts, tickling her waist, dipping between her legs where his seed leaked from her. "You are so lovely," he breathed. The smile he gave her was wistful. "Thank you for this week, Star. It'll be worth it." He brushed his lips across hers. "Remember that."

…when I'm gone.

The words were unspoken, but she heard them just the same.

Consumed by a sudden sadness, her spines retracted, and she slid easily to the floor.

A week.

She lowered her head. Only a week to find a way out of this mess without killing Roark or ruining her career. Star hoped that would be enough time.

Chapter Three

"DID YOU PICK THIS place because of that harness?" Star asked, lying flat on her back and staring up at the apparatus above the bed.

"Yes. A guy has to be creative when fucking a woman who gets prickly when aroused."

His smile curved against her shoulder. Roark had the oddest way of sleeping. He wrapped himself around her with their limbs tangled together. At the moment, his hand cupped her breast and his leg was slung over hers. After years of serving on the bench, a position which required frequent travel and killed any chance for a relationship, it was an intimacy that soothed her loneliness.

"Also it was the best way to get the 'drop on you.'"

"You know," she grumbled, "that tactic wouldn't have worked if I'd had any sleep the week before."

"You haven't had any sleep this week either," he said smugly. "Partly because of that harness, and its endless possibilities. Who knew the stern Huntress judge had a liking for such erotic play?" He caught her nipple between his thumb and forefinger. "You're just full of surprises."

So was he. Roark was a multi-faceted individual—one moment teasing and playful, the next abrupt and arrogant. He was still getting used to her disagreeing with him over simple things, like what vid station to watch or which restaurant to order food from. It was clear he'd never held a long-term relationship, but then he'd just turned thirty and he was exceptionally handsome. She wasn't surprised.

The comm link beeped next to her.

"Yes?"

"The clerk for Justice Yamada has been comm'ing you," Two-Thousand said.

"He's been doing that all week." Star gave a slight shrug, or as much of one as she could manage with Roark's head on her.

"He has tried several times today, and his last message was very clear—'Check in, or lose the robe.'"

So that was it then. Their time was up.

Star sighed, her hand stroking through the silky strands of Roark's hair. "Make the pre-flight arrangements. We'll be on board within the hour. Star out."

Roark kissed the tip of her breast and then rolled out of bed. He stretched, his beautiful skin moving sinuously over the muscle beneath. She watched him, as she had been all week, memorizing every line of his body, every smile, every heated glance.

"I'm not going to your ship, Star," he said in that deep voice she adored.

"What?" Sitting up, she gaped at him. "You promised!"

His mouth was taut with determination, his sapphire gaze intent. "Terminate me here."

"*What?* Are you insane?"

"It's best this way, and you know it."

After leaping from the bed, she began to pace. "I thought all-you-can-take sex was supposed to prevent madness. Isn't that right? Did I not fuck you enough?" She threw up her hands and then pointed a finger at him. "Just so you know, sometimes I was really sore, but did you hear me complain? No! I put out all week. You shouldn't be crazy."

Roark came to her and pulled her into his embrace. "I love it when you start with the humor. Especially when you do it because the situation is too uncomfortable, or you're facing questions you don't want to answer. It's one of your little quirks."

She buried her face in his chest, her own so tight she found it hard to breathe. "Don't ask me to do this, Roark. Not after this last week."

He tilted her chin up to look at him. "Did it mean something to you, Star?" His gaze searched her face. "Do *I* mean something to you?"

"Well, you're pretty to look at. And you're built in all the right places, and that thing you do with your tongue is awe—"

Roark lowered his head and took her mouth, one hand cupping her breast while the other moved away from her advancing spines. His touch was like fire, it always had been. Everything inside her came alive when he held her.

"Yes," she whispered when he broke the kiss. "It meant something."

"Then do this for me." He cupped her cheek. "If it has to happen, I would rather it be you."

She shook her head. "You haven't done anything wrong. No one got hurt, you passed through the cycle. Perhaps I can argue on your behalf."

"I fled my pre-assigned," he pointed out gently. "If I get away with it, others will try. It's a good system, Star. It's protected a large number of individuals. As the former Jacian Ambassador to the Interstellar Council, I know how important it is that the Jacian people retain their reputation."

"Yes, I know all that!" she snapped, pushing away and running her hands through her tangled hair. "But how would you feel if I asked *you* to kill *me*?"

Turning to confront him, she was startled to see her blade

in his hand. Roark held it out to her, his bearing as proud and noble as always.

"No." Star shook her head, her eyes wide with horror. "Your appointment is at risk."

Her hands clenched into fists. "I hate you."

He flinched, but kept his hand outstretched.

As she stalked toward him, her eyes narrowed and she swiped away the tears coursing down her cheeks. She drew her arm back when she reached him, and punched him in the shoulder. He took the blow easily. "You teased me for a week." *Punch* "You requested me to come here." *Punch* "You fucked me to exhaustion." *Punch* "And now, after I *like* you, you want me to *kill* you? Go fuck yourself!"

Roark caught her next blow as it came toward him, and held her hand. "I didn't request you, Star. I *hoped* you would be the one to come after me, but I didn't ensure it. With the sentence for rogues being death, I thought I had a pretty good chance of the Justices sending you, but I didn't ask for you. There was no way I could have without revealing my plan to run."

Crying silently, she stared up at him. "Your government requested me in particular. They insisted on it."

His frown and pursed lips told her that he was as clueless as she was. He released her fist and brushed the tears from her cheeks. "I think you better find out what Yamada wants."

Nodding, Star moved to the comm link on the nightstand and linked to Two-Thousand.

"Patch me through to the clerk." It took only a moment for the clerk's disapproving features to fill the screen.

"You should at least attempt to make yourself presentable before reporting in, Judge Star."

"You seemed like you were in a hurry," she pointed out, smoothing her hair with trembling hands.

"Your input was desired, but the Chief Justices moved forward without it when you could not be reached. Now they wish to know if you've terminated the Jacian ambassador yet." Star lifted her chin. "Not yet."

"Excellent, they will be relieved."

She froze, and felt the answering tension in Roark. "What?"

"The Jacians have requested a reduced sentence based on the ambassador's prominence and the fact that he did not injure anyone during his heat. The Interstellar Council has agreed that terminating a political figure with the popularity of Ambassador Teron would incite trouble they don't want. The Jacians pointed out that they agreed to the pre-assigns in a show of goodwill, and they are not obligated to follow the dictate."

"Can they do that?" she asked.

"Certainly. They would lose membership in the Council if they resisted the pre-assigns, but it seems they are willing to do this. In light of these machinations, the Chief Justices have ordered the ambassador to five years guarded incarceration."

"No." Star shook her head adamantly, her stomach knotted. "I'd rather kill him than send him to a penal colony."

"I haven't finished," the clerk said in a chastising tone. "The ambassador is to be placed on house arrest, and since you obviously deal well with him…" He paused. "You did partner him through his heat, did you not?"

"Yes."

Roark's arms came around her waist in a gentle embrace that offered needed comfort. He looked over her shoulder at the comm link.

The clerk smiled. "Greetings, Ambassador."

"Greetings."

"So, Judge Star," the clerk continued. "You are assigned to

five years house arrest guard duty in addition to your regular bench assignments."

Star's eyes widened. As her knees went weak with relief, she was grateful for Roark's steady embrace. "Five years."

"That's a lot of judicial credits, right?" Roark asked.

"Yes, it is, Ambassador. Upon your return, Judge Star, you are to meet with the Chief Justices to discuss your advancement. Congratulations. We'll have a drink when you get back." He smiled again. "See you then. Out."

The screen went blank.

"Oh, man…" she breathed, turning in Roark's embrace. "Oh wow." Her eyes narrowed. "But you're still a selfish bastard."

He laughed that warm laugh that made her shiver, and kissed her nose. "I know. I'll make it up to you, Chief Justice Star."

"Damn, that sounds good, doesn't it?"

"Yes, it does." He released a deep breath and his mouth curved in a wry smile. "I guess I wasn't as good at hiding my attraction to you as I thought."

"Yeah, it's pretty obvious someone knew you had the hots for me." Star brushed the silky skeins of Roark's hair over his broad shoulders. "And they set us up."

"My personal assistant, I bet. I'll have to reward him when I see him next."

"What's my reward for seeing you through your sex-a-thon? That was insane, you know." She shook her head. "Insane."

"For the next five years I'll be your sex slave. You can do whatever you want with me. *If* you can handle being with me that long."

"Slave. Yeah, right." She snorted. "You're too arrogant for that. And too used to getting your own way. You argue about what vid shows to watch!"

"But you like me," he pointed out softly, pulling her closer.

"And maybe, if I'm really good and really lucky, I can make you more than like me."

Star stared up into those beautiful blue eyes, and smiled. "Wanna start being really good right now?"

Stepping backward, she tugged him toward the bed. Her spines flared outward, and his gaze heated at the sight.

His smile was wicked. "Looks like I just got lucky."

About the Author

SYLVIA DAY IS THE #1 *New York Times* and #1 international bestselling author of over 20 award-winning novels sold in more than 40 countries. She is a #1 bestselling author in 28 countries, with tens of millions of copies of her books in print. Her Crossfire series has been optioned for television by Lionsgate.

Connect with Sylvia Online:

www.SylviaDay.com
Twitter: www.Twitter.com/SylDay
Facebook: www.Facebook.com/AuthorSylviaDay

CPSIA information can be obtained at www.ICGtesting.com
Printed in the USA
LVOW12s0922070615

441501LV00006B/695/P